P9-CDA-593

DATE DUE

GAYLORD

PRINTED IN U.S.A.

DISCARD

T.W. Phillips Memorial Library
Bethany College

813.54
T824N

THE NEWS FROM PARAGUAY

ALSO BY LILY TUCK

Interviewing Matisse, or the Woman Who Died Standing Up

The Woman Who Walked on Water

Siam, or the Woman Who Shot a Man

Limbo, and Other Places I Have Lived

THE NEWS FROM PARAGUAY

A Novel

LILY TUCK

HarperCollins*Publishers*

THE NEWS FROM PARAGUAY. Copyright © 2004 by Lily Tuck. All rights reserved. Printed in the United States of America. No part of this book may be used or reproduced in any manner whatsoever without written permission except in the case of brief quotations embodied in critical articles and reviews. For information, address HarperCollins Publishers Inc., 10 East 53rd Street, New York, NY 10022.

HarperCollins books may be purchased for educational, business, or sales promotional use. For information, please write: Special Markets Department, HarperCollins Publishers Inc., 10 East 53rd Street, New York, NY 10022.

FIRST EDITION

Designed by Elliott Beard

Map by Nick Springer.

Printed on acid-free paper

Library of Congress Cataloging-in-Publication Data
Tuck, Lily.
The news from Paraguay: a novel/Lily Tuck.—1st ed.
p. cm.
ISBN 0-06-620944-7
1. Lopez, Francisco Solano, 1827–1870—Fiction. 2. Lynch, Eliza Alicia, 1835–1886—Fiction. 3. Paraguayan War, 1865–1870—Fiction. 4. Irish—Paraguay—Fiction. 5. Women—Paraguay—Fiction. 6. Presidents—Fiction. 7. Mistresses—Fiction. 8. Paraguay—Fiction. I. Title.
PS3570.U236N49 2004
813'.54—dc22   2003062452

04 05 06 07 08   ❖/RRD   10 9 8 7 6 5 4 3 2

To my family

Paraguay is the most interesting, loveliest, pleasantest country in the world, I believe.

> —*from a letter written by*
> C. B. MANSFIELD, ESQ., M.A., *in 1852*

Stranger and visitor, she has written in her diary the news from Ireland. Stranger and visitor, she has learnt to live with things.

—William Trevor

"Paraguay," says Muratori, "means 'River of feathers,' and was so called from the variety and brilliancy of its birds."

"Paraguay," says P. Charlevoix, "signifies 'fleuve couronné' from Pará, river, and gua, circle or crown, in the language of the people around the Xarayes lake, which forms as it were its own crown."

"Paraguay," says Mr. Davie (1805), "would signify 'variety of colours,' alluding to the flowers and birds. Pará, in fact, may mean 'spotted,' as in the name Petun Pará, the speckled tobacco familiar to all Paraguayan travellers." Mr. Wilcocke (1807), who borrows, without acknowledgment from Davie and other authors, echoes "variety of colours."

"Paraguay," says D. Pedro de Angelis (1810), "must be translated, the River running out of the lake Xarayes, celebrated for its wild rice."

"Paraguay," which in some old MSS, is written Paraquay, says Rengger, "is simply 'sea-water hole,' from Pará, the sea, and qua-y, water-hole."

"Paraguay," says popular opinion, "merely expresses water of the (celebrated) Payaguá or Canoe tribe of Indians, corrupted into Paragua by the first Spanish settlers."

"Paraguay," says Lieut.-Col. George Thompson, C.E., "is literally, 'the river pertaining to the sea' (Pará, the sea, guay, pertaining to and y—pronounced ü—river or water)."

An eighth derivation, for which there exists no authority, is "Water of the Penelope bird" (the Ortalida Parraqua, still common on its banks).

Without attempting to decide a question so disputed . . . , I would observe, that even as late as 1837, a tribe of Guaranis had for chief one Paragua; . . . and that, both in Portuguese and in Spanish America, the conquerors often called geographical features after the caciques whom they debelled or slew. Paraguay therefore, may mean the river of (the kinglet) "Paragua."

—CAPTAIN RICHARD F. BURTON, F.R.G.S., *etc.*

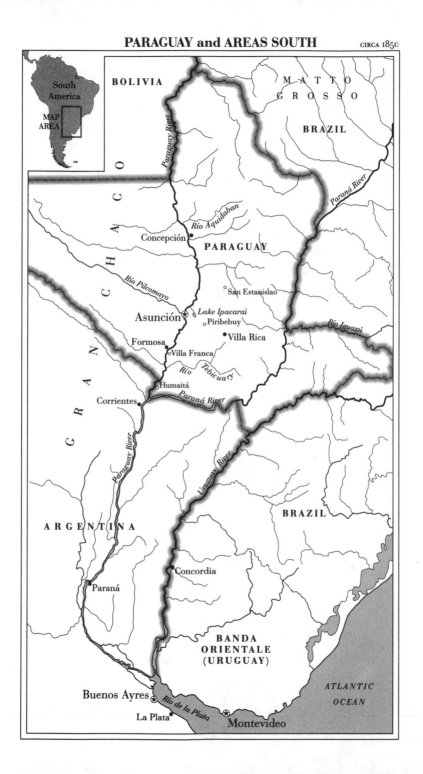

PARAGUAY and AREAS SOUTH

CIRCA 1850

South America

MAP AREA

BOLIVIA

MATTO GROSSO

BRAZIL

Paraguay River

Paraná River

GRAN CHACO

Río Aquidabán

Concepción

PARAGUAY

Río Pilcomayo

San Estanislao

Asunción

Lake Ipacaraì

Piribebuy

Río Iguazú

Formosa

Villa Rica

Villa Franca

Río Tebicuary

Humaitá

Paraná River

Corrientes

Paraguay River

Uruguay River

BRAZIL

ARGENTINA

Concordia

Paraná

BANDA ORIENTALE (URUGUAY)

ATLANTIC OCEAN

Buenos Ayres

Río de la Plata

La Plata

Montevideo

THE NEWS FROM PARAGUAY

One

PARIS

For him it began with a feather. A bright blue parrot feather that fell out of Ella Lynch's hat while she was horseback riding one afternoon in the Bois de Boulogne. Blond, fair-skinned and Irish, Ella was a good rider—the kind of natural rider who rides with her ass, not her legs—and she was riding astride on a nervous little gray thoroughbred mare. Cantering a few paces behind Ella and her companion, Francisco Solano Lopez was also a good rider—albeit a different sort of rider. He rode from strength, the strength in his arms, the strength in his thighs. Also he liked to ride big horses, horses that measured over sixteen, seventeen hands; at home, he often rode a big sure-footed cantankerous brown mule. Pulling up on the reins and getting off his horse, his heavy silver spurs clanging, Franco—as Francisco Solano Lopez was known—picked the feather up from the ground; it briefly occurred to him that Inocencia, his fat sister, would know what kind of parrot feather it was, for she kept hundreds of parrots in her aviary in Asunción, but it was Ella and not the feather that had caught Franco's attention.

The year was 1854 and the forty miles of bridle paths and carriage roads were filled with elegant calèches, daumonts, phaetons; every afternoon, weather permitting, Empress Eugénie could be seen driving with her equerry. Every afternoon too, Empress Eugénie, in fashion-obsessed Paris, could be seen wearing a different dress, a dress of a different color: *Crimean* green, *Sebastopol* blue, *Bismarck* brown. The Bois de Boulogne had recently been transformed from a ruined forest into an elegant English park.

Sent as ambassador-at-large to Europe by his father, twenty-six-year-old Franco was dressed in a field marshal's uniform modeled on Napoleon's, only his jacket was green—*Paraguayan* green. He was short, stocky—not yet grown stout nor had his back teeth begun to trouble him—and his thick eyebrows met in the middle of his forehead like a black stripe but he was not unattractive. He was self-confident, naïve, ambitious, energetic, spoilt—never had anything, except once one thing, been denied him—and he was possessed of an immense fortune. Franco put the feather in his pocket and mounted his horse again. He caught up with Ella easily and followed her home.

At age ten, Eliza Alicia Lynch had left Ireland; at fifteen, Elisa Alice Lynch married a French army officer; at nineteen, divorced and living with a handsome but impecunious Russian count, Ella Lynch needed to reinvent herself.

14 MARCH 1854

A lovely afternoon! I rode the little mare again in the Bois with Dimitri. *[Ella wrote in her diary that evening.]* Each day I grow fonder of her—her mouth is as soft as silk and a touch of the rein is sufficient. Her canter puts me in mind of sitting in a rocking chair! But how can I possibly afford to buy a horse? Already I owe John Worth a fortune! Oh, how I loathe worrying about money all the time!

Money and servants both! When I returned home and was changing my clothes, I once again had to listen to Marie complain about
Pierre whom she accuses of drinking my wine and who knows what
other thefts—servants are addicted to their tales of intrigue and to
their jealousies! Also, Marie's chatter nearly made me late—today
was the opening of the Salon! However, as it turned out, I was fortunate. The President of the Jury himself, the Count of Morny, was
the first person I met and he took me by the arm and recounted
how the day before, his half brother, the Emperor, had gone
through all the galleries never once stopping, never once glancing at
the paintings, until he arrived at the last gallery—the least important
gallery, the gallery filled with the most mediocre paintings—and
then the Emperor, out of duty, the count supposes, stopped in front
of a hideous picture of the Alps—the Alps looking exactly like a
stack of bread loaves!—and after staring at it for a good five minutes,
the Emperor turned to the poor count and said: "The painter
should have indicated the relative heights." I could hardly contain
myself and laughed until tears streamed down my cheeks! Rain was
falling when finally I left the exhibition to go to supper and of
course in my haste I had forgotten to bring an umbrella but, as luck
would have it, a gentleman smoking a foul-smelling cigar was
standing at the door and he offered me his.

From Paraguay, Franco had brought with him crates of oranges and
tobacco. On board ship, the oranges started to rot, the sailors squeezed
them and drank the juice; the tobacco fared better. The tobacco (the
Paraguayan leaves are allowed to mature on the stem and, as a result,
contain more nicotine) beat out the Cuban entry and was awarded a
first-class medal at the Paris Exhibition; the citation read, *Very good collection of leaves, especially suitable for cigars.* In addition to the tobacco,
Franco had brought dozens of ponchos as gifts; the ponchos were
made from a vegetable silk called *samahu* whose softness was much

admired. After he followed Ella home, he had one of the ponchos delivered to her house on rue du Bac with his card.

Pierre, Ella's valet de chambre, put Francisco Solano Lopez's card on top
of the other cards on the silver tray on the table in the front hall of the
house on rue du Bac; then he gave the package with the poncho in it
to Marie, the maid. The poncho was badly wrapped in brown paper and,
curious, Marie opened it. Also, the package smelled strange. Like tea. The
color of red soil, the poncho, although soft and no doubt warm, did not
look like the clothes Ella usually wore—her fur stole, her velvet cloaks
and paisley cashmere shawls. Holding the poncho in her arms, Marie
shivered a little and, glancing out the window, noticed that it had
begun to rain, a slight drizzle. *God knows, she'll never miss it, and anyway
she owes me a month's salary,* Marie said to herself as, without another
thought, she slipped the poncho over her head and went out the front
door to do her errands.

Everywhere he went—to the home of the Errazu sisters, who, like him,
were wealthy South Americans, to the home of Countess Walewska, an
Italian whose husband was Polish, to the Duchess of Persigny, married
to Napoleon III's minister of the interior, to the Duchess of Malakoff,
to the Marchioness Chasseloup-Laubat, a Creole whose skin was even
darker than his, or to the Maréchale Canrobert, who had a large goiter
on her neck—Franco took along his retinue of servants and his private
Paraguayan band. Invariably, halfway through the reception, his mouth
full of champagne and sticky petits fours, Franco motioned them to play,
and, invariably too, it took the assembled guests a moment to realize that
the tune the hapless Paraguayan band was playing on their wooden
harps was "La Marseillaise."
     Not only did Franco astonish French society, he impressed them with
his intellect. He had read Jean Jacques Rousseau's *The Social Contract* and
could discuss the difference between "true" law and "actual" law; he had

gone up in Monsieur Nadar's giant balloon, which carried a complete developing laboratory, and could discourse on photography; still better he was an accomplished and graceful dancer. *Un, deux, trois,* he waltzed the Errazu sisters around the ballroom, *un, deux, trois,* he swung the Countess Walewska in a mazurka, then whirled the Marchioness Chasseloup-Laubat around the room in an energetic polka.

Messy, messy bang, messy bang—the only French words Justo José, one of the musicians in Franco's band, had learned, he repeated. He hated France. Always cold, the food uneatable, and the people were pale and unfriendly. Worse still, there was no *yerba maté.* At home, he drank fifteen to twenty gourds a day, the silver straw never far from his mouth. The time he tried the French drink, a dark red substance the color of blood, he was sick to his stomach and the next day he felt worse—worse than when, as a boy, he was kicked in the head by the neighbor's old burro who was blind in one eye. Another thing that bothered Justo José was the women. He had gone with one, a little blond—he had never been with a woman whose hair was the color of a yellow parakeet—he could not say her name although she made him repeat it—*Eeyon.* She had taken him up several flights of stairs to the top floor of a building; her room had a chair and a bed and a basin in it, and the first thing she did was make him wash his member in the basin, then she had lain on the bed with all her clothes on, her legs spread, and during the entire act she never moved or made a sound. Afterward, she asked him for ten francs—twice the amount they agreed on, he had held up the fingers of one hand. When he tried to leave, she stood by the door and screamed and Justo José screamed back at her: *Puta, puta,* but, in the end, he gave her the extra five francs.

At supper in Princess Mathilde Bonaparte's house on the rue de Cour-celles, Ella drank too much champagne and ate too many oysters. The room was filled with Russians, Poles, Italians and filled with the noise of

silver knives and forks striking china plates, the noise of glasses clinking
and being refilled, and of everyone talking too loudly and at once in different languages. The room too, with its velvet drapes, heavy crystal chandelier and arrangement of sweet-smelling lilies, felt airless and hot.
Next to Ella, Jules de Goncourt was repeating the latest Paris gossip and
Ella only half listened as names floated by her—the Countess of Cas-
tiglione, the Count Cavour, Monsieur Viollet-le-Duc, the Duchess of
Alba, Monsieur Balzac, Monsieur Mérimée. On her other side, Adolphe
de Custine was repeating to her what the Emperor had told the Count
of Morny when he saw the painting of the Alps. But Adolphe de Custine was easy and charming and Ella could not help think it was a pity
that he preferred young boys. Mostly during the meal, Ella kept glancing toward the dining room door. Earlier Dimitri had sworn that he
would come and join her for supper but he never did. By the time she
was ready to go home, Ella had both a headache and a stomachache.

"*Ma chère,* are you not feeling well?" Princess Mathilde had asked her
as she kissed Ella good night.

With his unlimited bank account, Franco bought whatever took his
fancy—snuffboxes, ormolu clocks and silver candlesticks, fine clothes and
silk slippers, thoroughbred horses, carriages, and, more important, he
bought arms and munitions (already, in England, he had negotiated a
long-term contract with the Blyth Brothers, London's leading arms merchant, for the construction of an arsenal in Asunción). Also, Franco
bribed officials, shopkeepers, theater attendants. When a week went by
and Franco still had not heard from Ella, he went again to her house on
rue du Bac. This time, he gave Pierre, the valet de chambre, ten francs to
make sure that Ella received his card.

19 MARCH 1854

Last night Dimitri informed me that in a few days he will be leaving for the Crimean front to join Prince Menschikov who he

claims is his cousin (if I listened to him, Dimitri is related to all the Russian nobility including the Czar and Czarina!) *[Ella wrote]*. Still, I cannot believe it. Why? oh, why? I asked him. I tried to reason with him but that proved to be useless. I even got down on my knees, begging and pleading him to stay. All to no avail. Nothing I said or did could dissuade him. Dimitri is determined. He feels honor-bound, he says, to fight for his country. The truth is, I think, that Dimitri is bored with Paris. And bored with me. I know him well. Dimitri is the sort of man who needs constant challenge and excitement. I imagine he will find it quick enough in Crimea if one is to believe the most recent battle reports. How many dead thus far did Princess Mathilde say? Fifteen hundred? Fifteen thousand? She should know, she is in constant touch with her cousin, the Czar. But numbers mean nothing to me. When Dimitri tried to put his arms around me to comfort me, he even attempted to kiss me, I would not let him. Instead, in my distress, I reached up and scratched his face. My beloved's handsome face! I drew a little of his blood, which caused Dimitri to turn pale and push me away. Then—oh, I cannot bear to recall Dimitri's terrible words!—he called me a common whore, and without another word or glance, he left the room. I ran after him, I said how I was sorry, I said how I was out of my mind with grief and did not mean to harm him, but it was too late. I heard the front door close. Oh, what have I done? Damn Dimitri's cold heart and his hot blood. I love him.

A woman stood on the corner of rue du Bac and Boulevard Raspail—half her face was missing. Marie crossed to the other side of the street to avoid her. Still, the woman spotted her. "*Vieille conne!*" she screamed. With her fingers, Marie made a sign to ward off the evil eye. Farther down the street, she stopped at a fruit stand. She knew the fruit merchant, a big, good-natured man.

"So," he teased Marie, "what is Mademoiselle going to buy from me

today? Some strawberries, perhaps?" The fruit merchant held up a basket filled with the fragrant little *fraises des bois,* which were not yet in season in Paris.

Marie shook her head but she leaned down to smell the strawberries. "Where do they come from? The Americas?

"How much?" she also asked.

"Too much," she said before the fruit merchant had time to reply.

He laughed and offered the basket to another customer. While his
back was turned to weigh the *fraises des bois,* Marie slipped an orange
underneath her poncho and quickly walked away.

Marie liked the fruit merchant. He seemed like a solid and generous
man; he would not be the kind of husband who would make her
account for every penny she spent or every minute of her day. Also she
could imagine herself in bed wrapped in his big arms and how he would
smell of plum or peach or pear—depending on the season. Marie
smiled to herself, in the coming months she was determined to pursue
the man.

Turning around, the fruit merchant right away saw that an orange
was missing from the neat mound and he knew of course. He too smiled
and determined that the next time he saw her he would make Marie pay
for the fruit. Pay him with a kiss, pay him with perhaps more.

When Franco saw Ella again, she was wearing a blue silk gown that
matched her eyes. The dress was cut low and showed off the almost
translucent whiteness of her skin. She was leaning against a young
man's arm and standing with a group of people who were laughing and
talking. Each time Ella finished speaking, she ran her pointed little
tongue over her lips to wet them. The occasion was a reception at the
Tuileries and Franco, busy staring at Ella, nearly missed his much antic-
ipated and one chance to meet Napoleon III.

Although nearly spring, it was snowing by the time Franco left the
Tuileries and was walking back to his lodgings; the city streets were cov-

ered in a luminous white film. Snow was strange to Franco and he had no idea that it was not seasonal. Tilting his head back to the sky, Franco stuck out his tongue and let the snowflakes fall and melt on it.

22 MARCH 1854

Am I imagining this or is the man following me? I see him every-where—at the Louvre, in the Bois de Boulogne, the other day at the Tuileries. When he speaks French, no one understands him. Worse when he speaks English. He wears the most outlandish costumes— and the way he walks in his fancy high-heeled boots as if he were not used to wearing shoes. But there is something curious about him as well, he seems oblivious of what people think, he seems not to notice they are making fun of him. Perhaps he does not care. Princess Mathilde says he is American and the Americas, she says, are full of gold. One only needs to dig in the ground a little. Gold and silver. How I wish I could get my hands on just a bit of it! I had to put Marie off for the third time by telling her I would pay her next week for certain. (How?) This morning when she was brushing my hair she was brushing it so hard I swear she meant to pull it all out. Much, much worse—a hundred, a thousand times worse—Dimitri leaves tomorrow. I weep for him already. My handsome, unreliable Dimitri! Please, please, I'll do anything, Dimitri, stay—

"Ella, my love, open the door."

On the day he left for the Crimean front, Dimitri had knocked repeatedly on Ella's bedroom door.

"Ella, my darling, I am leaving now. I've come to say good-bye," he continued, knocking louder, harder. "Please, Ella, one little kiss good-bye. One little kiss for good luck," he added.

Too proud to beg and too vain to let him see her with her eyes swollen and red, Ella was lying on her bed, a pillow over her head, and she barely heard Dimitri's entreaties.

In the end, Dimitri had gone; his face expressionless, Pierre, the valet de chambre, had opened the front door for him.

Weeping, Ella stayed locked up in her bedroom for three days. When Marie, the maid, knocked, she yelled at her to go away. When Marie left trays outside her door, Ella threw the food on the floor. When finally Ella emerged from her room, she had lost two kilos and had resolved never again to lose her heart or a man.

But, at heart, Ella was a gambler. As a child in Ireland, she loved playing games. Her favorite was called Wanderers in the Wilderness, a board game that consisted of maps of exotic countries with numbered tracks printed on them. Each player had to move his marker in correspondence with the throw of the dice, and each number represented a site. Ella could still remember how vividly and alarmingly the sites on the map of South America were described:

> Site 10—*Look at the large creature swimming up the river! It is a water-serpent, 40 feet long at least.*
> Site 17—*What cry was that? So much like a man. O! there is an opossum with a crab he has jerked out of the water, pinching his tail in self-defense.*
> Site 22—*Hark at the horrid sounds which proceed from the forest! It is the death roar of the Jaguar which an immense Boa-Constrictor is in the act of crushing to a jelly.*

Site 66 was more dangerous still:

> *I see the track of* CAYMEN *in the mud. Ah! there is one. He plunges in the stream with an unhappy negro whom he has surprised in his tremendous jaws. Now the shrieks of his struggling victim are stifled beneath the waves.*

In Paris, games were fashionable; at parties, Ella often had to wear a mask. Now her favorite game was one in which each person was given a piece of paper with half a saying written on it: *L'amour est l'histoire de la vie des femmes* and the object of the game was to find the person who had the piece of paper with the rest of the saying on it that matched hers: *C'est un épisode dans celle des hommes.*

How she finally met Franco.

On his way to Ella's house, Franco was holding a large bouquet of roses when he saw a young woman on rue du Bac wearing the poncho made from *samahu* that he had sent Ella.

"But Mademoiselle—" Franco put out his hand to stop her—he was still holding the bouquet of roses—and the young woman reached up and took the bouquet. Franco started to protest—to tell the young woman that the poncho and the roses were not for her—instead he started to laugh—he understood that Ella was worth more.

The young woman turned and ran.

C'est un fou!

When Ella next went to the Bois de Boulogne, the gray mare she rode was gone. Furious, she waved her whip at the groom.

"You know perfectly well I always ride her," she shouted at him. "I have hired her for the season and just because I have been indisposed for a few days, you take advantage of me."

"I'm sorry, Madame, but Madame has not paid us and—" the groom tried to explain.

"Of course I will pay you!" Ella's voice was shrill. "But meantime I don't want anyone else riding her—is that understood? She is a sweet-tempered young horse and a bad rider could do her a lot of damage." Ella was close to tears. "Who did you say took her out?"

The groom shrugged. "A foreign gentleman."

"A foreign gentleman! You fool! No doubt you will tell me an American who is used to riding in the desert and chasing after cattle and has no idea how to ride a thoroughbred. Oh, how stupid, how unjust, how, how—"

Ella began to cry.

Franco had hired out the gray mare. He had bribed the groom. He trotted back to the stables, posting lightly, his reins loose and easy; he was not wearing his heavy silver spurs. The mare looked calm; she was not sweating or nervously bobbing her head up and down. "What a nice horse," Franco said, dismounting. "I think I'll buy her."

"My horse—" Ella tried to speak.

"Ah, your horse." Smiling, Franco turned to the groom. "Go ask your employer how much he will sell this horse for?"

Right away, the owner of the stables came out and named a price, a price higher than the mare was worth, and, without another word, Franco counted out the money and gave it to him. Then taking the mare's reins from the groom, he handed them to Ella.

Naked, Franco looked better than he did dressed. His big-barreled, hairy chest and his short arms and legs were strong and powerful; the rest of his skin dark and smooth. Also, he seemed more at ease. He was graceful in his movements and he was not self-conscious about his body; right away, too, without Ella having to move or touch him, he was aroused. And, it was clear too that Franco did not trouble himself greatly over his affairs with women. He was used to women. They were like bread or water for Franco. Not special but necessary. The thought of it, for a reason Ella did not try to understand, was a relief to her. It also made it easier.

Afterward, Ella did not toss and turn and worry about how to pay the rent, the servants, pay for her dresses; she slept better than she had in months. In the morning when she woke up, Franco was next to her. He was snoring lightly; his hand lay on top of one of Ella's breasts as if the breast belonged to him. It was Sunday and outside Ella heard a strange noise. A kind of music. Still dozing she listened to it for a while, then, quietly, without disturbing him, she removed Franco's hand and got out of bed. A small crowd had gathered in the street outside her house; the crowd was listening to Franco's Paraguayan band. This time the band was playing a native tune on their wooden harps and the music sounded both shrill and sweet.

A man in the band was singing:

> *Tovena Tupa~tachepytyvo~*
> *ha'emi hag~ua che py'arasy,*
> *ymaiteguivema an~andu*
> *heta ara nachmongevei*

Standing at the window, Ella listened.

Later, when Marie made up the bed, the sheets were covered with dark hairs. If she had not already known, Marie would have said a dog or an animal with fur had slept in Ella's bed. But Marie kept her mouth shut; she had been paid finally.

That spring Paris had never seemed more beautiful; the chestnut trees that bordered the boulevards and avenues were in full white bloom; from the flower stalls along the banks of the Seine the scent of lilacs and lilies of the valley filled the air. In the parks, elegant ladies wearing huge crinolines—the latest fashion—under their dresses strolled arm in arm with handsome young men. No word from Dimitri but for once Ella was not troubled. She was ready for a change. "'Europe's decrepitude is increasing; everything here is the same, everything repeats itself,'" Ella told her friend, Princess Mathilde—she was quoting Lord Byron for more authority. "'There, the people are as fresh as their New World, and as violent as their earthquakes.'"

Even while her music teacher played a new sonata on the piano, Ella, restless, fingered the gold earrings Franco had given her and tried to conceal a yawn.

Although never in his wildest dreams—and Justo José often dreamt strange dreams like the one where he was swimming in the ocean while, in fact, in his whole life Justo José had never stepped foot in any water, even bathwater, that reached above his knees—would he say this out loud nor did he dare even think it in case the woman Ella Lynch, like the woman in his village who was thought to be a witch, could read his thoughts, nevertheless she with her blond hair the same color as a yellow parakeet reminded Justo José of the woman whose name he could not pronounce properly—*Eeyon*—whom he had had to give the ten francs to.

Worse, the woman wanted the band to learn foreign tunes: tunes by composers Justo José had never heard of and whose names he was never able to say: Stross, Bisay and Waldtoofil.

Again and again Franco told Ella how, when he got home, he would transform Paraguay into a country exactly like France. "I will build an opera house, a library, a theater, wide avenues with paved streets, parks with tall trees. In addition," he said, "I will make Paraguay the most important, the most powerful country in all of South America.

"One day, you'll see, my dear," Franco continued, "I, Francisco Solano Lopez, will be so well-known, so popular, so celebrated and famous that I will be able to do anything I want."

"Anything?" Ella started to laugh. She was remembering how, according to Jules de Goncourt, Monsieur Balzac had wished for the same thing, only he had been more specific.

"You don't believe me!" Frowning, Franco raised his voice.

Monsieur Balzac had said that he wanted to be so well-known, so popular, so celebrated and famous that it would permit him to break wind in society and society would think it the most natural thing.

Still laughing, Ella went over and kissed Franco.

"Of course, I believe you, *chéri.*"

26 SEPTEMBER 1854

In any event if I am not happy there I can always come back to Paris. It is not "good-bye," it is merely *"au revoir!"*

TACUARI

On a rainy day in November, Ella set sail with Franco for Buenos Ayres on his five-hundred-ton steamer, the *Tacuari*. The other passengers on board consisted of Franco's retinue, his servants and his private band; the cargo included all the things Franco had acquired as well as all of Ella's belongings: her Pleyel piano, her furniture, her paintings, her carpets, several sets of Limoges and Sèvres china, her silverware, her household linens and dozens of trunks filled with her clothes. Also the gray mare—a gift from Franco—whose soft mouth and comfortable gaits Ella had admired, was in a box stall filled with straw in the ship's hold. In addition to her maid, Marie, Ella had engaged another woman, a woman to teach her Spanish during the voyage.

Doña Iñes Ordoñez came from the city of Toledo. However, the way she explained it, after her father, a cavalry officer and a member of the Progresista party, died saving the life of Colonel Garrigo—a fact she never ceased talking about—at the battle of Vicalváro, she and her mother had to flee Spain for France. Doña Iñes spoke *español* with the classic Castilian lisp. She had large dark eyes, an elegant long neck, and she walked with a pronounced limp—a childhood accident—even though she wore a bulky black shoe with a four-inch wooden sole. When a sailor tried to help Doña Iñes walk up the steep gangplank— she was carrying a heavy suitcase—she ignored his proffered hand and crossed herself.

When Ella first engaged Doña Iñes she asked her how old she was.

"I am twenty-eight years old," Doña Iñes answered.

At the time, Ella thought Doña Iñes was older.

"Have you ever been married?" Before Ella asked the question, she knew the answer.

The voyage across the Atlantic was to take approximately three weeks.

The first week the wind blew steadily from the northeast, the sea stayed a uniform gray color and was not high; most days it rained and the deck of the ship was slippery and wet. At night, colder, the rain turned into sleet. Except for the sailors, no one ventured out. Also there was a bad smell on deck—a mixture of burning coal, bilge water, and cooking odors from the galley; worse still, when the forecastle hatch was left open, the odor of burning fat from the forecastle lamp.

3 NOVEMBER 1854

I have been feeling ill from the moment I stepped aboard this stinking ship *[Ella wrote in her diary at the beginning of the voyage]*. And reading out loud for two interminable hours with Doña Iñes hardly helps matters. The basin is never far out of my reach. And how I wish she had chosen to read a book such as *Don Quijote de la Mancha*, instead of the dreary tomes on religion and mysticism that she keeps producing—and never mind that I've told her repeatedly that being Irish does not necessarily make me devout. The hope to convert me, I suppose, springs eternal in her breast—what there is of it, poor woman! To make matters worse, Doña Iñes never smiles or laughs the way Marie does, and if I have to hear about her father one more time, I will personally throw her into the sea! What do I care about the Progresistas and the Moderados! All in all, however, things could be a great deal worse; I have hardly given Paris a thought and I don't miss the balls, the receptions, the dinners—on the contrary, what a relief to do something different (although who knows what the outcome of this will be!)—and Franco is being most attentive—too attentive, I daresay! (I don't allow him to smoke his dreadful cigars inside my cabin.)

Housed underneath the ship's galley were a dozen bleating sheep, a sty full of pigs and several poultry coops. In the mornings, Gonzalo, the cook, a large, violent-looking man who wore a red knit stocking cap, sat by the door of the galley, peeling vegetables or plucking chickens. Regardless of the weather, he prepared huge meals for Franco. At a single sitting there was roast fowl, boiled pork, mutton, cheese, potatoes, turnips, which Franco washed down with wine, sherry, Madeira, beer and ale; Ella, on the other hand, picked at her plate and drank only a little arrowroot. At night, still wearing his red stocking cap, his greasy shirtsleeves rolled up to his elbows, Gonzalo sat by the galley door and smoked his pipe. He regarded everything and everyone—the sea, the sky, stars, women—with the same surly suspicion.

"*Hola,*" he called out to Marie. "*Hola, chica!*"

Franco was not a good sailor. The truth was Franco was afraid of the water and he did not know how to swim; at home the current of the Paraguay River was strong and the river was full of crocodiles. Nevertheless, despite the bad smells and the rain, he was more comfortable on the open deck than in his stuffy cabin. Wrapped in his cloak, Franco paced from stern to bow and back to keep warm and to forget the rumblings inside his stomach. Also he was restless, which made him bad-tempered. He shouted instructions at his servants, then, still shouting, he reversed them. He gave the boy in charge of shining his boots a bloody nose, he slapped a waiter for spilling gravy, he threw Justo José's wooden harp overboard. Only in Ella's cabin did Franco sit still for longer than a few minutes.

When Franco knocked on Ella's door, the maid and the Spanish woman with the short leg left immediately. The Spanish woman was always mumbling to herself: *Nuestras vidas son los rios, que van a dar en la mar, que es el morir.*

Marie and Doña Iñes shared a cabin but the cabin was so small only one person could stand and dress in it at one time. Because of Doña Iñes's leg, Marie slept in the upper berth and each time the ship pitched or rolled, she was afraid she would fall out. Worse, each time Marie sat up in bed, she hit her head on the ceiling. And Marie disliked Doña Iñes. Her superior airs; the oily lotion she put on her hair; her heavy suitcase, which took up too much space; her endless kneeling and reciting of prayers. First chance she got when she was alone, Marie went through Doña Iñes's suitcase. Not sure what she was looking for, Marie found books. Books whose titles she could not read: *La perfecta casada, Los nombres de Cristos, Camino de perfección, Libro de las fundaciónes, Moradas del castillo interior, Obras espirituales que encaminan a una alma a la perfecta unión con Dios.*

"Tell me the truth, are you a virgin?" Marie one time asked Doña Iñes, although, like Ella, she knew the answer.

From the deck of the *Tacuari*, Ella watched the Peak of Tenerife gradually appear on the horizon, it looked like a mirage as, for the first time since they had set sail, the sun came out. The ship was making steady progress through the waves, occasionally some spray hit Ella in the face. Instead of wiping off the spray, she licked it. She liked the taste of salt, also the salt settled her stomach. Leaning against the ship's railing, she watched a school of flying fish; the fish seemed to be following the ship. Their wings shone silver in the sunlight and, without thinking about it, Ella reached out to touch one. At that moment, abruptly, the wind died and, unable to change its course in time, one of the flying fish flew onto the deck. Stunned, the flying fish lay with its silver wings spread out like transparent sails. Before Ella could move or say anything, Gonzalo, the cook, was standing next to her, a knife in his hand. With one swift and expert motion, Gonzalo chopped the fish's head off.

"Bad luck," Marie, who was watching, said, "like when a bird flies inside a house, it means someone is going to die."

"You are worse than Doña Iñes always talking about death," Ella answered her.

Gonzalo winked at Marie. "I'll cook it for your supper." Already he had begun to filet the flying fish.

9 NOVEMBER 1854

What a relief to walk on dry land again. I had hoped to bring Mathilde ashore—I've named the mare after Princess Mathilde—and exercise her a little, but the tide was too low and the sailors could not get Mathilde to walk down the steep gangplank. The more they tried the more agitated Mathilde became, she reared and bucked in fright, so that I feared Mathilde would break her leg. Instead, she managed to kick one of the sailors in the head. To make matters worse, Doña Iñes, who happened to be on deck at the time, was seized with hysterics. The poor woman is afraid of everything—men, horses, she is afraid of her own shadow probably. Afterward I insisted on walking Mathilde around the deck myself for a few minutes to calm her before she was put back down in her stall. Poor

Mathilde, she has a nasty sore on her shoulder from rubbing against the stall door.

When at last we got ashore we visited the Marquis de Sonzal's beautiful gardens. I told Franco how I've never seen so many flowers: heliotropes, camellias, hydrangeas, fuchsias, amaryllis, jasmine, roses growing together in such profusion and Franco said: "Wait until you see the flowers in Paraguay!" Later, when I saw a palm tree that was over 100 feet tall and remarked on it to Franco, Franco again said: "Wait!"

We took tea at the French consul's house. The consul then insisted on taking Franco to look at the colors Lord Nelson lost in the battle of Santa Cruz—the colors, he said, were kept inside a nearby church. I told him that I would prefer to stay in the house and rest, which I did. Franco was in exceptionally high spirits when he returned. "A pity you didn't come with us," he said, "in addition to Lord Nelson's colors, we saw Lord Nelson's arm!"

When the *Tacuari* crossed the tropic of Cancer, the wind died down and it grew hot and still. The sea appeared motionless, no wave or ripple marred its flat surface.

"The horse latitudes," the captain explained to Franco. "Named for when, in the old days, they used to ship horses to the West Indies and the ships were becalmed for so long they had to throw the horses overboard."

When Franco repeated what Captain Ribera had said, Ella said, "If they threw Mathilde overboard, I would go overboard with her!"

Franco put his arm around Ella. "I would not let you."

Sometimes, before visiting Ella in her cabin, Franco masturbated. It gave him more time with her. He could sit next to Ella on the over-stuffed little sofa, one leg crossed on top of the other, and talk. He and Ella talked in French, a language that was not native to either one of them, although, sometimes, to express himself more naturally or more accurately, Franco spoke in Spanish and Ella answered him in English, but no matter what language they spoke to each other in, they managed to make themselves understood.

Franco described his family to Ella. First his father, Carlos Antonio Lopez.

"I was never close to my father but I respect him. My father is a very learned man, a lawyer. When I was growing up, I hardly saw him, he stayed locked up in his office, reading all day, reading all night as well. When the dictator Francia died, my father was made part of a ruling consulate, then he was elected president for a ten-year term; he has since been reelected. No man in Paraguay works harder than my father." Franco paused. "He has opened up the country, brought in foreigners, stimulated commerce, renewed our ties with Rome—" Franco shrugged. "More important, he has abolished slavery in Paraguay."

"And your mother?" Ella asked.

"My mother, Doña Juaña, is very ambitious. She is of Spanish descent and she considers her family vastly superior to my father's. She is right, it is. Her family is also much richer. As for my sisters," Franco continued, "they are fat and lazy. Rafaela especially. At least Inocencia takes an interest in something other than the food she puts into her mouth. She collects parrots, parrots from all over the Americas. She must have hundreds, which she keeps in an aviary in her house in Asunción."

"Your sisters won't like me," Ella predicted.

Ignoring Ella, Franco went on, "My brothers, Venancio and Benigno, are younger. Venancio considers himself quite the dandy; Benigno, my mother's favorite, is an inveterate gambler but he is the clever one. I don't trust either one of them. But enough about my family." Franco got up from the overstuffed sofa; he took off his boots, he began to undress. He could never resist Ella for long. Better yet, he did not tire of her. In bed, there was something unyielding about Ella, something withheld that was a challenge to Franco. A challenge *he* liked. Also, the sea air became Ella. She had never looked lovelier; her Irish complexion had never been more flawless.

At midday, Marie had no shadow. The sun was directly overhead and no matter where she stood on deck, there was nothing. It made her feel weightless. Tentatively, she twirled her skirt and took a couple of dance steps; a polka tune had begun to spin round and round in her head. In the galley doorway, she could see the whites of Gonzalo's eyes shining, watching her; she did not care. The tune was getting louder, livelier. Lifting her arms in the air, Marie sprang higher and wider to the insistent music in her head and spun herself quickly out of Gonzalo's sight.

Every Saturday night, in her village of Sens, the local band played in the town square; Marie and her sister danced together, they did not dance with the men. The men were rude and smelled of wine and if one tried to grab Marie by the waist and make her dance with him, Marie said, "No." Marie was a good dancer and she was not afraid to say no. But when Ella asked Marie to come with her to this new country, Marie said yes, and now she was afraid.

He did not care about the wooden harp—the precious harp made from cedar wood with thirty-six gut strings he had worked hard to buy. Luckily it was the harp and not he that Franco had tossed overboard into the sea. Food for the fish—God forbid—and hadn't he seen some strange fish, large whales and sea turtles poking their ugly heads out of the water? Justo José crossed himself again. If ever he got home, Justo José would, he swore—swore on his departed mother's head, God bless her soul—recite a thousand . . . no, five thousand, ten thousand—what did he care as long as he got home safe and sound?—Hail Marys, exactly the way the good missionaries had taught his forebears, and not only would he recite the Hail Marys, Justo José promised, but he would walk all the stations of the cross. He would walk them on his knees.

When they crossed the line, Captain Ribera, as was his habit, placed a hair across the lens of the telescope. Franco was not fooled; after all, had he not crossed the equator once before? Looking through the glass, Ella was not fooled either.

"It's a trick," she said, "the equator is an imaginary circle."

Doña Iñes was sitting on deck reading a book; Captain Ribera went over and asked if she wanted to have a look.

Squinting through the glass, Doña Iñes cried, "I see Him!"

"See who?" The captain frowned. All around, he saw nothing but water.

"*Jesù*," Doña Iñes whispered, before she fainted and fell, hitting her head hard on the wood deck.

Later, the sky turned dark. Captain Ribera ordered the skylights and hatches shut and fastened in anticipation of the squall. Except for the foresail and jib, he had the sails lowered. With the engines on, the heat below in the airless cabins was intense—worse than inside a furnace, Ella complained—forcing the passengers to come back on deck. At last it began to rain, first big drops of warm rain, then the wind picked up and the ship began to roll.

"A warning, I know." Doña Iñes's face was the color of dough.

Marie did not answer her. She was throwing up to windward, her vomit blowing back on her dress.

The sea was black, the waves, large arching ones, were veined and capped with foam. The booms swinging, the spars creaking, the ship bucked its way through the heavy sea: first landing heavily in a trough, as if to rest for a moment, before another wave broke over its bow, sending water rushing and swirling on the deck and forcing the passengers down below; then pitching up again.

Franco was inside the deckhouse with the pilot. His legs braced against a mahogany console, he rode the lurching ship as if it were an unruly horse. He was chewing on a cigar—in the wind, the cigar had gone out. He was less afraid of the bad weather than he was of the sea.

A bolt of lightning lit up the sky and Franco, anticipating the accompanying thunderclap, shouted to the pilot, "I know for a fact that lightning strikes Paraguay ten times more often than it does any other country." The storm made him feel expansive and Franco liked noises—the boom of cannons, the bang of musketry, the clang of metal hitting metal. "When I was a little boy," Franco went on, but, occupied holding the ship on a steady course, the pilot was not listening to him, "my nurse, an old Indian woman, told me that thunder is like a lost dog looking for a place in the sky to sleep and growling."

When the storm had subsided, Franco left the deckhouse and went below to find Ella. Her cabin was empty. "Ella!" he called. Now, Franco was afraid. "Ella!"

In the hold, Mathilde whinnied nervously; each time the ship rolled, she was flung against a wall. Ella opened the stall door and went in. Squeezing herself inside the manger for support and holding the mare by the halter, she stroked and spoke to the horse in a gentle and soothing voice: *Mathilde, my darling, wait until you see the green fields we will gallop on. Mathilde, my dear, fields so green and grand you have no idea, fields so green and grand you cannot imagine them in your wildest horse dreams.* Ella thought she was talking about Paraguay but she was thinking of Ireland.

Franco never looked back. He did not look back at the women he had loved briefly or the women he had slept with—nor did he ever give a backward glance to the one woman he did not get to sleep with, Carmencita Cordal. From the moment he saw light-skinned, graceful Carmencita, he had wanted her but Carmencita refused Franco; worse, she called him "an Indian pig." But Franco got his revenge—albeit a bitter revenge. The story went like this: Carmencita was about to marry handsome Carlos Decoud—the Decoud family, like the Cordal family, was an old aristocratic Spanish family and a part of the privileged Spanish aristocracy Franco's mother belonged to from which Franco felt excluded.

Carlos's brother, Juan Decoud, had been sent to Buenos Ayres by Franco's father, the president, to deposit some money there for future use; unfortunately, on the way, Juan gambled away most of the money and, too frightened to admit his mistake, fled to Europe with what was left. Furious and to retaliate, Don Carlos Antonio Lopez ordered his son Franco to arrest Carlos, the brother. When Franco went to do so, Carlos Decoud and Carmencita Cordal were celebrating their engagement at a ball in their honor, they were dancing together. In her happiness, Carmencita looked even lovelier and again Franco made advances to her, suggesting that if she accepted them he would be disposed to treat her fiancé leniently, but again Carmencita rebuffed Franco. This time she called him "a *fat* Indian pig!" Franco not only arrested Carlos Decoud but had him shot. He had the bloody corpse thrown in front of the Cordals' house for Carmencita to see. When she saw Carlos's corpse, Carmencita ripped out her long hair, tore the flesh on her face, she stopped eating. Even if Franco could have had Carmencita then, he would not have wanted her.

Marie had a nightmare—a dream that started out well enough before it turned bad. In the dream, Marie was walking down the rue du Bac, in Paris; ahead of her was the fruit merchant—she recognized his broad back, the way he held his head—and although Marie kept walking faster the fruit merchant too walked faster and she could never quite catch up to him. After a while, in the dream, frustrated, Marie called out to him— a name she could not remember but which she knew for certain was his name—and when the fruit merchant finally turned around it was not the fruit merchant after all but the beggar woman with half the face and Marie woke up. The cabin was hot and she was sweating; then she heard a strange sound. In her berth, Marie lay still and listened. The sound came from underneath her—a kind of muffled moan. When her eyes had adjusted to the darkness, Marie peered down through the space between the two berths. Doña Iñes was lying on her back, naked, her hands working in between her legs.

✗

22 NOVEMBER 1854

I swear to God none of the nuns in the convent can hold a candle to Doña Iñes! How she crosses herself all the time, like a tic. And how she makes me repeat and repeat: *"Sin arrimo y con arrimo"* until I have rolled my Rs properly—*arrrrrimo!* (Franco, I notice, does not roll his Rs, and when I asked Doña Iñes, she said Franco spoke low Spanish!) Useless to tell her that I need to learn practical phrases:"I am happy to be in your beautiful country." "What a lovely dress you are wearing!" "No, thank you, I have eaten enough oranges." When I asked Marie, Marie shrugged her shoulders and twirled her finger on her forehead. But enough about Doña Iñes. Captain Ribera assures me that we shall see the coast of South America within the next two days. What a relief and perhaps, at long last, I will be able to eat a proper meal and digest it properly. Franco is so impatient, he stands all day on deck scanning the horizon and smoking his cigars. I swear he must have smoked a hundred cigars by now. I too am *curious* to see this new land that I have heard so much about and where Franco has promised me I will be happy (and where he also promised to build me a palace—a pink marble palace filled with gold!).

The last night on board the *Tacuari,* Marie chose to sleep on deck in a hammock. The cabin, she told Doña Iñes, was too hot, and she liked looking at the stars—the Southern Cross. The Paraguayan band came up and played softly—without his wooden harp, Justo José hummed the tune along with the rest—and Marie swung back and forth in her hammock in time to the music. As always, Gonzalo sat at the entrance of his galley; tonight, he was mending a shirt; his fat fingers wielded the needle clumsily back and forth through the cloth. Marie watched him for a while, then beckoning to Gonzalo, she motioned that she would finish up the sewing for him.

X

Franco and Ella watched a faint streak of red on the horizon grow larger; they watched the color of the sea turn from dark blue to green. They watched as a dozen Cape pigeons flew out of nowhere next to the ship and skimmed the waves without appearing to move their wings. "Land ahead," a sailor high up in the crow's nest cried out; a few minutes later Franco and Ella saw the lights of the port city of Montevideo blinking ahead. Throwing his cigar into the water, Franco put his arm around Ella. He whispered something in her ear, but because of the wind and the noise of the engine, Ella could not hear—a promise? a declaration of love? in which language? She smiled, she nodded as if she had understood and, taking Franco by the hand, she led him down to her cabin. More likely, she guessed, Franco had said that he wanted Ella to put his *pene* in her mouth and suck it.

From Montevideo, Captain Ribera had to follow the written instructions from the river pilot, a man named Nuñez. (Nuñez, it was rumored, had contracted typhoid fever from one of the immigrant ships and was too ill and too contagious to come aboard the *Tacuari.*) The instructions were handwritten and full of misspellings—some words were illegible—often Captain Ribera either had to guess or rely on his instincts in order to navigate the ship up the north side of the Chico Bank of the Río de la Plata:

1. After leving Montevideo, steer S.W. by compas [illegible word] you run abut 30 miles.
2. After 30 miles, shift your corse to W.S.W. and run for Point Indio.
3. After making Point Indio, bring it to ber S.S.W. 8 or 9 miles distant.
4. Point Indio bering S.S.W. at the expresed [illegible word], steer N.W. by compas and run for the Ortiz Bank.

Less than a year since Captain Rodriguez, Captain Ribera's first cousin by marriage, had run aground on the Ortiz Bank; the ship had sunk and all aboard were drowned.

5. After making the Ortiz Bank, steer W. by compas until you make the Points of Santiago and Lara.
6. When 6 or 7 miles of Point Lara, steer W. by N. and you will see [two illegible words] Quilmes or trees on the hills; and by continuing the same corse you will see the steeples of Buenos Ayres, and afterward the vessels in the Outer Roads, and you may steer for them without danger.

"Ah, yes, without danger," Captain Ribera sighed to himself as he read over the instructions, "that would be good."

She knew of course. Marie did the laundry—she washed Ella's nightgowns, her petticoats, her underwear. And although Ella did not show yet—only her waist had thickened—Ella had missed three of her periods already.

Three

BUENOS AYRES

10 DECEMBER 1854

The Hotel de la Paix is situated on Calle Cangallo, a most convenient location, directly across from the Teatro Nacional. After my dinner, I only need dress, cross the street, secure a seat, and, each night, I can enjoy a different performance. The hotel contains 100 apartments that are well ventilated and spacious. Mine consists of a bedroom, a dressing room, a sitting room and a sleeping closet for Marie; we also have a splendid view of the harbor. Doña Iñes has a good-sized room on the first floor of the hotel but no view of the harbor. M. Maréchal, the proprietor, is French and he has been very helpful getting us settled here. I have most of our meals sent up; the food is quite good: mostly we eat beef, which I've been told is beneficial for my condition. Spanish, French and English are spoken in the hotel and the groom at the stable where I keep Mathilde is Irish! God bless him!

Besides the location, the Hotel de la Paix had another advantage, a special rate for extended stays; Ella was planning on staying six months, until after the baby was born.

After battling the current of La Plata and sailing past the islands of Martin García and Los Dos Hermanos, the *Tacuari*, with Franco, his retinue, his servants and band on board, entered the calmer waters of the Paraná River on her way up to Paraguay. Only since Juan Manuel de Rosas, the dictator of Buenos Ayres, had been deposed had the Paraná River been open to traffic and, as if to make up for the lost time, the river was crowded with ships. Although wide, the river was shallow and the ships had to follow shifting channels; they had to avoid sandbanks, floating islands of lianas and scrub. If the wind died down, the ships had to be poled up the river or else tied to a tree on shore and pulled along by the men on land.

Almost three years since Franco had left Asunción and he was impatient to get home. In his shirtsleeves, he paced the deck and urged the sailors on; he swore at Captain Ribera when twice the *Tacuari* went aground and they had to wait for the tide before they were afloat again. He took no interest in the flat wooded landscape that stretched on one side of the shore or, on the other, the unmapped Chaco, inhabited by cannibal tribes; likewise Franco paid little attention to the abundant wildlife: the cougars and tapirs that came down at dusk to the shore of the river to drink; the loglike crocodiles that dozed in the mud; the tremendous herons that, with a great clap of their wings, suddenly took flight; the flocks of parrots—sometimes hundreds of birds at one time—that flew, screaming, only a foot or two above his head. On one exceptionally hot and steamy afternoon, they ran into a swarm of locusts—brown-winged insects two to three inches long. Thousands of them dropped on deck; some of the locusts landed on Franco's French linen shirt and ate holes in it, but he hardly noticed.

In addition to the Teatro Nacional, Buenos Ayres boasted a number of other theaters, an opera house, a natural history museum, a public library and several clubs. The popular Club del Progresso provided members with a reading room, a billiard room, a conversation hall where the commercial news of the day was written on a slate and, best to Ella's mind, a monthly ball considered the most elegant in all of South America. The city, which was built according to an orderly grid, had plenty of parks and public spaces; the largest and most fashionable square, Plaza Victoria, commemorated the revolution and the independence of South America with a column to Liberty inscribed with *25 de Mayo 1810.* Not far from the Hotel de la Paix, Ella walked to Plaza Victoria each afternoon with Doña Iñes; together they sat in the shade of the large Paradise trees and listened to the band play and they continued her Spanish lessons in the open air.

Only when the wind blew in the wrong direction did Buenos Ayres no longer live up to its name. There were two abattoirs inside the city limits and hundreds of cows were slaughtered there each day—not for their meat but for their hides. The carcasses were left where they fell to rot or to be eaten by vultures and wild dogs. On those days, people rode through the city streets with perfumed handkerchiefs held tightly to their faces.

Up before dawn, Marie was quick to find her way to the markets: the Recoba Vieja at the corner of Calle Potosi and Calle Peru and the Italian market, Mercado del Plata, at the corner of Calle Artes and Calle Cuyo, where she bought vegetables. She was quick to learn that the best potatoes came from Baradero; the best peaches from Santiago del Estero; the best butter from English-bred cows and from the Swiss colonies of Entre Rios and Santa Fe; and the freshest milk was supplied by the Basque *lecheros* who rode in every morning on horseback, from Quilmes, Lomas de Zamora and Moron.

One morning, a young *lechero* brought Marie a gift, a cup filled with cream—*crème fraîche.*

X

"Who told you he was Jesus Christ?" Father Gaspar Alvarez, Doña Iñes's confessor, asked.

"He told me Himself," Doña Iñes answered, crossing herself.

Mathilde was stabled at the Allinson & Malcolm's livery stables on Plaza 25 de Mayo, not far from Plaza Victoria. The mare had lost weight during the ocean crossing, the sheen was gone from her gray coat; she tossed her head up and down restlessly, nervously. "Do not worry yourself over her," Patrick MacBride, the groom who took care of Mathilde, told Ella. "I'll look after her fine for you. You'll see, she'll be right as rain soon." Once a steeplechase jockey, Patrick promised to ride and exercise Mathilde every day for Ella now that Dr. Henry Kennedy, the young doctor from North America, had forbidden her to. And like Ella, Patrick was from County Cork—from Schull, exactly. He had left in 1847, at the height of the famine. "Not only in Schull but in Goleen as well, and as far away as Drimoleague, little children mostly died—twenty-five of them a day," Patrick told Ella.

Ella left Ireland when she was ten years old. One night, her father simply gathered as much of his belongings as he could carry and, abandoning his house and the rest of his possessions, he took the family to relatives in France. A doctor, her father had seen enough—not just famine but the fever and dysentery that followed. All the servants had fled and there was no food left in the house. Ella's mother, Adelaide, had to make soup from the roots she dug out of the garden, and as long as she lived, Ella said, she would never forget that feeling of emptiness—she was so hungry that she once ate seaweed and right away was sick from it—and of giddiness she associated with not having enough to eat, with starving nearly.

Ж

5 FEBRUARY 1855

I feel astonishingly well and have regained my appetite and Dr. Kennedy says that everything is progressing as it should and I should not worry. I told Dr. Kennedy that I was afraid the baby would turn into a circus acrobat the way he tumbles around inside my stomach but Dr. Kennedy did not appear to be amused. I believe he takes himself very seriously. Something else I have noticed about Dr. Kennedy is that he has very small hands, smaller than mine I daresay, but I suppose that is a good thing since he is a surgeon and has to perform delicate operations. Nevertheless, I feel there is something strange about him, but *"no importa!"* as people here are so fond of saying, as long as he delivers the baby safely.

(*"Quién sabe?"* is another favorite saying—I find the people in Buenos Ayres very kind but also quite lazy. Perhaps, it is the hot climate.)

Naturally I miss Franco but I believe it is for the best that he has gone on ahead. In my present condition, he would not find me very entertaining company. Also it allows Franco the time to make the necessary arrangements for my arrival in Paraguay!

A very elegant woman, Monsieur Maréchal, the proprietor of the Hotel de la Paix, observed to Madame Maréchal, his wife. Not only elegant but charming and well bred, even if she was *enceinte*. Monsieur Maréchal considered himself a good judge of people—after all it was his occupation, and here, in Buenos Ayres, he got to see all sorts of people passing through—rich landowners, engineers, naturalists, a lot of fortune hunters, too. Right away, as soon as someone walked through the hotel door, Monsieur Maréchal unerringly could tell, he said—and never mind how, an instinct perhaps—if that particular person would make trouble or complain about the food or the service. More important, Monsieur Maréchal could always tell if that particular person would pay his bill on time. Madame Lynch had a lovely smile, too, and when she spoke to him—not necessarily of anything of great importance—but only to say good day, or wasn't it a fine day?, Monsieur Maréchal was once again struck by the mellifluousness of her voice, the sweetness of her gaze. And such a talented woman besides! The other night after supper, at their repeated request, she had played the piano, a beautiful piece by Franz Liszt, who she said was her friend and her teacher, and everyone, including Madame Maréchal, agreed that Madame Lynch played just like a professional, a concert pianist. Yes, there was no doubt in Monsieur Maréchal's mind that Madame Lynch was a lady!

8 FEBRUARY 1855

Today, at last, I received a letter from Franco, who, since his arrival in Asunción, claims to have had no time to write. He describes the boat journey as long and hot and tedious and how he got bitten by at least a thousand different kinds of insects and that he missed me more than ever especially since there was no one there to scratch those bites for him. Ha ha! I am going to write back saying that I hope Franco's affection for me is not based entirely on my ability to scratch mosquito bites! Franco also writes that his father, Don Carlos, has gained an enormous amount of weight—so much so that Franco, at first, nearly did not recognize him. He looked like some sort of mastodon is how Franco described him in his letter. Apparently the old man cannot get out of his chair without the help of at least two men and he must be carried everywhere. Franco did not mention whether he has told his family about me and our child—my supposition is that he has not. Frankly I am not surprised, in my experience, even the most courageous men are cowards when it comes to discussing matters of the heart.

Speaking of the heart—I wonder what has become of Dimitri? I promised myself not to think of him but I cannot help myself especially since I am feeling alone. . . .

I try to keep occupied and in the afternoons either I go to Plaza

Victoria or I visit the sights and Doña Iñes accompanies me. Such a strange woman! Thus far I am prepared to swear that we have lit candles for the baby in every church in Buenos Ayres! Meantime, too, I have become acquainted with many of the local families, who have been most cordial and hospitable, and I have spent several pleasant evenings in their homes—however, I cannot help but take note of how never in my entire life have I seen people, women and children included, consume so much meat. Each person must eat at least several kilos of beef a day!

Tomorrow I plan to write Princess Mathilde and ask her for news.

In Buenos Ayres, only Doña Iñes went limping along on foot. Everyone else, including the beggars, the *pordioseros*—so called because when they begged they cried out: *por el amor de Dios*—rode a horse or rode in a carriage. Every day, she walked from the Hotel de la Paix to the church of Our Lady of Monserrat and back. Sometimes she walked back and forth twice a day, mumbling to herself:

> *Del Verbo divino*
> *la Virgen preñada*
> *viene de camino:*
> *si le dais posada!*

Dr. Henry Kennedy, technically Mr. Henry Kennedy, lived under a black cloud. A few years back, in Philadelphia, the city of brotherly love and his home then, a nurse had found Dr. Kennedy in bed with a patient— a twelve-year-old boy whose ethereal blond beauty and rosy cheeks were the result of a terminal case of tuberculosis—and immediately the nurse had alerted the entire hospital staff.

✗

Chère Yvonne, Marie was dictating a letter to Doña Iñes. *We have arrived in Buenos Ayres safely.* Marie stopped. She was unused to writing or dictating letters.

"Yes? What else do you want to write your sister?" Doña Iñes frowned, her dark eyebrows meeting.

"Wait. Let me think," Marie answered.

"Do you want to describe the climate to her?"

Marie shook her head.

"The countryside perhaps?"

Marie shook her head again. "No."

"What then?" Doña Iñes persisted, tapping her pen.

"I don't know."

If Marie knew how to write for herself she would have written her sister how, on the evenings Ella went to theater and Marie was free, she and the handsome gaucho *lechero,* who wore boots made out of horsehide that left his big toe exposed, went to a *pulperia* and drank *caña,* a fiery sweet rum, and she would also write how the *lechero* had taught her to play a game of heads and tails called *taba,* with the knee bone of a cow, and how the *lechero* always tried to kiss her and how, one of these evenings, she might let him. Instead Marie said, "Write that I miss her."

"Is that all?"

"Yes. That's all."

Afterward, it occurred to Marie that, like her, Yvonne could neither write nor read.

Early every morning Patrick MacBride, the groom and former steeplechase jockey, took Ella's gray mare, Mathilde, for a gallop. He rode out into the country at the same time as the gauchos were coming into the city from the *estancias* to sell their provisions of milk, meat, eggs, vegetables. Soon, Patrick was able to recognize some of the gauchos and he would greet them as they passed one another on horseback. The gauchos, Patrick felt sure—he could tell by the way they looked at her—admired Mathilde. A few times, because he enjoyed those admiring glances, Patrick gave Mathilde a little kick with his spurs or he flicked her with his whip so that she would quicken her pace and show off her power and grace.

One morning, Mathilde returned riderless to the Allinson & Malcolm's livery stables on Plaza 25 de Mayo; her gray coat was streaked black with sweat, her nostrils were flared and the skin inside was veined red. Her saddle had slipped and was hanging upside down; one of the metal stirrups had come off, the other dangled against the ground, setting off occasional sparks. A stable boy had a hard time catching her by one of the broken reins, then he had to walk her round and round to calm her.

20 May 1855

Last night I went to a ball at the Club del Progresso, and according to the ladies here I hardly look eight months pregnant. Naturally I did not dance; instead I sat and watched and practiced my Spanish. I also met a very charming Englishman named James White. Mr. White is said to be one of the largest landholders in the Río Plate district. Mr. White was most attentive, he spent the entire evening sitting at my elbow, bringing me plates of food and glasses of wine and I admit I did not discourage him.

Marie is certain Patrick was attacked by the gauchos. The gauchos are a lawless, violent bunch and one hears terrible stories about them—for instance, Marie told me one (she swears the story is true and that she heard it directly from a gaucho himself) about a gaucho who killed a man because he *dreamt* that man had slept with his wife! Hard to imagine! This time *I* asked Doña Iñes to light a candle for Patrick but I am afraid no amount of candles will bring Patrick back. Poor man, I shall miss him. He reminded me of home! Funny, I don't think about rue du Bac or Paris, but I do think about Ireland! I miss the gentleness of the landscape, the greenness of the countryside. Here everything looks so harsh. Perhaps, too, it is my condition which is making me sentimental but I find that in the morning, often, before I am completely awake, I feel as if I am back in my old room in our house in Cork, lying in bed, and thinking how if I were to lift up my head a little I could see out the window to the garden and to the tall fuchsia hedge by the road, and also thinking how it must be time to get up or else I shall be late for school and I start to call out to Corinna, who shares the room with me, when I remember that I am in Buenos Ayres instead. All quite silly, I am afraid.

The baby has dropped. Should I notify Dr. Kennedy, I wonder? Marie, too, has noticed, and she says that the way I carry it, the baby is sure to be a boy. Oh, I nearly forgot—at the end of the evening Mr. White invited me to his *estancia* in Belgrano next Sunday, to an "*asado*" to be cooked in my honor. Also, he promised to send a carriage for me.

In her room with no view of the harbor in the Hotel de la Paix, Doña Iñes was eating a pomegranate. If anyone had knocked or opened the door, she would have hidden the fruit. The *granada* was a luxury, something she indulged in from time to time. Not a sin exactly, only she did not confess the pleasure she experienced eating the fruit to Father Gaspar Alvarez. She sat at a table and sucked each individual kernel, then she spat out the seed into a plate. Pomegranates reminded Doña Iñes of Spain and while eating one, she closed her eyes and imagined herself back home—her father alive, and she, thirteen, sitting outside in the garden with a friend. They were eating pomegranates and having a spitting contest—seeing who could spit the pomegranate seeds farthest out into the garden—and for once she forgot about her short leg, as did her friend. Of course, her friend spat farther and won and, as a reward, he demanded a kiss. Afterward, when she returned inside the house, Doña Iñes had felt moisture in between her legs—the onset of her first menses—the result, she assumed, of the kiss. From then on too, Doña Iñes would associate blood and the kiss with the fruit—the inside part of the fruit with the little red gluey kernels and dark seeds.

Ⅹ

"An opera house."

In Asunción, the first time Franco officially went to see his father after he returned from Europe, he spoke to him of his projects.

"Like La Scala, in Italy."

Carlos Antonio frowned and shook his massive head; he had no idea what Franco was speaking about.

"A theater where people sing," Franco tried to explain.

"Sing? What do they sing? Here in Paraguay, people are happy to sing in their homes, to sing in the streets." Carlos Antonio was struggling to stand up.

"Rafaela and Inocencia are in favor of it." Franco tried to pacify his father before he changed the subject. "We must construct arsenals, shipyards, fortifications, we must build up the army to defend our country from our enemies."

"What enemies?"

Marie held a perfumed handkerchief up to Ella's nose as they drove past one of the city's abattoirs. Hundreds of carcasses of slaughtered cows and horses lay putrefied by the side of the road; large potholes contained their intestines. Hundreds of live animals were kept penned in corrals, they neighed and bellowed, pressing against one another and against the fencing that was made out of the dead animals' bones and horns. It was only after they had crossed the Barracas Bridge and had left the city far behind them and the unpaved road opened up to a wide green plain that Marie, taking a deep breath, finally removed the perfumed handkerchief from Ella's nose. Folding it carefully, she put the handkerchief away in her purse, then calling out to the coachman, *"Parar, per favor!,"* Marie got out of the carriage and threw up into the long grass.

※

On Mr. James White's *estancia*, wooden chairs and tables for the guests were set under a grove of orange trees; a few yards away, inside a pit, a whole lamb roasted on a spit. At the smell of it, Marie was afraid she would be sick again. Ella, on the other hand, had never felt better. She drank several glasses of imported French wine and ate two large helpings of the greasy lamb and listened attentively to Mr. White as he explained the breakdown of the Rivadavian land system; how the first fence built in 1844 changed the nature of cattle breeding in Argentina; and finally (since Ella showed so much interest), how he had imported the first Durham bull from England. The bull's name was Tarquin; and Tarquin, Mr. White also told Ella, would change the livestock industry in South America—change the value from hides, tallow, grease, to meat. Already, Tarquin's descendants, Mr. White added proudly—half criollo, half English shorthorn—were known throughout the country as *tarquinos*.

"*Tarquinos?*" Ella repeated. Instinctively, she touched her belly.

Embarrassed, Mr. White quickly changed the subject. Sheep farming in Buenos Ayres, he said, was a whole lot simpler.

It was late afternoon when they returned to Buenos Ayres. On the way, Ella saw a quantity of birds: wild duck, snipe, partridge, black starlings that looked exactly like the starlings at home; once a little owl flew up nearly from under the horses' feet, and she watched several hawks circling high up in the darkening sky. Also, there were some animals she had never seen before: they looked half rabbit, half badger, and as the carriage drove past, the animals stood up and stared at them before they bolted down into holes in the ground. When Ella asked the coachman what the animals were called, he said they were *vizcacha*.

"*Vizcacha*," Ella repeated dreamily.

Then, just as they were crossing the Barracas Bridge back to the city, Ella's water broke.

Four

VILLA FRANCA

During the hottest part of the day, José de Carmen Gomez, the handsome commandant of Villa Franca, was inside his house making love to a large-assed girl from the village—a girl he had pursued for several weeks. The girl was on her hands and knees on the floor and José de Carmen Gomez had just entered her when someone knocked on the door and shouted that Francisco Solano Lopez's mistress—Lopez's *querida*—had arrived and needed to be accompanied to the capital. Distracted and understanding only the word *"querida,"* José de Carmen Gomez shouted back, *"Momentito,"* and went on with what he was doing. The knocking continued, there was more shouting but, by then, José de Carmen Gomez was pumping himself back and forth into the girl and was near orgasm and the girl had taken José de Carmen Gomez's hand and put it in between her legs and was moaning and climaxing herself, so that neither one of them heard the door open.

X

A few miles north of where the Paraná River divides into the Paraguay River, Juan Francisco, aged six weeks, got his first look at Paraguay. Dark-haired and dark-skinned like his father, Juan Francisco was a healthy, noisy baby. Always hungry, he kept his wet nurse, a Guaraní Indian woman named Rosaria, up at all hours of the night breast-feeding him. Only then was he quiet; his eyes half closed, his lips sucking, his small hand resting on Rosaria's large breast.

When she was not feeding or looking after Juan Francisco, Rosaria made lace—a skill taught by the Jesuits, which had been preserved and handed down to each generation of her family. The lace was extremely fine, the pattern as intricate as a spider web.

As soon as she was able, Ella had boarded an American steamer to Asunción. Mrs. Charles Washburn, the wife of the American minister to Paraguay, who was joining her husband there for the first time, was a passenger on the steamer as well. When the weather was fine, Mrs. Washburn, who was blond and fragile-looking, had a chair brought up and she sat on deck reading; she was reading *The Last of the Mohicans*. From home, she had brought along a little dog, a terrier. The terrier's name was Bumppo—named, she said, after the hero in *The Leatherstocking Tales*. For his safety, Bumppo was tied to the ship's railing next to Mrs. Washburn's chair where he sat barking. Mrs. Washburn appeared oblivious of the sound but the barking irritated the other passengers and, when she was not looking, the sailors made it worse by teasing Bumppo—dangling food in front of him or making as if to throw a ball for him.

"How old is he?" Ella had tried to make conversation. "I love dogs, horses, all animals—I grew up in the country."

"He's just a puppy." Mrs. Washburn was less inclined to talk. She had heard rumors about Ella.

Bark, bark, bark—below in her cabin, Ella could still hear Bumppo. The barking got on her nerves.

The journey from Buenos Ayres to the frontier fort of Itapirú took the ship a week, then from Itapirú to Villa Franca, a distance of only seventy miles, another week. To Ella it seemed like a year. Nervous and impatient, Ella paced the deck of the ship. For no reason she slapped Marie, she could not concentrate on her Spanish lessons with Doña Iñes; even the baby did not hold her attention for long. The nearer they got to their destination, the more agitated Ella became. Also, as the steamer slowly progressed upriver, Bumppo's barking grew louder, more insistent. In her cabin, Ella lay on her berth, her hands over her ears, while, on deck in her chair, Mrs. Washburn, unperturbed, read on in *The Last of the Mohicans.* When at last they reached Villa Franca Ella could bear it no longer. She decided to leave the ship and go the rest of the way to Asunción on horseback. Quicker, she said. And she would not have to listen to a dog barking all day.

From Villa Franca, they rode through a forest thick with *rebora-hacho* and *algarroba,* a kind of mimosa, and thorn bushes that scratched their boots and tore at their clothes. Eventually the thorn bushes gave way to rushes and water plants and they waded in water up to the horses' knees through a marsh dotted here and there with giant fan palms. Marie had never ridden before and, on a lead rein, her horse was being pulled along by one of Commandant Gomez's soldiers. The soldier pointed things out to Marie—trees, birds, plants; in particular a spiky plant that had a pale blue flower with a bright yellow dot in the center of it—but Marie was too uneasy as she swayed uncomfortably in the saddle to pay attention to what the soldier was saying. A few paces in front of her, dressed in a Parisian riding outfit and sitting straight and tall in the saddle, Ella, on Mathilde, trotted abreast with Commandant Gomez; from the sound of their voices, the two were having a lively conversation.

"*Merde!*" Marie cursed under her breath as she slapped away a mosquito.

In the afternoon, they crossed a river; the horses were made to swim while, from inside the canoes, the soldiers held their heads. Marie's horse tried to turn back and the soldier splashed water in the horse's face to distract him and keep him swimming in the right direction. When Marie got back on, the horse was less docile; his ears were laid back. Instead of allowing himself to be led, he jerked his head up and reared; Marie screamed and the horse reared again, then finding himself free— the soldier had dropped the rein—the horse plunged forward and Marie fell off and broke her arm.

When Doña Iñes saw the man board the ship, she nearly fainted and Mrs. Washburn's terrier, Bumppo, started to bark. The man was a Payaguá Indian and he was naked; a long piece of wood dangled from his slit lower lip, a black bird's wing flapped from his pierced ear. He held a letter for the captain signed by Commandant José de Carmen Gomez that said to fetch Dr. Henry Kennedy right away. Speaking to the Payaguá Indian in Guaraní, Rosaria, the wet nurse, understood only a few words of what he answered: *Canaza hanauaki*—bad happenings. To whom? To Ella? The Payaguá Indian shook his head, making the black bird wing flap wildly. He could not say.

Doña Iñes stood at the ship's railing and watched Dr. Henry Kennedy get into the dugout canoe with the Payaguá Indian; in one hand Dr. Kennedy was holding his leather case full of instruments, in the other, his canvas sun hat. He did not think to step in the middle of the canoe, the canoe tipped and he dropped his sun hat. Making a lunge for it, Dr. Henry Kennedy set the canoe to rocking, then, trying to regain his balance and reaching for support, he lost his hold on the leather case full of instruments. Doña Iñes saw the sun hat get swept up in the current and disappear down the river, she also saw the Payaguá Indian lean over and grab the leather case just in time before it sank in the water.

As soon as she saw the dugout canoe reach the shore, Doña Iñes crossed herself and fell to her knees on the deck of the ship. She began to pray: *Oh, Mary, full of grace, mother of us all and blessed virgin, I pray you, save my dear mistress from any harm that might have befallen her. . . .*

Bark, bark, bark—Bumppo had not stopped.

X

The bone stuck out through the skin, Marie's arm looked to be hanging inside out, she had suffered a compound fracture. Someone strapped
her arm in a makeshift sling in between two boards, then she was put
back up on the horse. Two soldiers were on either side of her and, not
to jog her, they walked so slowly they soon lost sight of Ella and the others who were ahead. The soldiers gave Marie *caña* to drink out of a bottle and soon too, Marie had no memory of the ride to the next post
house. She remembered waking up later in a hammock and seeing Dr.
Henry Kennedy's pale face rocking back and forth above hers. Then she
must have passed out again. The next time she woke up, she felt as if not
just her arm but her whole body was wrapped in pain.

Holding his Bigg and Milliken saw in one hand and a manual entitled
Necessity of Amputation, in the other, Dr. Henry Kennedy stood over
Marie and read, mouthing the words to himself:

1. Cases where a limb is nearly or completely carried away, leaving
   a ragged stump, with laceration of the soft part, and projection of
   the bone.
2. Cases in which the soft parts of a limb are extensively lacerated
   or contused, the principal arterial and nervous trunks destroyed,
   and the bone denuded or fractured.
3. Cases in which a similar condition exists, without either fracture
   or denudation of the bone.
4. Cases of compound and comminuted fracture, particularly
   those involving joints.

The words blurred on the page. Overhead, a bird shrieked or was it
the woman?

Blinking, he skipped a few lines:

7. Compound fractures of the middle and lower part of the thigh,
   occasioned by gunshot, require amputation. As regards similar

injuries in the upper two-thirds of the thigh, the mortality following amputations has been so very great that army surgeons
have generally abandoned the operation. And finally,

8. Great care should be exercised, before proceeding to amputation,
   to ascertain whether a patient may not be otherwise mortally
   wounded.

Dr. Henry Kennedy had never amputated a limb before. Several
times during the procedure, he thought he himself would faint. Also, he
had never felt so hot in his life and he missed his hat. Every time he bent
his head, a stream of sweat fell into his eyes, the salt stinging, so he could
not see what he was doing properly. To make matters worse, the saw was
not sharp enough. The woman too was half conscious; she was screaming and struggling; then there was all the blood. Bright red blood from
the severed artery attracted a swarm of flies—Dr. Henry Kennedy had
never in his life seen so many: large filthy blue-black flies landing on
what was left of the arm and spreading infection.

Gaspar and Fulgencio, the two soldiers who had led Marie's horse, were
brothers. The following morning, barefoot and dressed in only shirts, they
walked down to the river together. They were going fishing. For several
hours they stood on the bank of the Paraguay casting their bamboo rods.
They hardly spoke—no need; since they were children they could read
each other's thoughts. Mostly thoughts of how the day before they had
to hold the poor foreign woman down, hold her legs and her good arm
and shoulders, her whole body bucking and resisting, her desperate
strength surprising and frightening them (one time Marie had managed
to sit up and looking Gaspar in the eye, she screamed, *"Voleurs!
Voleurs!"*). In the end both brothers had to use all their force—Fulgencio sat astride on top of her as if the screaming foreign woman was his
wife, his knees squeezing tight her soft hips—while the foreign doctor
sawed off her arm.

The Paraguay River was full of dorado, *manguruzu,* a sort of catfish, *pacu,* a type of turbot, pike, salmon and piranha. The fish that morning were not biting and after several hours, bored, Gaspar put aside his rod and sat down. After inspecting his toes, he took out a pocket knife and began cutting out jiggers. Absorbed, he did not right away hear Fulgencio yell. Fulgencio's line was straining under the weight of a fish. Dropping the knife, Gaspar ran to help his brother. Together they took turns playing in the big fish. It took them two hours.

The *manguruzu* was nearly three feet long—longer than Fulgencio's extended arm—and it weighed at least a hundred pounds. Exhausted—wrestling the huge fish made both Gaspar and Fulgencio think of wrestling with the foreign woman, although neither one spoke of it—they finally beached the fish. Picking up a stone from the beach, Gaspar struck the ugly whiskered head, killing the *manguruzu* instantly, then, taking the pocket knife he had used to cut the jiggers out of his toes, he slit the *manguruzu's* belly, lengthwise, from head to tail. In the stomach of the fish, Gaspar and Fulgencio found a whole and as yet undigested monkey—hair, tail, and pale blue eyes open wide.

23 JULY 1855

Oh, what a terrible thing has happened. Poor Marie. I should never have left the ship; I should never have told Marie to accompany me. She has lost so much blood and the infection has spread to other parts of her body. I am not sure she always recognizes me; when I tried to wash her face and tidy up her hair, she screamed and pushed away my hand. Also, each time Marie moves, the bleeding starts up again, I could see the blood seeping through the bandage and soiling the sheets. Poor Marie! So pale and pitiful, I can hardly bear to see her in such a state. When I think of how gay and good-humored she was, always gossiping and telling me jokes, always so full of life. How I wish I had never asked her to accompany me to the Americas! Please, please, God, make a miracle! Dr. Kennedy says a miracle is what is needed.

Oh, Marie!

X

Commandant Gomez was not an insensitive man, he was a lazy man. He was eager to return to Villa Franca and he spent a large part of the day swinging in his hammock, drinking *yerba maté* from his silver gourd and thinking about the large-assed village girl and the different ways he was planning to make love to her. Occasionally, when he caught sight of Ella, José de Carmen Gomez thought about what it might be like to make love to her.

Once he reached Asunción, he would return to Buenos Ayres, Dr. Henry Kennedy had decided, and from there go back to the States—not to Philadelphia, but to Baltimore or perhaps Washington—and begin his practice anew. Meanwhile, he would not worry; he had done the best he could for the poor woman. As everyone knew and as he had tried to explain to Commandant Gomez the time the commandant pulled down his pants and showed him the chancres on his penis, infection spread more rapidly in a hot, humid climate.

Still dressed in her Parisian riding habit—the skirt was torn and muddy—Ella never went far. There were poisonous snakes, man-eating jaguars and wild boar, the commandant had warned her from where he lay drinking *maté* and swinging in his hammock, and the woods were full of thorny mimosa thickets that made walking difficult; also the thick waterproof boots Ella wore were cumbersome and hot. One time she got as far as a wet meadow full of tall rushes and she watched a flock of wild ducks land—blue teal, she guessed; another time she scared up a family of wild turkeys whose sudden gobbling startled her. On the way back, Ella walked over to where the horses were kept hobbled and tied. She put her arms around the gray mare and buried her face in the elegant neck.

Oh, Mathilde!

In her dream, Rosaria was bathing the baby in the river. The baby was splashing water, gurgling and laughing. Rosaria was also laughing as she washed the baby's little legs and arms, his full little stomach, as she pushed up the foreskin to wash the little penis, as she washed the baby's back and behind. But slowly, slowly, almost imperceptibly, the current in the river got stronger, and Rosaria was having a harder and harder time holding on to the soapy, slippery baby; the baby too was no longer laughing but crying, and suddenly Rosaria was struggling with all her might to hold the baby against the current and, in the dream, the current had turned into a person, an evil person with superhuman strength, who was wrestling the baby away and Rosaria was no match for that person and she had to let the baby go. When she awoke Rosaria was soaking wet and it took her a few moments to realize that she was wet not from bathing in the river but from her sweat.

"Have you tried *maté*?" Commandant Gomez handed Ella his silver gourd. He also said, "As soon as I return to Villa Franca, I am going to marry my sweetheart." He had made up his mind all of a sudden.

The liquid was surprisingly bitter and Ella was tempted to spit it out, but the commandant was watching so she swallowed it.

"Her name is Maria Oliva," Commandant Gomez said.

The second time he handed her the gourd, Ella was prepared for the bitter taste. She took another small cautious sip.

"Maria Oliva comes from my village," Commandant Gomez told Ella.

By the fourth and fifth sip, Ella found she was getting accustomed to the *maté* and she liked the feel of the cool silver *bombilla* between her lips.

"Maria Oliva is a good girl, she is still a virgin," Commandant Gomez was saying.

Yerba maté was a mild stimulant and it might relax her muscles, Ella hoped, unused as she was to sleeping in the hammock the commandant had strung up for her. But sleep did not come. Every time Ella shut her eyes she heard Marie screaming.

Ella stayed at the post house five days. Most of that time, she sat at Marie's side. She held a cold cloth to Marie's hot forehead, she wet Marie's lips with water, she brushed away the swarm of flies that kept landing on the stump of Marie's bandaged arm. She tried to stop Marie from moving or from sitting up, so as not to start the hemorrhaging again.

Delirious, Marie called out: *"Yvonne! Yvonne!"*

"Ivan? Who is Ivan?" Ella bent close to Marie to hear. "Is Ivan Russian?" Ella thought of Dimitri, but Marie never answered.

On the fourth day, Marie was much weaker, she no longer recognized Ella or anyone.

"Look, Marie!" Ella told her. "Here is Ivan. Here is Ivan's hand," she whispered, giving Marie her own hand to hold.

When finally they got back to Villa Franca and their homes, the pretty thatched cottages on the bank of the Paraguay River, Gaspar and Fulgencio—without speaking or discussing it first with each other—never said a word to their wives, who likewise were sisters, about the foreign woman whom they had had to hold down while her arm was being amputated and who afterward died; nor did Gaspar and Fulgencio ever speak of the big *manguruzu* they had caught the next day with the hairy, long-tailed, blue-eyed monkey inside it.

When Commandant Gomez returned, he looked in vain for the large-assed village girl. Maria Oliva, he was told, had left Villa Franca in search of work—or so she had said. She had gone to Asunción, the capital.

Five

ASUNCIÓN

Asunción
4 December 1855

Ma chère Princesse,

    I cannot properly express the joy I felt when I received your letter and want to quickly reassure you that I am finally settled here in the capital after a rather difficult journey (I won't tire you with the details), and I hardly know where to begin or how to describe my adopted country. Perhaps I should start by answering your questions since you were kind enough to show such an interest, although I just lately have become acquainted with these matters myself. As you correctly surmised, the first surprise was the weather, which is most agreeable and warm at this time of year (it is our summer) and I need wear only my lightest cashmere shawl when I go out in the evening. The

*second pleasant surprise, and what immediately impressed me, is the bucolic
and peaceful nature of the countryside. (To be truthful, I had imagined
something quite different, indeed like the unmapped and wild area across the
river from us known as the Gran Chaco, which is made up principally of
swamps and marshes, large parts of which are quite impenetrable.) Instead we
are surrounded by gentle rolling hills, meadows dotted with orange and
mimosa trees, now in bloom, spreading their perfume in the air and affording
us with welcome shade. The cultivated land one sees is tidily fenced and
divided into fields where maize, manioc and sugarcane are grown. Everything
grows quickly and there is a great abundance of flowers, the variety and the
colors are quite extraordinary. How I wish I could paint you a picture—is
there not a Chinese proverb that says one picture is worth more than ten
thousand words?*

*Franco and I are in the habit of riding in the afternoons (one of my
greatest pleasures, as you know, dear friend, is horseback riding) and we ride
down long grassy lanes that stretch perfectly straight for miles—again I wish
you could see how green and lovely these lanes are! One would almost think
we were riding in an English park! And everyone we meet along the way is
very polite and takes off his hat and bows to us because—and this may amuse
you!—during the reign of the dictator Francia, Franco's father's predecessor,
everyone, on pain of death, was required to take off his hat to a superior, so
that even the poorest country boy who had no clothes and went naked was
forced to wear a hat for the sole purpose of taking it off! So far my impression
of the Paraguayan people is that they are quite friendly and a bit childish in
their habits and pleasures. The men are content to spend the day (and the
evening) swinging in their hammocks, drinking tea. The women are more
active and not unattractive to look at; they are slender and cut their dark hair
short. They wear white cotton dresses called* tupois, *the petticoats are flounced
with yards and yards of lace—they make the lace themselves (lace quite
different from Valenciennes or Chantilly lace but nevertheless quite well
made)—then the outfit is completed with a bright red sash tied around the
waist. And did I mention this?—all the women smoke cigars! Guaraní is the
local language (Juan Francisco's wet nurse speaks only Guaraní), which is
hard to understand and full of words with many syllables, as for example:*

"che oroipotáité cheribéricora," *which means "I should like you very much for my wife!" Thanks to my teacher, however, my Spanish is progressing splendidly and you would be quite pleased with my accent and how I roll my* Rs.

Now to return to your questions—yerba maté *(also known as Paraguay tea) is the principal export and you will no doubt be surprised to hear that I too, despite the bitter taste, have grown quite fond of it. Here, the people drink at least five or six gourds a day. Next, I believe, comes tobacco, then—I must ask Franco—although I do remember his saying that certain plant fibers used to make the dyes, such as indigo, are sent abroad. However, in my next letter, I promise you I shall be better informed.*

Meanwhile Franco has many plans for the modernization of his country and the beautification of the capital. He has already begun to build a railroad, a telegraph line—the first one in all of South America—a new cathedral, a customs house, a library, a post office, an opera house modeled on La Scala in Italy—I can hardly wait for the first opera to be performed—and also a lovely palace for me!

I try to keep up my practice on the piano but the days are full and there is little time. The baby, Juan Francisco, is thriving; he has started to crawl and his nurse predicts that he will be walking in no time.

I hope this letter finds you in good health, and please be so kind as to give my best regards to Monsieur le Comte.

> *Your most affectionate friend,*
> *Ella*

P.S. Along with the lace, as a Christmas gift (or more realistically a new year's gift), knowing how fond you are of animals, I am sending you a pair of parrots. According to Dr. Eberhardt, a naturalist who has lived in Paraguay for many years, these parrots (Psittacus passerinus is their Latin name) are among the smallest and rarest species. M. Bernard, the captain of the Flambard, which is due to sail from Asunción next week, has promised me that he will do his best to make sure the parrots survive the journey (even if, he has also promised me, it requires bringing the parrots inside his own cabin). One last favor I beg of you—in an earlier letter I believe I mentioned this—

*do you have any word yet of Dimitri? Or perhaps the Czar, your cousin, has
news of him—you remember my friend, the handsome young count, who left
for the Crimea?*

The first time they met, Inocencia and Rafaela, Franco's fat sisters,
would not speak to Ella. They turned their broad backs to her and
would not shake her hand.

"*Puta*," Inocencia had muttered loud enough for Ella to hear;
Rafaela had giggled.

Both sisters, however, took note of everything Ella wore.

"A lavender silk dress cut to here." At lunch later that day—Inocencia and Rafaela lived next door to each other and they regularly ate their
meals together—Inocencia pointed to her own heavy bosom and
added, "With black satin trim on the sleeves and on the hem. Who but
a woman of that sort would wear such an outfit?" Inocencia helped herself to more of the *puchero*—a beef stew with rice.

"Did you notice her shoes? The pointed toes? The high heels?"
Rafaela asked as she spooned *sopa paraguaya*—manioc soup the consistency of pudding—into her mouth. "How can the woman walk?"

"And such an ugly hat—with the dangling colored ribbons. She
looked like a parakeet." Inocencia smirked. Finished with the stew, she
reached across the table for the *dulce*, guavas drowned in a sugary syrup.

Asunción was built on a hill that rose steeply from the Paraguay River.
From afar, the city, with its red-tiled roofs and buff and violet-colored
houses decorated with pilasters and colonnades, its streets lined with
orange trees, looked nearly pretty. However, a lot of the plaster pilasters
and colonnades were crumbling, the streets were unpaved and made of
sand, and, in the winter when it rained, they turned into ravines
through which torrents of water flowed and became impassable. Most
of the city's population lived in miserable mud hovels. There were two
main squares, one was where Franco was building his palace, the other,

Plaza de Gobierno, was where at Christmas and during holidays circuses, fireworks and bullfights were held; it was also next to Town Hall, where congress met occasionally. One of the few two-storied buildings in the city, Town Hall bore two carved medallions on its façade: the one inscribed with the words *República de Paraguay,* under which were crossed branches of *yerba* and tobacco; the other medallion was inscribed with *Paz* and *Justiza.* Town Hall also housed the dungeons. The principal and only marketplace in Asunción was built on a marsh and was flooded most of the year; the women who came in from the country to sell their produce had to hike up their *tupois* not to get them soiled or wet.

When the dictator Don José Gaspar Rodríguez de Francia died at the age of eighty-four, news of his death, Franco told Ella, was kept secret from the people for three whole days, in case the announcement was a ruse.

"How do you mean a ruse?" Ella asked. "A prank?"

"The announcement of his death could have been a test to see who rejoiced and who mourned him," Franco answered. "Francia was obsessed with the idea that everyone wanted to kill him, to murder him. He refused to eat unless someone first tasted the food; when he rode through the streets, people had to go inside their houses, shut the doors and windows, otherwise they were beaten. No one was allowed to look at him, no one was allowed to touch him. To this day, people are still afraid to mention him by name; they refer to him as *El Difunto.*"

"The deceased," Ella said.

"The jails were full of innocent people; he imprisoned and tortured them for no reason, according to his whim. Francia kept Paraguay isolated. No one was allowed to leave or to come into the country. Monsieur Aimé Bonpland, the famous French naturalist who lived in Corrientes, is an example. Francia destroyed all of Bonpland's specimens and experiments, he killed Bonpland's servants and kept Bonpland prisoner for several years before he finally allowed Bonpland to go back to France. Curiously, however, in the end, Bonpland did not want to return to France."

"He liked Paraguay," Ella offered.

"In a way, Paraguay's isolation was not such a bad thing. It made Paraguay self-sufficient. Paraguay had to produce enough food for its people, enough homes, enough clothing. More important, it kept Paraguay out of wars, out of both foreign and domestic wars. It made Paraguay strong."

4 JUNE 1856

Each day I learn a little bit more about this country. I read the other day that one of the first governors of Paraguay was a man named Carlos Morphi, which stands for Murphy—an Irishman! The country is full of surprises and is as unpredictable as Franco! One day Franco is as docile as a child, the next he is as unreasonable as a wild animal. But I have learned to be careful with him and not to show him that I am afraid. He hates people who act timid or frightened, "cowering dogs" he calls them; he has no respect for them. And he does not like people to complain. I have made it a rule never to complain—not about his ignorant sisters, his arrogant brothers, the stupid servants, the flooded dirty streets, the manioc stews, the guava puddings (which I have actually grown to like!), the heat, the flies—*nada*. For him, no matter how I feel, I always—

Pen in hand, Ella paused. She raised her head from her diary and looked at herself in the dressing room mirror. She smiled at her reflection. She was now twenty-one.

"Ella!" Franco was waiting for her. "Come to bed."

Franco kissed Ella's mouth, her neck, he slipped the sleeves of her nightdress from her shoulders.

"Such lovely skin," he said.

Franco liked women and he liked to please them. If he had not drunk too many glasses of brandy, he was an attentive lover. More attentive than the Russian count, Dimitri, Ella had to admit.

While the baby, Juan Francisco, slept, Rosaria, his wet nurse, sat next to him with her lace pillow on her lap and a thick cigar in her mouth. In spite of its rough appearance, the cigar, a brand named *pety-hobi,* was mild and the lace pillow, packed stiff with straw, was filled with straight pins and bobbins made from bone. Wound around the bobbins was a linen thread so pale and fine it was nearly invisible; from time to time the thread broke. Except for those times—and then Rosaria had to stop and make a slipknot in the bobbin thread and hang it over a pin and bring the new thread next to the broken thread and fasten the two together with a half-hitch knot—Rosaria's hands never stopped moving. Her hands went from one pair of bobbins to the next: crossing right, twisting left and crossing right again, as the braid of lace pinned to the pillow lengthened and dropped neatly into a little cloth pouch pinned to Rosaria's skirt at the level of her knees. All the time too, as she made the lace, Rosaria was puffing on her cigar.

Bishop Basilio Lopez, President Carlos Antonio Lopez's brother, refused to baptize Juan Francisco in Asunción's Catedral de la Encarnación or, for that matter, in any church. In addition, Bishop Basilio threatened that any priest who performed the rite of baptism would be excommunicated. Franco appealed to his father, but Carlos Antonio was indifferent to Ella and did not want to get involved in his son's affairs; also he had been influenced by his wife and daughters, who did not want Franco's bastard son to be officially recognized and he sided with Bishop Basilio, his brother. Franco then sought out one of his schoolmates, Padre Fidel Maiz, but Padre Fidel was Inocencia and Rafaela's confessor. Already he had heard enough about Ella.

Father, forgive me for I have sinned, on her knees, Inocencia confessed, *I wished that a tiger might tear her limb from limb.*

Father, forgive me for I have sinned, Rafaela bowed her head and said, *I prayed that a crocodile might devour her.*

Instead of a baptism, to satisfy Ella, Franco commanded a 101-gun salute in honor of his son. The reverberations from the guns were so powerful that they caused several buildings under construction in Asunción to collapse; also one of the imported English field artillery pieces had not been cleaned properly and it backfired. The battery landed on the hospital and killed and injured a large number of the patients in their sickbeds.

Far from satisfied, Ella vowed to seek revenge: *May Inocencia and Rafaela break their stupid necks!*

After Marie's death, Doña Iñes found it harder and harder to pray. The difficulty appeared to be a physical one—something wrong with her mouth, with her tongue. On her knees, Doña Iñes would begin in the usual way, *Hail Mary, full of grace,* but heard herself say instead: *Hell Mary, full of lace.*

In the pocket of her dress, she kept a letter to Marie, written by someone who had answered for her sister, Yvonne. In the letter, Yvonne claimed to envy her sister: the unique opportunities, the adventures, the interesting people she was sure to meet. In an added postscript, Yvonne had asked Marie, please, to be certain to remember in her next letter to describe the taste of every fruit she had eaten in Paraguay. Doña Iñes had neither the heart nor the courage to write back to Yvonne.

Your Holiness—

When his brother died, President Carlos Antonio Lopez, an astute and clever lawyer, who ruled Paraguay efficiently and who usually got

his way, wrote Pope Pius IX in Rome, asking him to name a totally sub-
servient and ineffectual priest, Juan Gregorio Urbieta, as Basilio's suc-
cessor. Pope Pius IX refused and he was so outraged by the request that
he accused Carlos Antonio of not paying the church tithes. The accu-
sation was true, the tithes had not been paid in fifty years! Pope Pius also
wrote Carlos Antonio that the new bishop would not be a man from
Paraguay but a man of his own choosing. Finally, if these conditions were
not met, Pope Pius IX threatened in his letter, *he* would excommunicate
the entire Paraguayan population.

Your Holiness [Carlos Antonio wrote Pope Pius IX again],
    *I am quite confident that your holiness would not deem it necessary to
close the Gates of Heaven to your dutiful and loving Christian children across
the sea. However, should you feel compelled to do so, I am equally confident
that our Great Lord, Merciful and Just as He is, would find the means and
the space to allow His dutiful and loving Christian children across the sea a
bit of room in the Kingdom of Heaven.*

Before he left France, Franco had invited a group of agriculturalists to
colonize and to plant vineyards in the Gran Chaco, the large unmapped
and trackless area of forests, plains and marshes that lay west of the
Paraguay River. The group consisted of a few agronomists, a handful of
viniculturists, but was comprised mainly of displaced farmers and
unemployed laborers. The settlement was to be called Nuevo Burdeos,
in honor of their native Bordeaux. According to the agreement, Franco
was to provide each colonist with a house, as much land as he could cul-
tivate and the necessary provisions for the first eight months in the
Chaco.
    When, after a particularly rough ocean crossing, the two hundred
French colonists and their families finally reached Asunción, they were
treated with great fanfare. Balls and receptions were given in their
honor; Ella invited the entire diplomatic corps, including, of course, the

French envoy, Monsieur Cochelet, and his wife, to a *fête champêtre*—the last good meal, no doubt, the colonists were to enjoy—on the banks of the Paraguay River to celebrate the official opening of Nuevo Burdeos.

At the time of their arrival, the area designated Nuevo Burdeos was completely flooded. For the first three months, the colonists and their families were forced to live up in trees. Later, when the waters from the Río Pilcomayo—the water from the Río Pilcomayo was salty, and because of a juniperlike shrub that grew on its banks, foul—and its tributaries had receded and the burning sun shone day after day without respite, there was no water to be had at all—not a single drop or enough for a bird, one of the colonists complained. To make matters more difficult, there were armies of ants, gnats and flies; there were poisonous snakes, crocodiles, wild pigs, tigers, a whole host of animals none of them had ever heard of or imagined; and far more dangerous still, there were the inhabitants of the Chaco, the fierce, cannibal Guaycurú Indians.

In less than the allotted eight months, most of the colonists had died from heat prostration and starvation. Unfortunately for the remaining, hardier survivors, a worse fate awaited them at the hands and teeth of the savage Guaycurús. Too late, advised of their gruesome end, Monsieur Cochelet, the French envoy, sent Franco several indignant letters on behalf of his government and on behalf of Napoleon III; Franco ignored the letters.

9 OCTOBER 1856

I have hardly seen Franco all week, when I enquired I was told he had to spend time at the *quinta* with his father. By now I know Franco well enough to know that something else besides his father is the matter, although rumor has it that President Lopez is ill. Except for his family, President Lopez refuses to see anyone or go out into society. However he still manages to keep complete rule over the country and he alone is the supreme judge of every single crime and misdemeanor, no matter how petty. A shocking example of this occurred only a few days ago, when a gentleman who is an acquaintance of mine applied for a passport to go to Buenos Ayres and because something to do with the payment for the stamps was not to his liking he got angry and tore up the passport; the poor man was immediately arrested on President Lopez's orders and, without a trial or any sort of hearing, he was shot! To make matters worse, when Franco and I finally had supper together last evening and I described the terrible fate of this poor man, Franco did not appear in the least interested. "*Chéri*, don't you care about justice being done?" I asked as gently as I could. Instead of replying, Franco shouted at me: "Justice! What do you know about justice? And why do you care about this man? Was he your lover?" Then, without finishing his food, Franco stood up and left. I went to the window in time to hear Franco yell to his servant, then yell to his horse and gallop off. But this morning, early, to my great surprise, I woke up to find Franco standing next to my bed. He did not apologize and without a word he handed me a box that contained a necklace of aquamarines—the stones are the size of robins' eggs and the color he claimed matched my eyes! (I did not argue with him but I have always maintained that my eyes are not blue but gray.) "What's this?" I asked. Franco only shrugged and smiled. "It's not my birthday," I told him. "Put it on," he answered. The necklace also serves to confirm my suspicion that Franco must be the one to have a lover. A mistress he keeps in a house in Asunción. However the necklace is beautiful and I shall wear it with pleasure!

Franco took to calling his son Pancho and spent many hours playing with him. In their favorite game Franco got down on his hands and knees on the floor and Pancho climbed on his back and rode him. Pancho wrapped his fat little legs around Franco's sides and kicked his father in the ribs with his heels to make him crawl faster. Sometimes Pancho carried a little whip with which he hit Franco and then Franco would shake his head and neigh and rise up on his knees as if rearing while Pancho hung on to his father's neck and screamed half in fear. Hearing the commotion, Ella would come into the room and try to caution Franco, "Not so rough, *chéri*," or "Careful, *chéri,* you might hurt him," but Franco always waved Ella away as, laughing, he once more circled the room on his hands and knees, his little son clinging to his back like a monkey.

"*Profesor,* would you like something to drink?" Forcing herself to be attentive, Inocencia asked. Inocencia called Dr. Eberhardt *Profesor.*

Inocencia had to shout, "Tea? *Profesor?*"

Dr. Eberhardt was old and deaf, Dr. Eberhardt was also absent-minded. According to Inocencia, if she was not there to remind him, he would forget completely that it was teatime.

"Perhaps, I can bring you a little *dulce, Profesor?*" Inocencia had to yell.

Dr. Eberhardt had arrived in Paraguay years ago—how many years exactly he had forgotten—to work with Monsieur Aimé Bonpland in Corrientes. However, the two naturalists had disagreed. The disagreement occurred over a plant—Dr. Eberhardt could still recall exactly what the plant looked like, with its two sets of three leaves, its small thorns along the stem, its pink flower—that Monsieur Bonpland insisted was part of the mimosa family while Dr. Eberhardt claimed the plant was clover. Young and stubborn, the two men had come to blows over the specimen, and Dr. Eberhardt had left Corrientes with a split lip. Soon after, his interest had shifted from plants to birds. Twice a week now, he spent the afternoon inside Inocencia's aviary. He sat at a small table while parrots of different sizes and colors—green, red, blue, yellow—flapped all around him. The parrots were tame and unafraid—also, their wings were clipped and they could not fly. Several parrots were perched on Dr. Eberhardt's shoulders; one parrot—always the same little mean green one—flew straight to the top of his bald head and stayed there. Another parrot, by far the largest bird in the aviary and Dr. Eberhardt's favorite, a hyacinth macaw whose brilliant blue feathers never ceased to amaze and delight him, clung to the back of his chair and talked to him: *kráa! kráa!*, as still another parrot mimicked his mistress and, at intervals, screamed: *Tea? Profesor, tea?* All afternoon Dr. Eberhardt sat quietly; carefully and patiently he examined and classified each of Inocencia's birds, neatly filling page after page in his notebook:

> *Psittacus passerinus*—green; blue tail-coverts in male; blue wing-spot five inches long; blue under-wings; short tail.
>
> *Psittacus virescens*—green; yellow wing-spot; longish tail.
>
> *Psittacus mitratus*—green; orange-red on the top of head and forehead; blue under-wings, and blue tip to tail; shortish tail. The female has not the head red.
>
> *Psittacus cotoro*—green; dirty gray forehead and breast; bluish wing-quills; long tail, bluish near tip.
>
> *Psittacus aureus*—green; black head; dark black-blue wing-spot and quill ends; tail long, black beneath, bluish above; scarlet thighs, bluish breast.

When Inocencia brought him the plate of *dulce* and set it down next to his elbow, he was so absorbed in his work that he did not notice. Squawking and beating their wings, several parrots—including the mean one, who temporarily left his perch on top of Dr. Eberhardt's head—vied with one another and grabbed the *dulce* from the plate and ate it.

> *Psittacus menstruus*—green; head mottled with dark inky-blue; the edges of the feathers so tinted; breast inky-blue; under tail-coverts bright crimson.
>
> *Psittacus militaris*—green; forehead with orange-red spots; head inky bluish-green, shading off to green; dull red patch on belly; wing-quills and upper of tail blue; lower mandible very deep.

X

Often Ella rode Mathilde out alone. At the slightest pressure from Ella's knees, the mare broke into a smooth canter; if Ella applied a little more pressure, her canter quickened into a gallop. Likewise a light tug on the reins made the mare turn or stop so quickly that if Ella's seat had not been so secure she might have fallen off. And Ella was not afraid: the country farmers recognized her. If ever she needed anything, Ella only had to stop at a house and call out, *"Ave Maria,"* and invariably someone in the house called back, *"Sin pecado"* to which Ella answered, *"Por siempre"* and she was invited in, *"Adelante, Señora."* Always she was given a glass of orange juice and a cigar; Ella drank the orange juice and, not to appear rude, she took the cigar but did not smoke it. Back on the mare, either she threw the cigar in the bushes or she put it in the pocket of her riding jacket to give later to Rosaria. Then, off at a trot, Ella urged Mathilde, faster, "Let us go, my darling." Faster and faster they galloped through fields so green and vast there was no longer any need to dream of Ireland.

In addition to being a good dancer, Franco was musical and he had a good ear. He spoke fluent Spanish, French, English and Guaraní. Ella spoke fluent French, English and near fluent Spanish; she was learning Guaraní. But Guaraní was a difficult language and Ella had a hard time wrapping her tongue around the strange-sounding syllables and vowels. She was learning to speak in simple sentences to Rosaria and to her servants and, in turn, to understand, but the more complicated sentences eluded her. When, in bed, one night, Franco, in his passion, said to her, *"Nde pûgwéûghpe capüpécha, ndepópe rosa potricha"* Ella had to coax him to say it again later—more slowly. The moment had passed, Franco was less inclined to repeat himself. *"Nde pûgwéûghpe capüpécha, ndepópe rosa potricha."* Still Ella did not understand that Franco had said, "I am under your feet like the grass, and in your hand like a rose."

Six

OBISPO CUE

Ella's second child, Corinna Adelaida, named after Ella's sister and mother both, died five months after she was born. Rosaria found her lying on her stomach in the crib in exactly the same position she had left her the night before. Always a healthy and lively baby, Corinna Adelaida had showed no sign of illness or distress or why all of a sudden she had stopped breathing. Grief-stricken and in shock, Ella rocked Corinna Adelaida back and forth in her arms and tried in vain to bring her back to life.

"My lovely girl. My little beauty," Ella repeated through her tears as she stroked the baby's head. Already, Corinna Adelaida had a full head of dark curly hair.

When Franco tried to comfort Ella by taking her in his arms and promising her another child, Ella shook herself free of him and held the baby more tightly to her chest. It was only after night had fallen and after rigor mortis had set in that Ella finally consented to give the dead baby up.

Wearing a lace cap and a long white frock to which Ella attached lace wings—Rosaria had made the cap and wings—Corinna Adelaida was buried in the cemetery at La Recoleta. Lines from Coleridge's verse—one line was misquoted, and the engraver, unfamiliar with English, incised *made it beossom* instead of *bade it blossom*—were engraved on her tombstone:

> *Ere sin could blight or sorrow fade*
> *Death came with friendly care*
> *The lovely bird to Heaven conveyed*
> *And made it beossom there.*

Constructed according to her own design, Obispo Cue, Ella's pink palace, was one of the few buildings in Paraguay to have two stories— Town Hall was another—and the first to be made out of marble, instead of the usual mud brick. It was built by Alonzo Taylor, an English stonemason from Chelsea. During the entire building period, which lasted longer than it should have, Alonzo Taylor always spoke highly of Ella—Ella, he claimed, was gracious and polite. Even when the work on the pink palace was slow and seemed to be endlessly delayed by the weather or, more often, by the workers' ineptitude, she never lost her temper at him. She always addressed him politely and began her sentences to him with: "Mr. Taylor, if you would be so kind as to . . ."

Alonzo Taylor had signed up to serve Franco for three years and to teach the native Paraguayans his trade. He was a tall, affable man and he considered himself lucky to be in Paraguay, the pay was good and the work not too demanding. Already he had built himself a house, with a fireplace and a chimney, and as soon as he was completely settled he was planning to bring his wife and two daughters over from England to join him. Meanwhile, he and the other Englishmen—there were a large number of foreigners in Franco's employ: engineers, doctors, mapmakers, soldiers, chemists, shipyard workers and, like Alonzo, stonemasons—got together in the evenings, to drink *caña,* the local liquor, dance, sing and flirt with the girls. Dolores was the name of the girl Alonzo liked in particular. Dolores was of mixed blood—Spanish and Guaraní; she was nearly as tall as Alonzo. She was lively and she sang songs to him in both languages:

Tovena Tupa~tachepytyvo~	*Una noche tiia nos conocimos*
ha'emi hag~ua che py'arasy,	*junto al agua azul de Ypakarai*
ymaiteguivema an~andu	*Tu cantabas triste por el camino*
heta ara nachmongevei	*Viejas melodias en guarani.*

But best of all, in Alonzo's view, Dolores did not squeeze her eyes shut and look disgusted—the way Alonzo's English wife did—when Alonzo put himself inside her mouth.

26 JANUARY 1858

I crave oranges. I eat at least half a dozen a day! The Paraguayan orange most resembles the Seville orange in taste, it is small and slightly acidic and it neither cloys the palate nor sets one's teeth on edge, which is particularly welcome in this climate and in my condition! (Dr. Kennedy says that the juice is antiseptic, antibilious and hemostatic—my word, all those excellent things!) I should speak to the gardener about planting some at Obispo Cue—didn't the new chemist, Dr. Mora, tell Franco that orange trees have considerable tolerance to adverse conditions, to drought or to too much moisture, and that they adapt to a wide range of soils? I have not yet told Franco that I am pregnant again and he has not noticed. I still go riding every day although Dr. Kennedy says not to. My chief complaint is of another sort entirely—the lack of female companionship. Madame Cochelet, Mrs. Washburn and the other diplomats' wives think themselves superior and snub me. Arrogant bitches! As for Inocencia and Rafaela, the less said about those two fat, ignorant women the better! Last night I dreamt that my little Corinna Adelaida, looking so pretty dressed in her lace cap and white dress, stretched out her little arms to me, but when I leaned down to pick her up, she was gone. My little angel! And poor Marie—I think of her as well. Thank God for the colonel!

Colonel Enrique von Wisner de Morgenstern was a Hungarian engineer and Carlos Antonio Lopez's military advisor. He claimed to be fifty but he was older (he dyed his hair, beard and moustache a light brown). He made no secret of the fact that he had been forced to flee the court in Budapest because of a scandal and although the scandal he alluded to—the death threat of a cuckold husband vowing revenge— was in fact sexual, Colonel von Wisner, everyone knew, preferred young men. The colonel was elegant, well educated and clever; he fenced, he danced, he played chess; he was not a threat to Franco. He became friendly with Ella.

"Be patient, Madame," Colonel von Wisner advised her about her lack of friends.

"Will you teach me how to fence?" Ella answered.

"His house on the corner of the Market Plaza seems quite spacious and is painted yellow according to the current style. The drawing room furniture would be perfect in Paris. Lopez has gilded furniture, silk curtains, chiffoniers and cabinets of exquisite workmanship inlaid with ivory, mirrors in Florentine frames, paintings of distinction, rare bronzes and porcelains. His is the residence of a well-traveled man with a taste for good living . . ." was how Héctor Varela, a journalist from Buenos Ayres and a frequent contributor to the Paraguayan newspaper, *El Semanario,* described Franco's house. The house—Varela was probably unaware of this—was directly connected to Obispo Cue by a road built especially; at a gallop, Franco could be with Ella in twenty minutes.

But while his father ruled the country, Franco was discreet. He stayed clear of family gossip and social scandals. With his brothers, Venancio and Benigno, he was neutral and businesslike; with Inocencia and Rafaela, his sisters, he was distant and polite. Regularly on Sundays, he dined with his mother and father at their *quinta*; they discussed the harvest of *yerba* and tobacco, the breeding of cattle. Despite Franco's stylish European clothes, his embroidered linen shirts, his hand-tooled leather boots with the heavy silver spurs, he went out of his way—he got off his horse, shook hands, traded jokes—to show that he was one of the people. The Guaraní people, not the rich, superior Spanish people; and Ella's name never came up.

Instead the names on everyone's tongue in Asunción, that year, were those of Carlos and Fernando Saguier, two handsome and wealthy brothers of Spanish descent who were part of the small aristocracy in Paraguay, which did not include the Lopez family but whom they of course knew—Carlos, the older brother, had gone to France with Franco. Rafaela and Inocencia also could not stop talking about them.

"Carlos and Fernando sent their millions to Argentina," Inocencia said. The sisters were eating again.

"To a bank in Buenos Ayres," Rafaela added, reaching for more *sopa paraguaya*.

It was true that in order to secure their considerable fortune, which was based on an export business licensed to sell *yerba* and other local products abroad, Carlos and Fernando made huge deposits to a bank in Buenos Ayres; in addition, when the Brazilian Navigation Company, which operated the steamship line between Montevideo and Matto Grosso, offered Carlos and Fernando a contract to supply the boats that stopped to refuel with coal at Asunción, they sought and got the approval of President Lopez (a Paraguayan citizen could not enter into a contract with a foreigner without government permission); then the two brothers went a step further. In secret they negotiated with an Englishman named William Atherton and sold him their business assets in Paraguay; next, wasting no time, they applied for passports and left the country.

"Carlos and Fernando said they wanted to go to Buenos Ayres to dance at the carnival. Liars! Traitors!" Her mouth full of food, Inocencia spat out.

Once Carlos and Fernando were gone, William Atherton had announced that he was the new owner of their properties. Immediately Franco, acting on behalf of his father, had him arrested and put in prison. William Atherton appealed to the British Consulate; outraged, the foreigners in Paraguay complained to President Lopez directly. The president was unwell, he did not want to be disturbed by scheming businessmen, and his son, Franco, was more than ready to teach the haughty Spaniards a lesson. "I don't give a damn if that fool William Atherton rots in jail," Franco was supposed to have shouted to an aide. "As for Carlos and Fernando, if ever they dare show their arrogant faces in this country—"

"Death is too good for the Saguier brothers," Rafaela said, agreeing with her sister. Despite their show of outrage, both Inocencia and Rafaela were delighted. They felt their brother's action was justified— and foreigners were not to be trusted. William Atherton had got what he deserved.

In August, Ella gave birth to a second son, Enrique Venancio—named after her new friend, the colonel. Enrique's birth was long and difficult and Dr. Henry Kennedy, who was away tending to a sick farmer in the country or-so-he-said, arrived only after Rosaria delivered the baby. At the last moment, Rosaria had reached inside Ella's womb with her hand and turned the baby around. Dr. Kennedy arrived in time to give his hand—the hand, he noticed, was shaking again—to Doña Iñes, who was on her knees, outside Ella's bedroom, and help her back on her own unsteady feet.

2 AUGUST 1858

Everyone says how one forgets the pain of childbirth but I swear on the head of little Enrique himself that I will not forget. The closest I can come to describing it is two huge horses setting their enormous weight on my belly and pulling me asunder—

Exhausted, Ella briefly noted in her diary that night.

Outside the rain fell in sheets, the road from Obispo Cue to Asunción would soon be a slippery river of mud. Every few seconds the sky was illuminated by a flash of lightning, the accompanying roll of thunder was almost continuous. Ella's bedroom was damp and moldy and the smell of ozone filled the air; Ella shut her eyes and tried to sleep.

"Fencing," Colonel von Wisner explained to Ella, "is chess with muscles. Like chess, fencing has a limited number of moves and an almost infinite number of combinations."

"Foil, epée or sabre?" At the start of the lesson, the colonel had asked her.

"Sabre."

With the foil and epée, Ella could score with the point; since the sabre has a point and two cutting edges (the full length of the blade on one side, a third the length of the blade on the other) Ella could score by both thrusting and cutting.

"Stand in first position with your heels together and your right foot pointing toward your opponent." The colonel demonstrated for Ella. "From first position, move your back foot eighteen inches and bend your knees. Your weight should be evenly distributed on each foot— pretend you are sitting on a stool. Raise both your arms, your fighting hand should be about chest high, the other hand slightly higher, elbows are pointing downward—" The colonel adjusted Ella's elbow slightly. "Hold your sabre hand flat, palm upward, your wrist should be like this. Now you are in what is called the second stance: guarding/inviting Sixte. If you move your sabre hand to the height of your elbow, you are in guarding/inviting Octave."

Slender, coordinated, with strong thighs from horseback riding, Ella learned the basic moves of fencing quickly. Fifty times a day, her arms folded behind her back, she practiced advancing, retreating, lunging, recovering, hopping forward and hopping backward, advance-lunging, retreat-lunging, hop-lunging and appel-lunging—tapping the ball of her foot on the floor so that the lunge was done in two parts.

Only one thing troubled Colonel von Wisner: Ella fought left-handed.

ASUNCIÓN
12 June 1859

Ma chère Princesse,

At long last my beautiful new house is completed and I am happily settled. How I wish you could see the fruits of my labor: the mirrors, the wall hangings, the furnishings, the fabrics, the wall clocks; I saw to every detail and you cannot imagine some of the difficulties I encountered. The workers—mere children some of them!—were neither experienced nor skilled but they tried nevertheless to follow my instructions (a case in point was my bedroom, which had to be repainted three times before the proper color, the palest of pinks imaginable, was found!). How I wish, dear friend, you were not so far away and we could exchange ideas on decoration and painting and gardening (Dr. Mora, a Chilean gentleman of my acquaintance, is assisting me with the garden) and I could benefit more easily from your good taste—could you perhaps send me a picture of Saint-Gratien?

Lately Franco has been very occupied with matters of state since his father has not been in good health and much of the burden of governing has fallen

onto Franco's shoulders. Also, to much popular acclaim, Franco was able to
mediate a peace in the Argentine between the two warring factions of General
Mitre and General Urquiza—names probably not so familiar to you.
Afterward, a Te Deum was celebrated in Buenos Ayres in Franco's honor,
banquets were held and a military march was renamed for him. In addition,
Franco is engaged in many important projects of his own: railroads, a telegraph
system, several new municipal buildings; one project that might be of interest
to you involves the colonization of the Gran Chaco, the area across the
Paraguay River from us. Although rich in many resources, the area is not yet
populated or well cultivated and Franco's goal is to encourage farmers from
France to colonize and plant vineyards there. Thus, we too will be able to
produce our own wine.

I was much amused by your description in your last letter of the Duchess
of Alba's costume ball and of you dressed as a Nubian woman. How I wish I
could have seen you with a blue tattoo painted on your forehead! No wonder,
dear friend, you caused a sensation and I would certainly have agreed with M.
Mérimée on the subject of your authenticity! Here as well, the ladies of
Asunción enjoy going to balls. (Some of them last several days!) The most
recent ball I attended was held at the quinta of Doña Eusebia Fernandez, a
Paraguayan lady, and was in honor of her niece. The dancing, which began at
sunset, lasted long into the next day, and, except for once at around midnight
when supper and refreshments were served, never ceased. The orchestra
consisted of half a dozen musicians with harps and guitars who performed
mostly popular Spanish dances—the montenero, the media caña and a very
odd dance indeed called pishèshèshè in which the right foot of the dancer is
dragged across the floor making the sound the name of the dance implies.
According to the custom of the country, and this will amuse you! everyone
dances barefoot.

In addition to horseback riding every day, I have taken up fencing lessons
as a form of exercise; my teacher is a most distinguished and charming
Hungarian colonel who is Franco's father's military advisor. The diplomatic
community is quite large and varied and my acquaintances include the French
minister's wife, Madame Cochelet, and Mrs. Washburn, the American

minister's wife; we meet often to exchange our views on literature and the arts.
We are very much looking forward to the opening night of our Teatro
Nacional—the building is nearly completed—modeled on La Scala, and the
performances by the well-known Argentine artists Señor Bermejo and Doña
Pura. I promise to give you a full account of the evening!

Meanwhile, my children, Pancho and Enrique, are very well indeed and I
am expecting another child (I pray it is a girl!) early in the new year.

With my most affectionate good wishes, I remain your devoted friend,
Ella

P.S. Looking back at your letters, I see that I neglected to write how sorry
I was to hear the news of the one little parrot not surviving the journey. As
soon as I am able I will send you a new mate for the other—however, you did
not indicate whether it was the male or the female parrot who died. Parrots are
said to live as long as we humans do!

Ella was right, Franco kept another woman in a house in Asunción. In
fact, he kept a succession of women, women with names like Juañita and
Carmelita, names Franco promptly forgot. Was Carmelita the tall one
who had sat on his face and Juañita the one who had knelt on the floor
in between his legs? Nor did the women seem to mind what Franco
called them; they giggled. If Franco had had to give a reason for the
women, he would have said that Ella was always pregnant or pregnant
a lot of the time. Another reason, a more truthful one, was that the
women were a physical need, like eating or drinking or going to the toilet—Franco would only admit to the last crude comparison after several glasses of brandy. Women like Juañita and Carmelita did not matter
to him. Rarely did he talk or make any conversation, he was not interested. If one of the women tried to tell Franco some fact about herself
or her life—about how for instance Carmelita had a little brother who
was ill or how Juañita started to tell him that she was born a twin but

unfortunately the twin had—Franco right away cut her off and told her to be quiet unless she wanted to leave. Also he paid the women and, to him, it was like a business transaction.

Federico Noel was born in 1860, Carlos Honorio was born a year later, and Rosaria had her hands full. And she did not have enough milk. To help her, Ella hired a girl from Villa Franca named Maria Oliva.

"Are you married?" Ella asked. Something about the girl seemed familiar but Ella could not remember what.

"Yes," Maria Oliva lied.

"And you have children?"

"Yes." Maria Oliva was telling the truth, in part.

"Are you married?" Rosaria had also asked Maria Oliva the same question.

"Do you have children?" Only Rosaria had asked the questions in a different tone of voice.

"On the opening night of the Teatro Nacional, the high society of Asunción attended. In the box of honor, the broad-faced and corpulent dictator sat with his wife and two daughters. In the next box sat General Francisco Lopez and Colonel Venancio Lopez, sons of the dictator," the Argentine journalist Héctor Varela was again there to report. "Madame Lynch was seated in the center box, gorgeously dressed and displaying many jewels. The gentlemen all watched her with definitely respectful admiration. The ladies gave her hostile looks, the meaning of which was perfectly obvious."

Varela continued:

President Lopez is a really imposing figure. One rarely sees a more impressive sight than this great tidal wave of human flesh. During the entire performance, the president ostentatiously wore an enormous hat, quite appropriate to him and equally suitable either for a museum of curiosities or for the Buenos Ayres carnival.

During the evening, which seemed an eternity, I watched Lopez for a sign of any impression produced upon him witnessing a play for the first time in his life. It was like watching a stone in the field. He is the master in the art of concealing emotions. At the end of the tedious proceedings, without any display of either approval or disapproval, the old monarch of the jungles glared momentarily at Madame Lynch and, with great difficulty, rose and left, ponderously followed by his wife, his daughters and the soldiers of the Praetorian Guard.

The performance of the players can be dismissed with a line. It was as ludicrous as Lopez's hat.

That evening, Ella noted in her diary, in perfect agreement with Héctor Varela:

The play was ludicrous and vulgar, and no wonder it appealed so to Inocencia and Rafaela. Frankly, I had to keep myself from laughing out loud. And never in my life have I seen such a silly sight as Doña Pura playing a maiden in love with a lion cub (the lion cub played by no other than her husband, Señor Bermejo!) I noticed that Mr. Varela, the handsome Argentine journalist, was busily taking notes. No need to ask what he wrote—shortly he will be here for supper.

At supper, instead of discussing the play, Franco discussed the situation of the Argentine Confederation: how through his own intervention, a few years earlier, he had brought the civil war there to an end; how he had persuaded Justo José de Urquiza to retire as president and let Bartolomé Mitre become governor of Buenos Ayres.

"You brought both stability and peace to the region," Héctor Varela, a diplomat as well as a journalist, told Franco.

"Doña Pura in her role as a Paraguayan maiden could stand to lose a few kilos," Ella tried to change the subject.

"A distinct political victory," Héctor Varela also said.

"Not only should Doña Pura lose a few kilos, she should learn how to act," Ella said.

Later, Héctor Varela could not conceal his admiration for Ella: "She was tall," he wrote in his journal, "and of a flexible and delicate figure with beautiful and seductive curves. Her skin was alabaster." Perhaps he was a bit in love with Ella himself and could not help exaggerating a little: "Her eyes were of a blue that seemed borrowed from the very hues of heaven and had an expression of ineffable sweetness in whose depths the light of Cupid was enthroned. Her beautiful lips were indescribably expressive of the voluptuous, moistened by an ethereal dew that God must have provided to lull the fires within her, a mouth that was like a cup of delight at the banquet table of ardent passion." Even the smallest detail about Ella did not escape his attention: "Her hands were small with long fingers, the nails perfectly formed and delicately polished."

A lie, Doña Iñes knew, was a mortal sin; she wrote anyway:

Dear Yvonne,

Do not worry about me, I am happy and well. Since I last wrote you I have married a ranchero, his name is—

Pen in hand, Doña Iñes paused. She was not good at making up names, then she remembered the priest, Padre Fidel Maiz.

Fidel. We have a very nice house with a garden and I grow vegetables and flowers. In summer, instead of a bed we sleep in a hammock as it is cooler. Fidel is very strong and handsome; when he is finished with his work in the evening he takes me out horseback riding. I sit in the saddle in front of him and he holds me tightly so I am not frightened as we gallop across the fields to inspect the cattle. Every night for dinner we eat beef and corn and a bread I bake myself called chipa; *afterward, if the evening is fine, we sit outside and I look at the stars while Fidel plays songs on his harp for me. If we have a child and it is a girl, I will name her Yvonne, after you.*

> *Your loving sister,*
> *Marie.*

P.S. You asked me to describe the fruit in Paraguay. The oranges and pomegranates are my favorites!

On September 10, 1862, Dr. William Stewart, Carlos Lopez's personal physician, held the president's wrist and studied the steady progress of the second hand of his pocket watch, while the president, a mountain of flesh, lay on his bed breathing his last rattling breaths. His eyes shut, his face the color of putty, Carlos Lopez's heavy head was supported by his favorite son, Benigno. Sitting next to the bed, his wife, Doña Juaña Carillo Lopez, sobbed uncontrollably while, standing behind her chair, Venancio, Carlos Lopez's middle son, shifted his weight nervously from one foot to the other. In the street, a dog could be heard barking and the priest, Padre Fidel Maiz, moved closer to the foot of the president's bed and raised his voice louder in prayer; looking up at him, Inocencia and Rafaela, Carlos Lopez's two daughters, murmured back the responses. The dog continued his frantic barking until someone was heard to shout, "*Zorra!,*" and then that person must have either thrown a stone or kicked the dog because the dog could be heard yelping. Franco was the last to arrive; he walked into the room at the exact moment that his father died.

In her pink palace, Obispo Cue, in her palest of pinks imaginable—painted room, Ella was lying in bed as well; she was giving birth to her fifth son, Leopoldo Antonio. This time it was a bright sunny day and her labor was short. In between contractions, Ella could hear the bells tolling.

Seven

LAKE IPACARAÌ

January 1, 1863

General,

I have been touched by your personal letter and its warm recollections of your visit to My Imperial Court. Believe me, I assure you, that I too remember them with pleasure. I have had occasion to appreciate your noble qualities which do you honor and therefore it is with that knowledge that I congratulate your country in electing you to safeguard her destiny.

It has filled me with great pleasure to look with admiration at the remarkable progress which Paraguay made under the rule of your illustrious father, may he rest in peace, and I have no doubt that under your wise and patriotic direction, your country will continue her progress along the path of civilization.

In expressing my cordial best wishes for your personal happiness and for the dignity of your office, it pleases me to offer you my personal esteem. Insofar as I can, I pray to Almighty God to bless and preserve you.

Given by my hand in the Palace of the Tuileries,

Your good friend,

NAPOLEON

Franco was unanimously elected Gefe Supremo y General de los Exercitos de la República del Paraguay by the ninety-two deputies who were too afraid to speak out or to vote against him. His first official act was to put his younger brother, Don Benigno Lopez, along with Padre Fidel Maiz and Chief Justice Pedro Lescano, on trial for conspiring against him. Padre Maiz was sent to prison; Chief Justice Lescano was tortured to death; and Benigno, the one who fared best among them, was banished to his *estancia* in the north.

Benigno's mother, Doña Juaña, tried to intervene on his behalf. "On my knees," she begged Franco. "Please. Show your own flesh and blood a little compassion." She started to weep. "Benigno is not strong like you. His health has always been poor. He suffers from affections of the lungs. Up north, the dampness will surely—"

"Enough," Franco told his mother.

"Wait, Franco, I pray you." Doña Juaña joined her hands together and continued to plead. "Since you were small boys, Benigno has always looked up to you—not only because you were older—but don't you remember the day you and Benigno were swimming in the river and the current was so strong that if you had not swum after poor Benigno and pulled him in, he would have—"

"Bah, enough of these lies! You know perfectly well I don't know how to swim," Franco said, turning away from his mother.

"Franco, may you—" Doña Juaña started to call out but she changed her mind. She could not bring herself to put a curse on her eldest son.

On the way to his exile at his *estancia* in San Pedro, in the carriage, loaded with trunks and all of his belongings, bumping and swaying along roads that were no more than dirt tracks and that threw up so much dust, making Benigno cough so hard he thought he would cough up his lungs, Benigno blamed Ella.

5 JANUARY 1863

How fortunate I am to have three ladies-in-waiting! Señora Juliana Echegaray de Martinez, Doña Dolores Carisimo de Jovellanos and Doña Isidora Diaz. My favorite, Señora Juliana, is the prettiest and the kindest; every morning when she comes into my room she has something sweet to say: "Señora, do you hear the birds singing this morning? They are singing just for you!" or "Do you see the beautiful flowers in the garden? They are blooming only to please you, Señora!" She is also the most outspoken by far—she is not afraid to make fun of certain people, like those two ignoramuses, Inocencia and Rafaela. Also, the way she laughs reminds me a little of Marie. Poor Marie! How I wish she was here still! Doña Dolores is lazy and too fat and Doña Isidora is sweet but absentminded. This morning, after my bath, Doña Isidora forgot to put out my shoes and when I pointed this out to her, she blushed and ran off; when she returned she brought two mismatched shoes: a green shoe in one hand and a blue shoe in the other! But enough about my shoes! Franco has never been happier. His dream of ruling the country has come true. (I must, however, try to persuade him to lose weight. Also, to drink less!)

At Obispo Cue, to celebrate, the banquet table was set for the guests with a dazzling white embroidered Belgian linen cloth and gleaming silverware; fine French wines were poured into Baccarat glasses and a ten-course meal was served on Ella's Limoges china; huge bouquets of orange blossoms decorated the room and sweetened the air with their scent. Dressed in white satin—the waist of her gown squeezed tight (only a few months since she had given birth to Leopoldo Antonio)—the aquamarine necklace sparkling at her throat, Ella presided. On her right, Franco looked elegant in evening clothes, also squeezed tight, with the presidential tricolor sash spread across his chest; on Ella's left sat Franco's brother Venancio.

Vincente Barrios, Inocencia's loud-mouthed husband, and greedy and opportunistic Saturnino Bedoya, Rafaela's husband, were there; so were the vice president, old and feeble Señor Sanchez; Antonio Estigarribia, arrogant and by far the handsomest man in the room; Wenceslao Robles, Mariano Gonzales, and the well-meaning but foolish Gumesmindo Benítez, editor of *El Semanario;* also invited were a number of foreigners, including: Colonel von Wisner, dressed in his Hungarian hussar uniform; Mr. Frederick Masterman, an Englishman, recently hired by Franco to be apothecary general to the Paraguayan Army and the British minister, Edward Thornton (hard to know Englishmen, Ella warned Franco, always polite, always condescending); Monsieur Cochelet, the French minister, and his wife; a new engineer, Lieutenant-Major George Thompson—less than a month since he had arrived in Asunción and already it was reported he was complaining about the heat, the food, the dirty streets; sitting next to Lieutenant-Major Thompson, the American, Charles Washburn, and his wife, whom Ella disliked; and, finally, at the other end of the table, Baron von Fischer-Truenfeld, a Prussian, who had a long dueling scar across one cheek and hair so blond it looked white, and who was Franco's newly appointed director of telegraphs and communications.

"*Votre robe est très belle, Madame,*" Ella complimented Madame Cochelet.

"Next to Asunción, London is my favorite city," she said to Mr. Thornton.

"*Los articulos publicados en su peridiodico por el Señor Varela me parecen muy interesantes,*" Ella spoke to Gumesmindo Benítez.

"Presently I am reading *The Last of the Mohicans,* a most edifying book about your country," she told Charles Washburn.

After dinner, Ella and Franco led the way into the next room; all but Inocencia and Rafaela followed. (To better enjoy their meal, Franco's sisters had kicked off their shoes; now, in the rush and confusion of everyone getting up, they could not find them. In the end, Vincente Barrios, Inocencia's husband, had to crawl under the table and get the shoes while Rafaela's husband, Saturnino Bedoya, stood by cursing his wife under his breath.)

Uno, dos, tres, uno, dos, tres, Franco began the dancing; despite his having gained weight, he was quick and agile. He twirled Ella so fast she had to hold him tightly to keep in step. The orchestra had learned to play Johann Strauss's "Loreley-Rhein-Klänge"—and when was the last time she had waltzed? Many years ago with Dimitri, whose face she could barely recall. Smiling, Ella spun around the room faster, the aquamarine necklace catching and reflecting the festive candlelight.

Edward Thornton never once took his eyes off Ella during the dinner. Later, when he got home to the one-story house he shared with Frederick Masterman, he could hardly wait to begin a letter to Lord Russell, the head of the British Foreign Office. "The Paraguayan Pompadour is the name I am obliged to assign to an Englishwoman calling herself Mrs. Lynch, who possesses considerable influence with the President." Half-asleep, his houseboy stood behind him ineffectually waving a palm leaf to ward off the flies. "Her orders, which are given imperiously, are obeyed as implicitly and with as much servility as those of His Excellency himself."

At the same time, in the adjoining room, Frederick Masterman, who likewise had stared at Ella all evening, was writing in his journal: "She is a tall and remarkably handsome woman, and I can well believe the story that when she landed in Asunción the simple natives thought her charms were of more than earthly brilliancy, and her dress so sumptuous that they had no words to express the admiration they both excited. She has received a showy education, speaks English, French and Spanish with equal facility, gives capital dinner parties and can drink more champagne without being affected by it than any one I have ever met with."

On a Saturday evening, in late April, Dr. Henry Kennedy, his young servant, Antanasio, and their guide set out—Dr. Kennedy had obtained a five-day leave of absence from Asunción in order to see more of the country before returning to North America. All night, under a full moon, the three men rode in companionable silence through fields of green and pink manioc leaves; in the morning they stopped at the town of Ituguà for refreshments—in addition to orange juice, Dr. Kennedy drank several glasses of *caña*—then they changed horses and rode on. Their next stop was harder to reach. The road had washed away and they had to make their way through dense woods in the bed of a stream. The stream was rapid and narrow and they had to ride single file; sometimes the water rose up to men's knees while, overhead, the branches from the trees—tall *cedros* and *lapachos* whose trunks were covered with climbers—hung down so that they had to keep their heads low, along their horses' necks. Dr. Kennedy kept falling asleep and his body lurched from one side to the other in his saddle and his servant had to stay attentive and quickly kick his horse forward, abreast of Dr. Kennedy's, and either push or pull Dr. Kennedy upright again; each time Antanasio did, Dr. Kennedy mumbled something and tried to grab Antanasio's arm.

On the third day, they crossed the Cordillera Azcurra and reached Lake Ipacaraì. Lake Ipacaraì, the guide told Dr. Kennedy, was where the Jesuit missionaries were said to have planted the first Cross in Paraguay. According to the legend, the guide said, the site of the lake was once a village full of lazy, thieving Indians who preferred to remain heathens and refused to be converted, so that eventually the Jesuits had to go. However, on the very night the Jesuits left the village, the single well, and the only source of water for the Indians, overflowed. There was no stopping the water; the water kept flowing, faster and faster, spreading everywhere, flooding the roads, the fields, flooding the village and the houses, and drowning all the lazy, thieving Indians who were sleeping in their hammocks—all the Indians, that is, but one. The one Indian who was saved had given a loaf of *chipa* to the half-starving Jesuits and his parrot woke him up screaming: *Terri-ho! Terri-ho!* (Begone! Begone!), warning him in time to leave for higher ground.

"And is Lake Ipacaraì still rising?" Dr. Kennedy was laughing.

The guide crossed himself. "No, *Señor,* the Jesuits came back and sprinkled the ground with holy water to stop it."

That night the three men camped out on the shore of the lake. After they had eaten supper, the guide played the guitar and sang:

> *Ay Cielo! ay Cielo! esto cruel amor,*
> *Es mia, es mia, Cielo estoy feliz!*

Dr. Kennedy stamped his feet and hummed in time to the music, he drank *caña* straight from the bottle. A few feet away, Antanasio lay on his back looking up at the stars and smoking a cigar.

"Antanasio, dear boy! Come sit here, by me!" Dr. Kennedy patted the ground next to him.

Antanasio puffed on his cigar, he did not reply.

"Do you hear me, Antanasio? Or have you gone deaf all of a sudden?" Dr. Kennedy took another drink from the bottle of *caña.* "Or perhaps you'd like to try some of this?" Dr. Kennedy waved the bottle in Antanasio's direction, spilling some of it.

"Antanasio, my *querido.*" Dr. Kennedy giggled and slid himself closer to Antanasio. "I order you to sit next to me."

Antanasio moved farther away.

When the time came to go to bed, Antanasio had to help Dr. Kennedy into his hammock; only first, Dr. Kennedy said, he had to pee. Dr. Kennedy was so unsteady on his feet that Antanasio had to hold on to him while he opened his pants and pulled out his penis.

"Wait! Wait, Antanasio!" Dr. Kennedy called out to him. "Don't be in such a hurry, I want to take a piss in the lake. In the goddamn holy lake!" Already urine was dribbling from Dr. Kennedy's penis on his hand and, as he turned to face Lake Ipacaraì, a sudden stream of urine hit Antanasio on the leg. "Look out there, my boy!" Too late, Dr. Kennedy warned Antanasio just as Antanasio let him go. Dr. Kennedy fell backward and hit his head hard on a stone.

Dr. Kennedy did not move or make a sound; blood began to seep from under his head on the ground. After standing over and watching him for a few seconds, Antanasio and the guide, without saying a single word to each other, picked Dr. Kennedy up—Antanasio took Dr. Kennedy's arms, the guide took his legs. Neither Antanasio nor the guide looked down at Dr. Kennedy or at his penis which was still spilling urine but at something invisible overhead as together the two men walked Dr. Kennedy as far as they could into the water of Lake Ipacarai and dropped him in there.

As if he had read his mother's mind—he would be damned if he drowned!—Franco decided to learn how to swim. Swimming, he knew, was both cleansing and good exercise. (In Europe, it was the rage—even women swam, and in the city of London alone there were six permanent pools and Franco had watched dozens of boys swim from floating baths under Waterloo Bridge.) At the suggestion of Mr. Frederick Masterman, the apothecary general to the Paraguayan Army, who also had assured Franco that he had seen this practiced successfully in his native town of Croydon, Franco put a frog in a large basin full of water, then lay naked on his bedroom floor and copied exactly the frog's screwlike movements. Mañuel, Franco's servant, acted as swimming instructor, urging Franco on and observing the frog's actions, occasionally goading or prodding the frog with a little stick—most of the frogs were sluggish (or else the opposite was true and they leaped out of the basin and escaped and Mañuel had to replace them). For a month, Franco spent an hour every morning on the floor on his stomach doing the breaststroke; he lost weight, he became fit. When, at last, he felt ready to swim in actual water, the Paraguay River, Franco had soldiers in canoes beat the water to make certain there were no crocodiles or other harmful fish in the area; the shores were lined with curious well-wishers, and standing on the bank Franco's band was all set to begin to play. Dressed in his wool bathing *calzoncillos,* Franco stepped into the fast-moving muddy river and, without appearing to hesitate, he took a deep breath and plunged in. In the water, he moved his arms, his legs, the way he had taught himself, but to no avail. Franco sank like a stone.

23 SEPTEMBER 1863

Thank God I did not witness the ridiculous swimming perfor-mance—I have never heard of such nonsense and what could have Franco been thinking of? And he tells me he nearly drowned! If only he had consulted me! And of course I will be the one who will be blamed for importing strange and dangerous European customs! Do none of the Paraguayan people know how to swim? I will make cer-tain the children learn; swimming is such a healthy exercise! Speak-ing of exercise, I must return to my fencing. Ever since I received the new piano sonata in the last mail packet, I have been busy practic-ing it. Strange how absorbing music is. When I play I stop thinking about everything—the children, the housekeeping, the servants, Franco. Especially Franco.

Among the difficulties that beset Alonzo Taylor, the stonemason, was his wife's unhappiness. She and their two daughters had arrived in Paraguay six months earlier and, although the daughters had adjusted—they were learning to speak both Spanish and Guaraní—Emily had not, and the new house with the fireplace and chimney meant nothing to her. Emily lay in bed all day, the bedroom dark and hot, the curtains tightly drawn; she would not get dressed or leave the room. She refused to look after herself, to wash or to brush her hair—her fine auburn hair, which had once attracted Alonzo, became matted and stiff—and Emily herself started to smell like old dead fish. When, every evening after work, Alonzo went to her bedroom, Emily turned her face to the wall and sobbed. Most nights then, after his two daughters were in bed, safe, Alonzo went out on his own looking for Dolores. Each night he liked Dolores more and if Alonzo had not been so attached to his daughters, he would have asked Emily for a divorce and told her to go home.

Another difficulty Alonzo Taylor encountered, and one which kept him from completing construction on Franco's large and ornate palace modeled on Buckingham Palace and situated right on the bank of the Paraguay River, was the growing lack of a workforce. Soon after Franco became president, he began building up his army; he recruited and conscripted every able-bodied man between the ages of eighteen and fifty. As a result, most of Alonzo Taylor's workmen were twelve- and fourteen-year-old boys.

Franco was proud of his five sons; he spent as much time as he could with them. Also he liked to watch Maria Oliva, the new wet nurse, feed Leopoldo. He liked to watch how greedily the baby sucked on her big breast; one time he saw some of Maria Oliva's slightly grayish-looking milk spill from Leopoldo's mouth and dribble down the baby's chin. In spite of himself, Franco had to swallow, he could not help being aroused. More than anything at that moment he had wanted to lean over and suck on Maria Oliva's breast.

Maria Oliva was oblivious of Franco's desire and, except for her occasional blinding headaches and Rosaria's occasional cruel remarks, she felt content. She loved the children and the children loved her. More patient than Rosaria, she told them stories. Most of the stories were based on Guaraní legends: the one Enrique and Federico liked best had to do with two brothers, the sun and the moon, and how the moon got smeared with *genipa* when the moon had pederastic relations with his brother, the sun.

"What is *genipa*?" Federico asked Maria Oliva.

"A type of tree," Maria Oliva answered.

"What is pederast?" Enrique asked.

"A type of person," she answered.

The story Pancho liked best was about the celestial jaguar who could cause an eclipse by gnawing on either the moon or the sun.

"As no doubt you must have already heard, I want to marry Isabella de Braganza," Franco announced to Ella one evening. "I've written to Dom Pedro asking for her hand."

They were playing chess and Ella did not look up; she appeared to consider her move. No matter what Franco proposed, Ella had to remain calm and not show him her distress or anger. Also she had heard rumors. "What about our sons?"

"Nothing will change between us. The marriage will merely serve to bring our two countries together." Franco continued, "My sentiments for you remain the same. We will go on as before."

"Thank God for that." Ella paused and moved a pawn. "I've heard from a very reliable source that Isabella is pleasant enough but not very pretty. I've heard she has something the matter with her lip—a harelip—which I believe is congenital." She looked up and smiled at Franco. A dazzling smile.

"I know you." Franco scowled. "You are making this up to punish me. Who is this reliable source?" Although he was not faithful to Ella—Ella was pregnant a lot of the time; also she did not expect him to be—Franco relied on Ella more and more for her advice and support.

Ella shook her head. "I promised not to say."

"Promised who?" Getting to his feet, Franco leaned against the table, tipping the chessboard. Most of the chessmen fell to the floor.

"Oh, look what you have done to our game!" Ella exclaimed as Franco took her arm and squeezed it.

"Who?" he repeated. "Tell me who said Isabella has a harelip."

"Your mother, Doña Juaña, who told your sister Rafaela, who told my lady-in-waiting Señora Juliana," Ella answered evenly. Gently, she disengaged her arm and took Franco's. "Come, *chéri*. Let's go upstairs."

✗

"What would you do if your husband left you for another woman?" Ella asked her favorite lady-in-waiting, Señora Juliana—Señora Juliana was so kind and pretty it was hard to imagine her husband, or any man, leaving her. The two women were walking arm in arm in the garden.

Señora Juliana stopped walking. "Oh, Señora, how can that be true?" She could not hide her sudden distress from Ella. "Francisco swore to me on our wedding day that he would always remain faithful—" Señora Juliana was nearly in tears. She had dropped Ella's arm and had put her hands up to hide her face. "It is hard for me to believe. We have only been married a few years."

"No, no—I was not speaking about your husband," Ella tried to take her by the arm.

"What should I do if this is true? Oh, Francisco, Francisco, I cannot go on living," Señora Juliana wailed. "After all you said, after all you promised me!"

"Please, Señora Juliana, you have misunderstood me."

Her face wet with tears, Señora Juliana looked up at Ella. "You did not mean what you said? You were only jesting?"

"Yes, my dear," Ella did not know how else to explain. "I was jesting."

"Thank God! How relieved I am! Although I suppose one never knows for certain, even such an honorable and good man as Francisco—" Señora Juliana had dried her eyes and was trying to smile again.

"I was speaking hypothetically," Ella also said.

"Well, in that case, my answer to your question is—" Pausing, Señora Juliana leaned down to examine a flower and give herself more time before she replied, "I would take a lover. Yes, a lover. Your roses smell so sweet, their scent is for your delight only, Señora," she also added.

Both women laughed.

✗

Diligently, Ella practiced her footwork: she ran forward and backward, she extended her arm, her leg as far as she could until she felt as if she were going to fall over. Each time she leaned a bit farther out, stretching her arm and her leg more, as if she were suspended in the air and floating.

"Flèching," Colonel von Wisner told her, "is a total commitment to attack. You cannot protect yourself and you cannot turn back. Smoothness is the key."

She practiced holding the sabre the way the colonel had shown her: the handle sitting in the crook of her last three fingers, the thumb and first finger loosely curled against the pad inside the shell, then rolling and flipping the sabre left and right, clockwise and counterclockwise, in wide ovals and arcs.

"As a left-handed fencer against a right-handed fencer, you must be careful to cover the elbow of your fighting arm. As a left-handed fencer you can often score with strong cuts to the cheek or the shoulder," the colonel both warned and advised Ella. "But, mainly—and don't forget this—" he instructed her, "as a left-handed fencer you have the initial advantage of looking strange to your right-handed opponent."

In his exile at his *estancia* in San Pedro, Franco's brother Benigno, his breathing labored and sounding harsh, spent most of the day sitting at his card table playing solitaire. If the cards did not turn out right, he cursed and shuffled and reshuffled them until they did.

"Federico, darling." Ella was sitting at her dressing table, doing up her hair. "Can you hand me one of those pins."

Standing in front of the mirror next to his mother, Federico was staring at their reflections. He watched himself pick up a hairpin and give it to his mother; he watched his mother smile at him and he smiled back into the mirror.

"Good boy," she said.

Of her five sons, the third, Federico, most resembled Ella. He had fair hair, gray eyes and his nose was straight and fine like hers; also, he was small for his age and not as robustly built as his brothers; his health too tended to be delicate. When Pancho, Enrique and Carlos Honorio—Leopoldo was still too small—teased him, Ella usually sided with Federico.

In the mirror, Federico watched his mother put on her earrings, then he watched her reach for the necklace of aquamarines. He put out a hand and touched one of the blue stones.

"Lovely, isn't it? Your father gave me the necklace."

Federico nodded.

"Here, you try it on." Federico looked at himself in the mirror as his mother clasped the necklace of aquamarines around his neck, then as she touched up his blond hair with her brush. "Don't you look pretty," she said, adjusting the collar of his blouse so that the necklace lay flat, "as pretty as a picture." She laughed into the mirror at him and Federico laughed happily back at her.

Dom Pedro, the Emperor of Brazil, was fastidious. It was rumored that he was in the habit of making everyone kiss his hand then, immediately after, having a servant wipe his hand with a clean handkerchief. However Dom Pedro did not appear to think it was necessary to reply to the letter Franco had sent him—the letter in which Franco asked for the hand of Isabella de Braganza, Dom Pedro's daughter.

Eight

CERRO LEÓN

One of Franco's earliest memories—he must have been five or six years old—was of being at his father's *quinta* and trying to pat a dog, a mixed-breed, brown-and-white working dog, and the dog, without giving him any warning, biting him. Years later, when Franco was riding back to town one day, he saw the same kind of brown-and-white dog trotting along the side of the road, and he caught up with the dog and whipped it. Brandishing his whip, Franco continued to chase the dog on horseback, and each time he overtook it, he whipped the dog some more, until, bleeding and whimpering, the dog fell down by the side of the road. Then Franco dismounted and walked up to the dog—the dog was a bitch—and very deliberately, Franco whipped her again. Franco knew perfectly well that this dog was not the same dog that had bitten him, but he did not care. For him, justice was served.

✗

"The mingled feeling of enmity and contempt felt by the people toward Paraguay and especially the Lopez dynasty," Charles Washburn, the conservative American minister, who disapproved of Franco from the start, wrote to U.S. Secretary of State William Seward, "has been greatly intensified lately by the rumors that the form of government here was to be changed to that of Empire. Nevertheless the indications here are that that change will be made. The President is building a new palace of grand dimensions which it is supposed is to be the imperial residence, and Buenos Ayres papers report the purchase of a crown in Paris, giving particulars of its cost and design. But as it is said that it is the same crown made for His Ethiopian Majesty, Faustin the First, it may be that the report is only got up to burlesque the whole affair. . . ."

British Minister Edward Thornton's report to Lord Russell, in a "Confidential Dispatch," was more critical: "The great majority of the people are ignorant enough to believe that they are blessed with a president who is worthy of all adoration. The rule of the Jesuits, of the Dictator Francia, and of the Lopezes, father and son, have imbued them with the deepest veneration for authorities. There may be three or four thousand who know better and to whom life is a burthen under such a government. . . . His Excellency's system seems to be to depress and humiliate; if a man shows a little more talent, liberality or independence of character, some paltry excuse is immediately found for throwing him into prison. . . ."

Aiii! Aiii de mi! The headaches were bad and Maria Oliva was afraid she would go blind or pass out or, worse, drop Leopoldo while she was feeding him. All her joints ached. She was afraid to tell Rosaria for fear Rosaria would tell Ella, and Ella would dismiss her, then where would she go? Back to Villa Franca? No, never. She had wanted to ask the American doctor, Dr. Kennedy, but it had been several months since she had last seen him. Another foreign doctor had come to the house the time Enrique fell out of a tree and cut his head. Maria Oliva would never forget the amount of blood and how it took both her and one of the gardeners to hold the screaming boy down while the doctor stitched up the cut. An older man, the doctor had a kind face; he spoke good Spanish and was married to a Paraguayan lady. When he noticed how pale Maria Oliva looked, he told her to sit down. If ever she saw him again, Maria Oliva was determined to gather up her courage and ask him about her headaches. In the meantime, she would have to bear them.

11 MARCH 1864

The boys are growing so fast! All of them, thank God, sturdy and strong (Federico appears delicate but is not; he is the quickest and most agile of all the boys). This afternoon we went riding and we made quite a handsome little group if I do say so myself! Federico and Enrique rode their ponies and Pancho, who claims to have out-grown ponies, insisted on riding a horse. He is so much like his father! We went all the way out to Campo Grande and rode past fields of manioc and corn, bordered on each side by lemon trees— the fragrance of the lemons at this time of year is indescribably deli-cious. Again, I was enchanted by the simple beauty of this country. We stopped briefly for refreshments at the ranch of Don Mauricio, a very charming old man. (In parting, he gave Pancho and me cigars—and Pancho insisted on smoking his!) On the way home, Enrique's pony shied suddenly—a rabbit ran in front of him—and poor Enrique was thrown. Luckily, the child was not hurt except for, I daresay, his pride (although of all the children, Enrique seems to be the one most accident prone) and we rode on without further incident. Only—and this was very strange—just before we reached home, I saw a figure limping along the road and when we approached I recognized Doña Iñes. I could hardly believe my eyes! We stopped and I asked her where she was going and she said she was on her way to the market to buy pomegranates. I fear she may be going mad: not only is it not the season for pomegranates but there is no market within walking distance of Obispo Cue. Dismounting, I told her to get on Mathilde and I myself would lead her home. At first Doña Iñes refused—she said she had never ridden before and she was frightened of horses—but the children and I somehow managed to persuade her, and between the four of us we got her up on Mathilde's back (I must say Mathilde behaved very well, she only tossed her head a bit to show her impatience). Poor Doña Iñes, she clutched both the reins and Mathilde's mane and giggled nervously all the way home but, in the end, she seemed to enjoy her ride on Mathilde. However, I must think what to do with her—I cannot send her back to Spain or France on her own.

The farmers of Cerro León were surprised to suddenly see a steady stream of war supplies and armaments, troop instructors and officials arrive and take up residence in their beautiful, peaceful valley. Sober and thrifty, they had not changed their ways much in the last two hundred years: tilling their soil, growing corn and manioc, tending their livestock, picking the plentiful oranges and drinking several gourds of *yerba maté* a day for their refreshment. But by the end of June, Franco had created a vast military training camp that numbered thirty thousand soldiers, and built both a railroad that linked the fifty or so miles from Cerro León to the capital and a telegraph line—the first telegraph line in South America, installed by Baron von Fischer-Truenfeld. Even so, the now familiar sight of their president, who spent days reviewing his troops and conferring with his officers Vincente Barrios, Antonio Estigarribia and Wenceslao Robles, and riding around on his big mule, did not reassure the farmers of Cerro León completely.

Franco's big-gaited mule stood over sixteen hands and was much taller than the native Paraguayan horse. Headstrong and hard of mouth, the mule was also difficult to handle and not friendly. At the sight of another horse, the mule rolled his eyes and laid his ears flat back on his large head and tried to kick; before the stable boy realized what he was up against, the mule had kicked and bitten him both. But Franco found the mule a challenge and he liked to sit taller in the saddle than anyone else.

"Oh, what an ugly animal," Ella remarked the first time she saw the mule. "What do you call him?"

Perversely, Franco had named the mule Linda.

Taita guazú was how, in Cerro León, all the farmers, including Julio Ignacio, called Franco. In turn, he called Julio Ignacio *mi hijo*—my son— as he listened to him tell about the lack of water that year for his manioc crop, how the corn had grown only to waist height and how his youngest son, who was eleven, coughed so hard he coughed up blood. When Julio Ignacio was finished listing his troubles, Franco told him how all his problems would be attended to and solved once Franco had dealt with their next-door neighbor, the Argentine Republic, whose revolutionary parties were in a constant condition of civil war and who, with their other neighbors, those *macacos*—the Brazilian monkeys—were plotting to take over all of Río de la Plata, and how it was Paraguay's duty to stop them. Afterward, Julio Ignacio's wife came out of the house and Franco complimented her on her embroidered dress and on the ornaments in her hair. He also thanked her as, smiling shyly, she presented him with a loaf of freshly baked *chipa* and a bouquet of flowers. Before he left, Franco did not forget to lean down from the big mule and pat the heads of Julio Ignacio's children—including that of the eleven-year-old boy who coughed up blood—then, flicking his whip and kicking the mule with his heavy silver spurs, Franco rode off at a quick and smooth *paso fino*. When he was out of sight of Julio Ignacio and his family, Franco threw away the bouquet of flowers and took a large bite out of the freshly baked *chipa*—the rest he would give to the mule, Linda.

Franco trusted Dr. William Stewart. A Scot, Dr. Stewart was senior medical officer in the Paraguayan Army and had been Franco's father's personal physician; now Dr. Stewart was his. Dr. Stewart was married to Venancia Baez, a Paraguayan lady, who was lively, slim and rich. Venancia Baez liked to travel and she had many friends in Buenos Ayres.

Several times, Venancia tried to entice Ella. "Come with us. Next week is *carneval.*" Or she tried to tempt Ella with talk of the monthly ball at the Club del Progresso. "This month's ball will be the most elegant, the best attended."

Several times, too, Franco asked Dr. Stewart and his wife, on their frequent visits to Buenos Ayres, to oversee the proceeds from the sale of large quantities of *yerba* that were exported to Argentina and, on Franco's behalf, to deposit the money (a sum total of 212,000 gold pesos) in the Royal Bank of Scotland, where Dr. Stewart's brother was a director. Dr. Stewart and his wife were more than happy to oblige and to make matters official, Dr. Stewart signed a letter to confirm the transactions.

"You should have been there with us," Venancia Baez reported back to Ella as, laughing, she did a graceful twirl in place to demonstrate. "We stayed up half the night dancing."

Pancho, the eldest, was a strong sturdy boy; he smoked cigars and knew how to read and write. He teased his younger brothers, especially Federico, who retaliated by calling him *un matón,* a bully. But Pancho was oblivious of insults, he was oblivious of most things and persons— already he showed a lack of emotional attachment, except to his father. He manifested this attachment by trying to imitate his father exactly: the way Franco walked, a rolling sort of gait; the way Franco talked, gesticulating with both hands; the way Franco puffed on his cigar, tilting his head back to exhale a thick cloud of smoke.

Pancho's favorite game was one he had invented. In the game he played Paraguay and he always won. His brother, Enrique, just six, was Brazil, Federico was either Argentina or Banda Oriental and three-year-old Carlos Honorio was the country Federico, at the time, was not; Leopoldo, asleep in his carriage and too small to play, was assigned the distant role of Spain or France or England.

While Pancho shut his eyes and counted out loud to ten, the three boys, without a word or a look at one another, their hearts pounding, raced off as fast as they were able. Enrique went to the stables, where there were a lot of places to hide, inside stalls or up in the hayloft; the quickest, Federico sped in the opposite direction, toward open country and fields where, even if Pancho spotted him, Federico could dodge and outmaneuver him and where Pancho could not catch him; genuinely panicked, little Carlos Honorio headed in a frantic zigzag toward the garden and the orchard.

Diez!

Once Pancho had captured Argentina or Banda Oriental—it was always poor Carlos Honorio, who could not run as fast as Federico or hide as well as Enrique, or if Carlos Honorio did hide, a part of him, an arm or a leg, always stuck out—Pancho would invent a new torture. He tied Carlos Honorio to a tree and pelted oranges at him; he stripped off his clothes, blindfolded him and spun him around so many times that, dizzy, Carlos Honorio fell down; one time, Pancho buried Carlos Honorio up to his neck in the flower-cutting garden and left him out there among the rows of gladiolas, zinnias and asters, his head broiling in the hot midday sun.

Dios!

Doña Iñes was the one who found him. Dropping her scissors and the red gladiola she had picked, she got down on her knees and with her bare hands, she began to dig.

Ella spoke fluent Spanish and she had no time for lessons; if truth be told, most days she did not think about Doña Iñes. On the few occasions when she did run into her, the time on the road when she made Doña Iñes ride Mathilde, outside in the garden or walking in the upstairs corridor, Doña Iñes looked thinner, her limp was more pronounced.

"Doña Iñes, wouldn't you like to return to Spain?" Ella stopped and remembered to ask her one day.

Mumbling to herself, Doña Iñes looked distracted; for a moment it seemed as if she had not understood Ella. "No, Señora," she finally answered, "I cannot go back to Spain. Have you forgotten that my father—God rest his soul"—Doña Iñes crossed herself—"was a member of the Progresista party and that he died saving the life of Colonel Garrigo at the battle of Vicalváro?"

"Ah, yes. You are right," Ella answered, "I must have forgotten."

"Then how about returning to France?" Ella started to ask, but Doña Iñes had gone. Ella could hear the wooden sole of her shoe thumping along on the corridor floor.

19 July 1864

I perfectly understand the animosity the Paraguayans feel toward the Brazilians—what do they call them? *macacos*—monkeys!—the result of the endless border disputes in Río Grande do Sul and Matto Grosso provinces. As for the others—the colonel has done his best to try to explain the situation to me—the alliances keep shifting and are confusing: there are the Blancos and the Colorados, the whites and the reds of the Banda Oriental and the Confederados and the Unitarios in Argentina. Franco has offered to mediate again between them and the fools have turned him down and now, too late, Dr. Octavio Lapido is here, whining and begging Franco to join forces with Berro and the Blancos in Montevideo. Let him beg, I say! I agree with Franco that Paraguay must be treated with the respect the country deserves and its important position in Río de la Plata must be acknowledged. But enough about dreary political matters— I must get ready for dinner. I will wear one of my new dresses— luckily they arrived along with Franco's latest shipment from France—although the shoes I had also ordered with the dresses were nowhere to be found, which I find most distressing. When I questioned the ship's purser more closely on the subject, the man swore up and down to me that he had never laid eyes on a box of shoes and that he had searched everywhere on the ship and had gone through all the boxes full of bayonets, guns, cartridges and whatnot, but the whole time he was speaking to me he was sweating so profusely that it was hard for me to believe he was telling the truth. Instead I imagine all the ladies in his family staggering around on my new high-heeled silk shoes—my hope is that they will break their silly necks! Another unpleasant bit of news is that Rosaria tells me that something is the matter with Maria Oliva, the young wet nurse. Hard to believe—never in my life have I seen a healthier-looking girl. My instinct tells me that Rosaria is jealous of Maria Oliva, who is young and very pretty. But what should I do—dismiss them both? Poor Franco, he has been so preoccupied lately and he has enough on his mind without listening to me complain about the loss of my silk shoes and the troublesome servants. Tonight I want him to enjoy dinner; the cook is making his specialty: *carne con cuero*—beef cooked in its own hide—Franco's favorite dish!

"Give me that *caudillo* Urquiza any day. He and his band of gaucho assassins!" His mouth full of *carne con cuero*, Franco was discussing the struggle between the Confederados and Unitarios in the Argentine Republic and how Venancio Flores had taken refuge in Buenos Ayres from where he was conducting raids against Montevideo with the help of General Bartolemé Mitre.

"Speaking of Buenos Ayres, Franco, *chéri,* Señor Varela was just describing a new Italian opera which has been an enormous success. What was the name of it, Señor Varela?"

The talk at dinner, despite Ella's efforts to turn the conversation toward lighter and more amusing topics, was always the same: politics.

"Any fool can see that Mitre owes his victory over Urquiza to Flores." Franco ignored Ella and helped himself to more red wine. "Which of course is the reason Mitre is helping Flores with the raids against

Montevideo." Franco turned to his brother-in-law Saturnino Bedoya, whom he had just appointed minister of the treasury. "What do you think, Saturnino?"

Caught off guard, Saturnino hastily swallowed his food and stuttered, "I think our duty—"

"Yes, yes, I agree. Our duty lies with Berro and the Banda Oriental. Until they show their good faith, I will never sign an agreement with the Argentines. And you, Venancio, did you read what that faggot Andres Lamas said?"

Venancio Lopez had been appointed minister of war and marine by his brother. He had just spilled some of the *carne con cuero* gravy on his best silk shirt. Busy rubbing the stain with water, he did not right away answer Franco.

Franco glared at his brother. "I'll tell you what Lamas said! He said, 'One might as well ask China to mediate as Paraguay.'" Shaking his head, Franco helped himself to more meat. "And look who they ask instead—that incompetent, rude monkey, Dom Pedro of Brazil!"

Still wiping the stain, Venancio finally replied, "In my opinion the Banda Oriental must accept mediation or face a Brazilian attack."

"*La forza del destino,*" Héctor Varela, who continued to be a frequent guest in Ella's house, was finally able to say.

"Speaking of Brazil, Vincente, have you told Franco about my new parrot from Matto Grosso province?" Nudging her husband, Inocencia suddenly spoke up. "The *Profesor* says it is a very rare species, a species that is nearly extinct."

"Be quiet, Inocencia." Frowning, Vincente Barrios turned his back on his fat wife.

"A new parrot?" Ella smiled brightly at Inocencia. "Oh, that makes me think of my friend, Princess—"

But Franco interrupted her. "The newspapers in Buenos Ayres print nothing but lies. They are influenced by those Spanish traitors, the Decouds, the Saguiers—and what do you people mean by liberty? The kind you have in Buenos Ayres?" Franco had turned in his seat and was shouting at Héctor Varela. "The liberty to insult one another in the

press, to kill one another in the district assemblies for the election of
deputies, to keep the nation divided, for everyone to do what he
pleases without respect for anyone else?"

"*La forza del destino?*" Again Ella tried to change the subject from
politics. "Next season we must perform the opera in Asunción."

Under the table, Rafaela was desperately searching with her bare feet
for her shoes.

Four or five times a week, Franco rode his big mule, Linda, back and
forth from Asunción to Cerro León. In the evening, when he came to
visit Ella, he was tired. His body was sore, his muscles ached. Taking off
his boots, lighting a cigar and setting his brandy glass on a table near him,
Franco, for once, was perfectly content to stretch out on Ella's chaise
longue and listen to Ella read out loud to him:

> "I scent the Hurons," he said, speaking to the Mohicans; "yonder
> is open sky, through the treetops, and we are getting too nigh
> their encampment. Sagamore, you will take the hillside, to the
> right; Uncas will bend along the brook to the left, while I will try
> the trail. If anything should happen, the call will be three croaks
> of a crow. I saw one of the birds fanning himself in the air, just
> beyond the dead oak—another sign that we are approaching
> an—"

Looking over at Franco, Ella saw that his head was thrown back, his
mouth was open and he was snoring softly. Shutting the book, Ella
leaned down and picked the cigar up off the floor, she did not have the
heart to wake him.

Modest and kind, Frederick Masterman, the apothecary general to the
Paraguayan Army, was popular with the Paraguayan people. By nature
solitary and by habit eccentric, he liked the freedom a foreign country

afforded him. Every Sunday morning he rode off in a different direction until he found a comfortable spot under an orange or a mimosa tree, where he then sat content all day with his sketch pad and pencils. He gave most of his sketches away—if he drew a little girl he gave the sketch to her mother, if he drew someone's house or someone's cow he gave the sketch to the owner of the house or the cow—and he sent the rest back home to his own mother in England. An only child, he was very attached to his mother, who was a widow and lived alone. Along with the sketches, he wrote her regularly, long letters filled with descriptions of Paraguay. When he was not sketching or working in the hospital, Frederick Masterman liked to scour the countryside for medicinal herbs. He found plenty of astringents among the mimosas, the castor-oil plant grew wild, and there were many different types of carminatives and euphorbial purgatives, which he picked and transplanted in his own small garden along with a row of poppies. He grew the poppies for opium, which he needed for some of his patients—soldiers in pain who had suffered from accidents during maneuvers. Frederick Masterman also spent many solitary hours studying the native wildlife—from the fierce puma, *Felis caguar*, to the lowly sand flea, *Pulex penetrans*. (In fact the sketch he considered the most successful and lifelike and that he planned to keep for himself—his mother, he knew, preferred portraits and landscapes—was of a female sand flea. He had sketched it at the top of the page, then, right underneath, on the same sheet of paper, he had drawn the same sand flea distended to three times her size with eggs; in the corner, at the bottom of the page, as an afterthought, he also had drawn a sand flea egg).

In the mornings, when Frederick Masterman inspected the wards on his rounds in Asunción's General Hospital, a gloomy, damp, barracklike building that had once been the dictator Francia's palace, the sick soldiers lying in their beds—unless a man was too ill—greeted him warmly: *Buenos días, muy señor mío!* They held up their arms to him so that he could feel their pulse—the soldiers thought that it was a kind of magic charm. If they got well, out of gratitude, the soldiers brought Frederick Masterman gifts—a basket of oranges, a loaf of *chipa*, a jar of honey. One time, a soldier brought him a huge tame heron. The heron was nearly five feet tall with a foot-long bill. Frederick Masterman kept the heron outside the hospital so he might observe him. The heron was tied with a hide rope, a heavy brick fastened to the end of it. Frightened by a barking dog one afternoon, the heron flew up and the brick hit the wall and broke off from the hide rope—the falling brick nearly hit a soldier who was having a siesta near where it fell. Hearing the clatter of wings, the crash of the brick as well as the startled yell of the soldier, Frederick Masterman ran outside just in time to see the heron fly across the Paraguay River, the hide rope trailing after it.

"What a pity," he sighed to himself as he watched the heron disappear in the Gran Chaco. He had hoped to sketch the big heron and now it was too late.

When Franco and Ella went out riding together in the afternoons, Franco no longer rode his mule, Linda. The one time he had, the mule had tried to mount Mathilde. Busy talking and pointing out the site for a new paved road, Franco was riding with a loose rein and it took him a minute to recover his seat and pull in the rearing, screaming mule; meanwhile, as soon as she felt the mule's hooves on her hindquarters, Mathilde bolted. Ella fell off. Luckily, Ella did not hurt herself. Jumping to her feet right away, she brushed off her riding habit, patted her hair back into place, retrieved her hat. Then, she went after the mare who was standing fifty or so yards away, whinnying and shaking her head up and down in an agitated way.

"Whoa, whoa, there, my darling." Ella talked as she walked. "It's all right, my love, he won't hurt you." In her hand, she held out a bit of sugar she kept in her pocket. "Don't worry, I'll protect you from that ugly old mule." When she reached the mare, Ella picked up the reins that were dragging on the ground and gave her the sugar. Gently, she stroked Mathilde's head and neck before she put her foot in the stirrup and quickly climbed up on the mare's back again.

"Stay away from us," Ella called out to Franco, who was watching her. "That ugly old mule of yours is crazy." Then turning Mathilde around and making clucking sounds with her tongue, Ella urged Mathilde into a fast canter. "Faster, my darling," Ella whispered, leaning far forward in the saddle and burying her face in Mathilde's mane. "Faster."

Behind her Franco kept his distance, but he was also laughing as he shouted after Ella, "In case you didn't know, my dear, this ugly old mule is sterile."

Nine

MARQUEZ DE OLINDA

"If we do not strike now," Franco told Ella, "we will have to fight Brazil another time, a time less convenient to us."

"You are right, *chéri*."

Franco's breath, Ella noticed, smelled sour.

"The only way that Paraguay can gain the attention and respect of the world," Franco continued.

"Napoleon himself would have done the same thing."

A rotten tooth, Ella guessed, but Franco seldom complained.

"Only by a show of strength can Paraguay compel other nations to treat her with more consideration. Come, let's go upstairs," Franco said.

"Wait," Ella said.

On a November day so hot the sky looked white and the Paraguay River was the color of mud, the *Marquez de Olinda*, one of the regular Brazilian steamers en route from Rio de Janeiro to Matto Grosso province, stopped to coal at Asunción. On board, the new governor of the province, Camheiro de Campos, lay dozing and sweating in his hammock, which hung motionless in the stern of the ship. Several hours later and fifty miles north of Asunción, the *Marquez de Olinda* was overhauled by the *Tacuari*. The Paraguayan crew was armed and, without firing a single shot (and without giving the governor time to leave his hammock) they forced the *Marquez de Olinda* to turn around and go back to Asunción. The following day, the Brazilian minister received a note from the Paraguayan foreign minister saying that diplomatic relations between Paraguay and Brazil had been severed and that the Paraguay River was closed to all Brazilian vessels. Meantime, Camheiro de Campos, the crew of the *Marquez de Olinda* and the passengers had been sent north to a prison in the interior.

Next, under the command of General Vincente Barrios, Franco's brother-in-law, a force was sent upriver. General Barrios had never fought a battle and, during the voyage, he never once left his cabin. Frightened, he drank himself into a stupor. By the time he crossed the border into Brazil, he was so intoxicated that his orders were unintelligible and his men were leaderless and disorderly. Meeting with little resistance—most of the Brazilian troops were *cambâs*, black men and slaves, who did not want to fight and who ran away—the Paraguayan soldiers raped and pillaged their way to Corumbá, the capital of the province.

Baron de Villa Maria, one of the richest *estancieros* of Matto Grosso province, owned an enormous amount of land, eighty thousand head of cattle, a fine house with valuable European furniture, and he had just enough time to pocket a handful of diamonds and get out before the Paraguayan soldiers attacked. His two sons were shot trying to escape, his wife and daughters were beaten and turned out into the jungle, where, without food, shelter or clothing, they perished. When, still drunk, General Barrios entered Baron de Villa Maria's house, he ordered that all the curtains be torn off the windows and sent back to Inocencia, his wife; he then helped himself to furniture, paintings, china, silver—enough to outfit an entire house. General Barrios especially fancied the marble statue in Baron de Villa Maria's front hall. The statue was of a life-sized woman lying on her back, naked (except for one leg that had a piece of cloth draped over it); the woman had just been stung by a serpent, but her attitude and the expression on her face was one of total sexual abandon. The woman was having an orgasm and General Barrios could not take his eyes off her. The moment he found himself alone in the front hall, General Barrios could not resist caressing the statue—first the woman's marble feet, then running his hand up her marble leg, fondling her marble breasts, and wrapping his hands around her flung-back marble neck. He could hardly contain himself or keep from throwing himself on top of the statue. Even the thought of it made General Barrios feel hot, turn red in the face and come, almost.

In the middle of the night, Frederick Masterman was awakened by loud knocking and by someone shouting, *"Vamonos, Señor!"* After dressing quickly and packing his bag with medicine and instruments, he mounted the waiting horse. Luckily it was a clear night with nearly a full moon and the road was plainly visible. On the way, in spite of himself, he thought *miscarriage*. More accustomed to tending sick men, he tried hard not to picture Ella, whom he had last seen resplendent in a ball dress, a glass of champagne in her hand, lying in the bloody mess of her torn placenta. He shut his eyes but even so, the word in his head blended in with the rhythmic pounding of his horse's hooves: *malparto, malparto, malparto.*

Ella—not so resplendent, for she too had dressed hurriedly—met him at the front door. "Quick. President Lopez," she whispered.

"Is he ill?" Frederick Masterman tried to ask.

Franco was lying on Ella's bed; his head was propped up against several pillows and wrapped in wet towels. The lower part of his face had swollen to nearly twice its size and Franco's lips were so distended, they had split and were bleeding. The smell of rot coming from his mouth filled the room. When he caught sight of Frederick Masterman, Franco tried to sit up; he tried to say something but his words were unintelligible. To calm him, Ella tried to take his hand, but Franco drew the hand away. To reassure Franco, Frederick Masterman leaned over and started to tell him how once the tooth was pulled the pain and swelling would quickly subside, but midsentence he stopped and stepped back. He felt he was looking into the eyes of a wild animal. It took several men to hold Franco down, but as soon as Frederick Masterman extracted the tooth, a bicuspid, the huge abscess surrounding it burst. Groaning and cursing, Franco sat up and spat a cheesy, puslike liquid into the basin that Ella held out to him. In spite of herself, the reek made her draw away and some of the cheesy, puslike stuff fell on Ella's silk shoe. Kneeling down at Ella's feet, Frederick Masterman tried to wipe away the stain on her shoe, but he only made the stain worse.

At the front door, Maria Oliva was able to stop Frederick Masterman on his way out. Before she could speak, Maria Oliva began to weep. Putting his hand on her arm, he spoke to her kindly in Spanish. Still weeping, Maria Oliva tried to describe her headaches, how debilitating they had become, how she could hardly walk because her joints were sore. Frederick Masterman listened and when Maria Oliva finished, he told her that he recognized the symptoms and that she should come see him at the hospital and he would give her medicine. Relieved, Maria Oliva tried to get down on her knees to thank him but he would not let her. Maria Oliva, Frederick Masterman guessed correctly, had syphilis.

From Villa Franca, Gaspar and Fulgencio had been sent downriver to Humaitá. The fort lay slightly north of where the Paraná River divides into the Paraguay River and slightly north of Corrientes, Argentina, a most strategic and crucial spot where huge iron chains had been placed across the river to prevent ships from sailing. Damp and humid, Humaitá was built on a malarial swamp, and each day, along with the twenty thousand other soldiers, Gaspar and Fulgencio had to march for eight to ten hours in marshland and mud that often reached up to their knees. The drill was made more arduous by having their accustomed weapons, knives and lances, replaced with heavy French bayonets (a part of the large store of arms, gunpowder and ammunition that Franco had ordered and that had been shipped from France).

Padre was how the two brothers always had to address their superior officer. In turn, the officer called Gaspar and Fulgencio *mis hijos*—my sons. If, for a reason or for no reason, Gaspar was flogged, he consoled himself by telling Fulgencio, "If my father did not flog me, who would?" A corporal, the brothers knew, carried a cane and could give a soldier three cuts, a sergeant, they also knew, could order a soldier to receive twelve blows, and an officer could order as many as he wished. Typical of the fortitude of the Paraguayan soldier, neither Gaspar nor Fulgencio ever complained.

Worse than the weather and the drilling was their diet. Both Gaspar and Fulgencio were used to eating maize, manioc and fruit, with the occasional fish—after catching the *manguruzu* with the monkey inside it, however, neither brother could eat fish—but since all the men in Paraguay had been conscripted into the army, none were left to till or plant the fields, and grain and vegetables had become scarce. The great hunks of undercooked bloody barbecued beef, their sole diet (large herds of cattle had been captured in Matto Grosso province and brought back to feed the army), gave Gaspar and Fulgencio acute and debilitating dysentery. No matter how many gourds of *maté* they drank a day to try to stop up their bowels, after each meal their stomachs cramped and, bent nearly double and barely able to contain themselves, they ran into the woods to relieve themselves—their shit a stream of malodorous yellow water.

At night, the two brothers hardly slept; they swung in their hammocks swatting at mosquitos and thinking about their wives, who cooked, cleaned the house, made *chipa* and bore Gaspar and Fulgencio many children. Gaspar's wife was older and not as good-natured or amiable as Fulgencio's wife, her sister; at times she was reluctant to have sex with Gaspar—she was pregnant or else she was menstruating—and, however frustrated he might be, Gaspar respected her wishes and never forced himself on her. Younger, prettier, Fulgencio's wife had no such reservations; she often wore a flower in her hair, a signal to Fulgencio, and, less fastidious than her sister, she did not mind if Fulgencio took her outdoors in the fields or on the banks of the river. Sometimes, to relieve the monotony of the nights at Humaitá, Gaspar and Fulgencio played a game among themselves—the game was simple, it consisted of who could get off first. In his hammock, Gaspar, more often than not—although he did not admit it to Fulgencio—thought about how he was making love to his wife's sister, Fulgencio's wife. He fantasized how Fulgencio's wife's body, although familiar and shaped like her sister's, was smoother and firmer, he also fantasized how she was more easily satisfied. Next to Gaspar, in his hammock, Fulgencio was also thinking about his wife and imagining her smooth dark skin and the flower in her black hair but then, without his hardly noticing it, the picture in his head of his wife invariably changed and turned into a picture of a much paler woman with blond hair and Fulgencio thought about how he was sitting astride her and how he could feel her soft hips between his knees and that thought more than any other made him come and he always won.

When Inocencia received the curtains from Baron de Villa Maria's house, she was delirious with happiness. She spent entire days in her bedroom in front of the mirror sifting through the heavy silks and brocades, draping each piece of cloth over her broad shoulders and around her thick waist to see which color suited her best—yellow? pink? crimson? blue? She pored over the candy-box illustrations of insipid-looking doll-women in outdated fashion magazines that Ella had discarded: *Le Journal des demoiselles, La France élégante, La Mode illustrée.* Out loud to herself, she read and reread the descriptions of plunging bodices, pagoda sleeves, hems trimmed with flounces, bows and ribbons, lace collars and cuffs.

Envious and resentful, Rafaela watched her sister. "Can I have a little of the pink silk?" she asked Inocencia finally.

Exhausted and emaciated, Baron de Villa Maria reached Rio de Janeiro months later on foot. He was the first to inform Don Pedro that Brazil had lost its richest province.

Meantime, a relieved and finally sober General Barrios returned to Asunción, bringing home, at great expense and inconvenience, the marble statue; several soldiers had to carry it and one, clumsy, let drop his portion of the statue, breaking off a foot of the woman stung by a serpent.

Irate, Charles Washburn, the United States minister, had already written a letter home complaining about Franco's actions in regard to the Brazilian steamer the *Marquez de Olinda*: "I told him that such a proceeding in time of peace was unprecedented in modern warfare; and that, as there had been no declaration of war, and the Brazilians had not expected such action, there could be no justification in such proceeding."

To Mrs. Washburn, during supper, he complained as well. "When I advised President Lopez today to release the new governor of Matto Grosso province, Camheiro de Campos, along with the crew and the passengers of the *Marquez de Olinda*, who I have heard are being kept in appalling circumstances in a prison in the interior, he would not listen to me. Again and again, I tried to explain how the seizure of the vessel would not provoke Dom Pedro nearly as much as the seizure of his own subjects, but I might as well have been talking to myself or talking to the wind for all Lopez heeded me."

"A prison in the interior? How dreadful—no doubt they will all perish! But never mind, dear, I am sure you did the right thing. As you well know, the only person the president will listen to is that awful, ambitious Irish woman, Madame Lynch," Mrs. Washburn answered.

"I even reminded President Lopez that the United States might eventually be willing to help him in a war against Brazil, and to furnish him with the tools to do so with greater dispatch," Charles Washburn said.

"I have no doubt that the president will soon come around to your way of thinking. Are you not hot, dear?" Mrs. Washburn made a fanning motion with her hand. "Hush," she also said to Bumppo, her terrier who, for no reason she could see except that he was greedy, had started to bark.

2 JANUARY 1865

What I wonder will the new year bring? I know that the Brazilians and the Orientals, like the Spanish and the Portuguese, loathe each other and the two countries are always on the verge of war. One of the reasons, the colonel was able to explain to me, is the Brazilian cattle owners who have established themselves in Banda Oriental and are engaged in smuggling cattle into Brazil, thus evading the import duties the Banda Oriental government has imposed. When called to account for this by the government of Banda Oriental, the Brazilians sided with General Flores, a revolutionary gaucho chief. More recently, according to the colonel, the Brazilians and the gauchos invaded and captured the Banda Oriental town of Paysandú. When the people from that town surrendered, the gauchos slaughtered them all anyway. Difficult to imagine such unprovoked violence!

Yes, definitely, there is something wrong with that girl, the wet nurse. When I walked into the nursery this morning, she tried to get up from her chair and nearly fell. I suspect she had been drinking. I will have to make inquiries.

The Banda Oriental minister in Asunción flattered Franco. The time for Paraguay to play a decisive role in the politics of the Río de la Plata had

come, he told him. As a result Franco sent a note of protest to the
Brazilian minister in which he said that he would regard any occupation
of Banda Oriental territory by the Brazilians as disturbing the equilib-
rium of the states of the Río de la Plata. He wrote that the matter was
of great concern to the Republic of Paraguay as a guarantee of its secu-
rity, peace and prosperity, and such a hostile action would have serious
consequences.

Franco's protest was not perceived as a declaration of war. Nor did
he act upon it. Instead Franco waited. Montevideo fell in February, and
Venancio Flores became the new president of Banda Oriental so that all
of a sudden, instead of being Banda Oriental's ally, Franco found himself both Brazil and Banda Oriental's enemy.

One afternoon while Ella was out riding alone, she rode past a group of
soldiers who, because there were not enough horses, were riding double and one of them had called out to her in an unpleasant way, and she
was reminded of the Irish groom in Buenos Ayres—what was his
name?—Patrick MacBride. Poor Patrick. Ella also remembered how at
the *asado* in her honor, Mr. James White, the rich landholder, had told
her that Patrick was probably killed by the gauchos while they
attempted to steal Mathilde from him. The gauchos, Mr. White said,
were a wild bunch who had little regard for human life. Forgetting her
condition, no doubt, he had gone on to describe to Ella the gauchos'
favorite method of disposing of their victims—"playing the violin," they
called it. "First, the gaucho throws the victim down on his face," he said,
"then the gaucho seizes him by the hair and plunges his knife into his
neck, just below the right ear and across the throat—" To illustrate, Mr.
White, who was holding a greasy lamb chop, sliced the air with his
hand. "So that the blood flows more rapidly, the gaucho wrenches the
victim's head back—" At the thought, Ella shuddered. Gathering the
reins and kicking Mathilde, she urged the horse into a canter. "Let's go,
my darling." Ella had to kick Mathilde twice. The mare was getting
older; she was no longer so quick to respond.

X

Baron von Fischer-Truenfeld was inspecting the telegraph line from Cerro León to Asunción. The line seemed in good order and the sun shone pleasantly in Baron von Fischer-Truenfeld's face as he rode on the hard-packed clay road. As he approached a village, he could hear the voices of children playing, then the voice of a woman calling to them. From his horse, he caught a glimpse of the woman, a pretty, dark-haired young woman, and for a moment he was tempted to get off his horse and go to her—he could flirt with her, kiss her, perhaps sleep with her. Instead he merely waved at her. Smiling, the young woman waved back. Paraguay, Baron von Fischer-Truenfeld knew, was preparing to go to war as was, he also knew, Prussia. Suddenly, more than anything, Baron von Fischer-Truenfeld wanted to go home.

In his hurry one morning, as Franco was leaving Ella's bedroom—late, he had scheduled for congress to convene—he bumped into one of the ladies-in-waiting, who was standing in the hall. Franco had seen Ella's ladies-in-waiting on many different occasions—Señora Juliana, Doña Dolores and Doña Isidora—and he employed their husbands in the army, but he got the three ladies confused. This one was pretty and plump; she had been leaning over, her skirt was hiked up, adjusting something—her stocking perhaps—and as Franco opened the door and stepped out, he nearly knocked her down. To keep her from falling, Franco grabbed her arm. Digging his fingers into the soft flesh, he held on to the woman's arm a little longer than necessary.

"*Muchas gracias, Señor.*" Unafraid, the lady-in-waiting looked him in the eye and smiled.

6 MAY 1865

According to the colonel, who did not have a chance the other day to finish telling me everything that occurred in Paysandú, the real reason that General Leandro Gomez, although he surrendered and waved a white flag, was taken out and shot against a wall was that he and General Suarez, the head of the Oriental forces, had a long-standing personal feud. Something to do with a woman! How typical and banal! Nevertheless it is an outrage and cold-blooded murder! *[Ella underlined these last three words "cold-blooded murder."]* And war, I am certain, is now inevitable.

Poor children! They have come down with the measles! Federico has the worst case, he is covered from head to toe with spots. When I consulted Dr. Stewart he informed me that several cases of the measles have been reported among the soldiers at Humaitá—and the infection he also said was brought over deliberately by an Argentine soldier! I hope and pray Franco does not contract it and when I inquired as to whether he had had the measles as a child, Franco said he could not remember. No use asking Doña Juaña, she would not deign to answer me. And she only cares for Benigno.

But I must not forget yesterday we had glorious news! Congress unanimously conferred the rank of field marshal on Franco (he was also given a most splendid diamond encrusted marshal's baton!). From general to field marshal—what next? I asked him. Emperor?

The next time Frederick Masterman went out to collect the opium that he had planted and that he had promised to give to Maria Oliva, he discovered that the neighbor's cattle had pushed through the fence and gotten into his garden. The cattle had eaten all the poppies; he could see them, spread out like dirty, blown sheets in the field, lying on their sides. One cow was trying to stand up. Each time she got herself up on two legs, she fell down.

Ten

CORRIENTES

Rosaria and Maria Oliva, the wet nurses—by then the youngest boy, Leopoldo, was weaned—also came down with the measles. First Rosaria, a week later Maria Oliva, who developed such a high fever that she went to lie down in a tub of cold water in an attempt to bring down her temperature. Just over the measles himself—his body was still covered with scabs—Federico was the one who found Maria Oliva curled up like a baby, her skin blue. Throwing down the bunch of flowers wrapped in newspaper that he had picked to give Maria Oliva, Federico ran to fetch Rosaria. Rosaria felt for Maria Oliva's pulse and, finding none, she crossed herself, then, reaching for the nearest thing at hand, she quickly covered Maria Oliva's naked body with the newspaper that was wrapped around the flowers Federico had wanted to give her.

Citizens! The course of the war in which our Fatherland is engaged against the triple alliance of Brazil, the Argentine Con-

federation, and the Banda Oriental no longer allows me the self-
sacrifice of absenting myself from the seat of war and from my
companions in arms, who are in campaign, as the public order
and the unanimous enthusiasm of the nation permit me to go
where the soldier's duty calls me—

Printed in bold type on the sheet from *El Semanario* was Franco's
proclamation to the Paraguayan people. The rest of the article (except for
a few more lines on the corner of newspaper covering Maria Oliva's
shrunken ass, which read, "Every citizen in his heart believes in the holiness of the cause, which has forced us to leave our peaceful and labori-
ous life, and the God of armies will watch over our fate!") was wet and
illegible. That hardly mattered; neither Rosaria nor Maria Oliva—had
she been able—could read.

Franco's troops, under the command of General Robles, occupied the
town of Corrientes. Already Paraguay was at war with Brazil and Banda
Oriental, and now Paraguay had started a battle with Argentina by asking for permission to march through the province of Misiones—a disputed territory on which both Argentina and Paraguay had claims, and
of which Corrientes was the capital—permission that Argentina, at
peace with Brazil, had refused to give.

"You may count on us for putting ourselves in a position to make
the voice of the Paraguayan government heard in the events that are
developing in the Río de la Plata," Franco told U.S. Minister Charles
Washburn.

As yet unaware—the news did not reach Paraguay for six months—
that President Lincoln had been assassinated, Charles Washburn lost no
time in reporting Franco's words to Secretary of State William Seward.
But William Seward had been stabbed in the throat by one of John
Wilkes Booth's fellow conspirators and was in no state to reply.

Bartolemé Mitre of the Argentine Republic replied immediately by declaring war on Paraguay. A few days later, on the first of May, he met with Dom Pedro of Brazil and Venancio Flores of Banda Oriental to sign the Treaty of Triple Alliance.

"None of our three countries should seek a separate peace." Impartial and just, Venancio Flores was adamant.

"A state of war with Paraguay will continue to exist until the abdication of Francisco Solano Lopez." Dom Pedro disliked Franco for both personal and political reasons.

"Paraguay will have to pay the entire cost of the war," always practical, Bartolemé Mitre insisted.

Again, Venancio Flores persisted, "All warships and war materials possessed by Paraguay will be divided equally among the three signers of the treaty."

"Paraguay will be forbidden to rearm within a generation." The most confident, General Luis Alves de Lima y Silva, Duke de Caxias, the new Brazilian commander in chief of the Allied forces, was certain the war would not last long. Paraguay, he predicted, would soon be defeated.

"Tell me, how does the electric telegraph work?" Curious, Ella was also flirting a little. Out riding one afternoon, she had happened to meet Baron von Fischer-Truenfeld.

Doffing his cap, Baron von Fischer-Truenfeld rode over to her. During the years he had spent in Paraguay, his face had tanned a dark brown, which made the scar on his cheek more prominent. Baron von Fischer-Truenfeld's knee brushed up against Ella's.

"No reason for a beautiful lady like yourself to concern herself with such dull matters," the baron had answered.

"I'm practical. I like to know how things work."

Ella and Baron von Fischer-Truenfeld's horses were trotting side by side.

"The telegraph is made up of electromagnetic impulses. The telegrapher sends the code by tapping on a spring-loaded brass key that opens and closes the electrical circuit. The impulses are then translated into dots and dashes—your hat is very fetching."

Ella did not reply.

"As you no doubt know, Morse Code consists of signs of different lengths. We Prussians improved on the system—three points now result in one line. Also, the words that are most often used have the shortest signs and thus are transmitted quickest." Baron von Fischer-Truenfeld kicked his horse to keep up with Ella's. "Blue becomes you," he also said.

Ella still did not speak.

"The next step is to find a way to use one telegraph line to send signs in both directions," Baron von Fischer-Truenfeld paused; he worried Ella was making fun of him. "For instance from Asunción to Cerro León and back again to Asunción. An Austrian named Julius Gintl invented how to do this with two batteries—are you certain this interests you?"

"Absolutely certain." At last Ella smiled.

Reassured, Baron von Fischer-Truenfeld continued, "Julius Gintl's method is called the method of compensation. Here, in Paraguay, I have been able to apply his method with only one battery. When I go back to Prussia, I will register the patent." Then, whipping his horse hard on the rump, he said, "Shall we gallop, Madame?"

Doña Iñes had become more and more reclusive, more silent and secretive; some days she hardly left her room. Other days she prowled up and down the corridors of Obispo Cue or she worked quietly in the garden. Sometimes, she walked over to the stables. (If it were not for the noisy thump, thump of the wooden sole of her shoe, she could have been a ghost.) In the stables, the grooms ignored Doña Iñes or gave her a just perceptible nod as they continued mucking out the stalls, raking up straw, polishing leather. They paid no attention to her as she limped from stall to stall handing out sugar cubes to the children's ponies, to Pancho's horse, to Ella's Mathilde; even as she grew more confident and stopped to rub a nose or let a pony nuzzle her hand with his lips. However, the ponies and horses were always attentive to her. Pricking up their sensitive ears, they could hear Doña Iñes coming from a distance, they could even hear her as she crossed the garden, as she walked through the orange grove and up the path to the stable courtyard, and, when they did, the ponies and horses went and hung their heads out of their stall doors, and neighing softly, pawed the ground with their hooves, in anticipation of Doña Iñes and her sugar cubes.

16 JUNE 1865

The children and I went to watch Franco embark on the *Tacuari*. What a splendid sight! The sun was just going down, the band was playing and the riverbanks were lined with people—all of Asunción must have been there. Before setting sail for Humaitá, Franco made a speech in which he spoke about the holiness of the cause and how the God of armies will watch over our fate! Never in my life have I heard such cheering. It brought tears to my eyes and the children could hardly contain themselves they were so excited. Four other steamers filled with soldiers sailed right after Franco and then, as if on cue, the moon came out and shone down on us. A good omen, I believe.

The one thing that distresses me greatly is that Pancho insisted on going with his father. Nothing I said to him—the danger, the discomfort of camp life, the lack of companionship—could dissuade him. He was determined. He is such a strong-willed child! And since Franco did not disallow it and Pancho took his father's silence as a form of consent, there was nothing more I could say. But Pancho is only ten years old!

On account of all these events I forgot to mention that Maria Oliva, the children's young wet nurse, died of the measles a few weeks ago. Dr. Stewart, who examined her, asked me if she had been ill for a long time and I told him that I did not know but that Maria Oliva was always complaining and that, frankly, I thought she was lazy. Poor Federico—it was he who found her lying naked in a tub of water. He was quite upset, now all he talks about is death. Children are so impressionable. I have asked Baron von Fischer-Truenfeld to dine with me tomorrow evening.

The entire Paraguayan fleet, the *Tacuari*, the *Paraguari*, the *Ygurei*, the *Ypora*, the *Marquez de Olinda* (the Brazilian steamer the Paraguayans had overhauled), the *Jejui*, the *Salto-Oriental*, the *Pirabebé*, the *Yberá* (the *Yberá* lost its screw and was obliged to stop at Tres-Bocas), and six flat-bottomed boats called *chatas*, under the command of Captain Mesa, set out to capture the Brazilian fleet. The ships got off to a late start—the plan was to sail at night—to Riachuelo, nine miles south of Corrientes, where the Paraná River is two miles wide and divides around an island, then to sail past Riachuelo and turn the ships around. Only it was morning and bright daylight when the Paraguayan fleet arrived at Riachuelo and the Brazilians saw the ships and had plenty of time to get ready and take action.

Mr. Gibson, an English engineer on board the *Paraguari*, watched as the Brazilians shot through the *Jejui*'s and the *Marquez de Olinda*'s boilers—the Brazilian ships were screw-propelled and more maneuverable while the Paraguayan ships (except for the *Tacuari* and the *Yberá*, which was out of commission) were merchant vessels and carried their boilers above the waterline, which made them more vulnerable and more exposed to enemy fire. Mr. Gibson also watched as the *Marquez de Olinda* drifted downstream and as a large number of the crew were scalded to death—he could hear the poor men's screams. (A few days later, when the Brazilians went to pick up the survivors, the captain of the *Marquez de Olinda*, who had lost his arm in the battle, ripped off the bandage and said that, rather than be captured, he preferred to bleed to death and die.) Meanwhile, Captain Mesa was hit in the chest by a rifle bullet and Captain Cabral, his second, had to take over the command. Next the *Salto-Oriental*'s boiler was knocked off and all the crew was shot and killed; finally, the *Paraguari* was struck broadside and the ship ran aground. A Brazilian steamer came alongside and ordered Mr. Gibson, the only remaining officer on board, to take down the flag or else he would be fired upon. Mr. Gibson complied but then, rather than be taken prisoner, with what remained of his crew he jumped overboard and swam to shore.

Three days later, after walking forty miles through the Chaco, barefoot—his boots had been swept away in the current—and without food or clean water, Mr. Gibson and three sailors, the only men left from the *Paraguari* (one man drowned trying to swim across the river, a second, who had tried to help the first man, was attacked and dragged underwater by a crocodile, a third man ate a *mio-mio,* a poisonous mushroom, and after suffering severe stomach cramps, died) arrived back at Humaitá. When Mr. Gibson was brought to Franco, instead of congratulating him on his escape and survival, Franco ordered him and the three sailors put in prison for a week.

The handsome and arrogant Colonel Antonio Estigarribia and his 12,000 men crossed the Paraná River to Uruguayana to wait for General Wenceslao Robles and his troop of 25,000 soldiers to arrive. Together, the two forces would invade the Brazilian province of Río Grande do Sul and destroy the Allied army at the Brazilian–Banda Oriental border, but General Robles never arrived. Instead, when General Robles got word of the defeat at Riachuelo, without informing anyone, he decided to return to Corrientes; and Colonel Estigarribia, while waiting in vain for Robles, made the mistake of dividing his troops on either side of the Paraná. Immediately, the Allied forces took advantage and massacred the troops on one side of the river as the rest of Estigarribia's soldiers, who were outnumbered as well as starving to death, watched helplessly from the other. Refusing to surrender, Estigarribia, who in addition to being arrogant was well read, wrote the Allies long pompous letters justifying himself:

If Your Excellencies open any history, you will learn from the records of that great book of humanity, that the great captains, whom the world still

remembers with pride, counted neither the number of their enemies, nor the
elements . . .

And another saying:

Recollect that Leonidas, when he was keeping the pass of Thermopylae with
300 Spartans, would not listen to the propositions of the King of Persia, and
when a soldier told him that his enemies were so numerous that their arrows
darkened the sun, he answered, "So much the better—we will fight in the
shade."

Only in the end Colonel Estigarribia did surrender; and, in Corrientes, General Robles was arrested and put in prison on charges of
insubordination and treachery.

For propriety's sake, Ella asked a lady-in-waiting to join her for dinner.
First she asked Señora Juliana, but Señora Juliana had a migraine; next
Ella asked Doña Isidora, but Doña Isidora was away visiting her
mother. In the end Ella had to ask silly, plump Doña Dolores. Wearing
a red dress that revealed too much of her breasts, Doña Dolores arrived
late—too late to help Ella dress, to lace up her stays and do up her
hooks—and Ella was irritated. Also, during the meal, Doña Dolores
hardly said a word. Instead, in between mouthfuls of the French food
Ella had chosen especially—*vol-au-vent, soupe à l'oignon, coq au vin, sorbet,*
Camembert cheese, and for dessert, *poires belle-Hélène*—and in between
sips of Ella's good French wines—*Château Margaux, Château Yquem,*
champagne—she giggled. No matter what Baron von Fischer-Truenfeld
talked about—the disastrous defeat at Riachuelo; the thousands dead at
Uruguayana under the command of Colonel Estigarribia—Doña
Dolores giggled, and each time her breasts inside her red dress jiggled.
Across from her, Ella frowned at her—the baron was looking down at
his plate, eating—Ella shook her head at her, Ella even tried to kick

Doña Dolores under the table, but whatever she did made no impression. Oblivious, Doña Dolores continued to laugh and giggle. When dinner was finished, unable to bear it any longer, Ella sent Doña Dolores home. Then, after offering Baron von Fischer-Truenfeld some Armagnac she had brought with her from France, Ella went and sat down next to him on the sofa, where she let Baron von Fischer-Truenfeld put his arms around her and pull her closer to him.

All night, Mr. Gibson, the English engineer, remained awake; he could hear the prisoner in the next cell screaming. The prisoner, Mr. Gibson guessed, was being tortured. Shutting his eyes, he could well imagine the sort of ordeal the man was going through.

"Is it not true that General Robles agreed to sell the Paraguayan Army to the enemy?" Mr. Gibson heard the interrogator ask.

"No!" screamed the prisoner.

No doubt the prisoner was sitting on the ground, his legs and arms bound together, with a musket barrel tied behind his knees and with several more bound in a bundle on his shoulders so that his face was forced down against his knees.

"Is it not true that General Robles was sending his family, his household possessions, all his belongings, to Argentina?"

"No!"

First the poor man's feet would go to sleep, then his legs and arms, next his torso, until the blood had no place to go and the pressure became intolerable.

"Is it not true that General Robles put all his money in a bank in Buenos Ayres?"

Since there was no answer, Mr. Gibson guessed that the prisoner had either passed out or had died.

Even in the sudden silence, Mr. Gibson could not go to sleep.

18 SEPTEMBER 1865

If only Franco had listened to the colonel! He should have marched directly to Buenos Ayres and taken advantage of the situation in Argentina, the state of revolutionary chaos and their complete lack of preparedness for war, and then Urquiza would have joined him. Instead Franco sent that fool Robles to cross the Paraná and that arrogant double fool Estigarribia to Río Grande do Sol, where he immediately surrendered! How many men were lost? Colonel von Wisner says at least 20,000 and our Paraguayan soldiers, he also says, fought like wolves! Franco is furious. I am told he refuses to see or to speak to anyone—nor will he listen to dear Dr. Stewart—and he has not eaten in several days (each time his servant brings him food on a tray, Franco throws the tray back at Mañuel along with several empty bottles of brandy!). No one will go near Franco; not even little Pancho. Must *I* then go to Humaitá?

In bed with Baron von Fischer-Truenfeld, Doña Dolores was giggling again. They had been lovers for only a few weeks and only since Doña Dolores had received the news that her husband, a lieutenant in Colonel Estigarribia's army, had drowned when his canoe tipped over in the Paraná River. But time enough for Baron von Fischer-Truenfeld to have stopped trying to comfort her—when Doña Dolores received the news she had been inconsolable—or to have stopped trying to please Doña Dolores in the usual way. Instead, Baron von Fischer-Truenfeld put Doña Dolores over his knee, hiked up her dress and several layers of petticoats, unlaced her corset, pulled up her chemise and spanked her. When he was finished, Baron von Fischer-Truenfeld handed Doña Dolores his riding crop and she in turn had to whip him.

Dressed in a diminutive version of the same uniform—a crimson cape with a stiff lace collar bordered in gold—and wearing the same shiny patent leather boots, ten-year-old Pancho had followed Franco to Humaitá. Like a small shadow, Pancho never left his father's side: he sat next to him while he ate supper, knelt beside him during mass, rode abreast of him while Franco inspected the troops—he copied just how his father ordered, yelled, joked (when Franco lit up a cigar, so did Pancho). Like his father too, the little boy could be arrogant and cruel or, at other times, kind and generous. Always he was unpredictable. The Paraguayan officers were careful with Pancho: they spoiled him; they deferred to the little boy; they brought him presents. Colonel Fernandez gave him a new chess set, Major Hermosa a handmade jigsaw puzzle, Major Sayas a picture book of wild animals. When word got around that Pancho collected them, several soldiers brought him enemy ears. Pancho strung the ears on a rawhide string, like a necklace, and kept them under his bed inside a wooden toy chest.

Ta dum ta dum ta dum dum dum, wherever Franco went, the band followed him and played the same tune. Each day, as Franco reviewed his troops, *ta dum ta dum ta dum dum dum,* and as Franco made a special point of addressing each soldier personally and by name, *ta dum ta dum ta dum,* and while he told the soldiers jokes—off-color, racist jokes, the butt of the jokes was always the Brazilians, whom he called "*macacos*"—Justo José never stopped playing *ta dum ta dum dum dum.*

Since his return from abroad, Justo José had married and had fathered four daughters—one daughter, the youngest, was born with arms that looked like wings, and the chances she would marry were slim. Nevertheless Justo José felt he was fortunate. Each time he thought about his trip to France, the awful journey on board the *Tacuari,* the bloodlike substance he drank that made him sick to his stomach, the woman who had lain motionless on her back on the bed and whose hair was the same color as the feathers on a parakeet—what was her name, *Eeyon?*—Justo José crossed himself and thanked his lucky stars. Also he had managed to save enough money to buy himself a brand-new thirty-six-string cedarwood harp so that he could continue playing in Franco's private band.

Justo José played when Franco withdrew his troops from Corrientes and when he had General Robles executed, *ta dum ta dum ta dum dum dum* (if Captain Mesa—lucky for him—had not died first of his chest wound, Franco would have had him executed as well, *ta dum ta dum*). Although the colonel was safe in Brazil, after he had surrendered, *ta dum ta dum,* Franco made sure that Estigarribia's entire family was punished; his sons—the youngest was ten, Pancho's age exactly—were imprisoned, tortured and shot, *ta dum ta dum,* his wife and daughters were robbed of all their possessions—including the little girls' freshwater pearl earrings—then beaten and sent out to perish in the jungle, *ta dum.*

Ta dum, Justo José did indeed feel fortunate.

The day after Franco promoted Frederick Masterman from apothecary general to assistant military surgeon, Frederick Masterman, for the first time in his career, had to amputate. In fact, he had to amputate the soldier's leg twice, first the foot, then since the gangrene had spread, the leg. Both times, Frederick Masterman was able to amputate quickly, the soldier was so emaciated there was little flesh on his bones to cut through.

The hospital had had three hundred beds but now that number had grown to a thousand beds, makeshift beds made out of strips of rawhide, beds made out of sacking filled with moss, that were jammed side by side in a single ward. Sent to Asunción from the front by steamer—a journey of at least two or three days—the sick and wounded soldiers received neither food nor medical care. Most of them died on the way and their bodies were thrown overboard before they reached their destination. When those who were still alive arrived, they were naked and famished but they rarely complained or cried out. They suffered in silence.

Already Frederick Masterman had counted 50,000 dead; after he had finished amputating the soldier's leg a second time, Frederick Masterman counted 50,001.

Asunción
20 October 1865

Ma chère Princesse,

    Thank you for your letter of July 28, which I only now received—the mail has been unusually slow these past months—I am delighted to have your news. I especially enjoyed your description of your friend Monsieur Sainte-Beuve, whom you brought most vividly to life. In my mind's eye I can see you both conversing in his "nest" full of books, papers and pens. How fortunate you are! I confess Monsieur Sainte-Beuve has always been a great favorite of mine. I vividly recall how I looked forward to Les Causeries du lundi *and how I read* Portraits de femme *with the greatest of pleasure. In particular, I remember how moved I was by Monsieur Sainte-Beuve's description of Madame de Sévigné's love for her daughter, and how their separation only deepened this love. Now, of course, I cannot help but think of my own little Corinna Adelaida, who would be nearly ten years old if she were alive today. (In my head, I write her letters as well, however instead of addressing them to Provence, I address the letters to Paradise!)*

    Every day I thank the Lord for my good fortune and for my family and my friends. You no doubt would be surprised at the number of foreigners who now reside in Paraguay—engineers, architects, physicians, all eager to make their fortunes in this rich new world. Recently, I made the acquaintance of a Prussian baron who is most charming and who has taught me a great deal about this new telegraph system that he is installing in Paraguay; another new acquaintance is a distinguished and well-regarded journalist—he and Franco have the most lively conversations! His appreciation of music is a source of great pleasure to me and I particularly value his suggestions, such as La forza del destino, *by Giuseppe Verdi—do you know it?—which will be performed during our next opera season; in the coming week, a Paraguayan lady whom I am quite certain you would like as much as I do—she is very lively and speaks half a dozen languages fluently and is married to a eminent Scottish physician who has made his home in Asunción—will accompany me to a ball in Buenos Ayres. So you see, dear friend, I hardly lack good company or entertainment! (I also look forward to receiving the books you so kindly promised to send me. I am particularly curious since Madame Cochelet, the wife of the French minister here, is of the opinion that* Salammbô *is vastly superior to* Madame Bovary, *which she found quite shocking and upsetting. Naturally I am much more inclined to share your opinion than hers!)*

I must also tell you of my surprise and joy last week when I went to Humaitá (a fort south of the capital, which is beautifully located on a bend of the Paraguay River where Franco is presently stationed with his troops), and on my arrival—I barely had time to remove my hat and cloak—Franco greeted me with the news that he had managed to obtain a new piano for me! (The Pleyel I brought with me from France is over ten years old and is perpetually out of tune.) And you can imagine my further surprise and joy when I saw the piano—no ordinary piano, but a Bechstein! (The Bechstein belonged to a Mr. Delphino who, on leaving Corrientes, had to abandon his possessions.) More than ever, I feel inspired to practice, practice, practice. . . . Also, rather rashly, I have promised to give a few piano lessons to the daughter of the architect who designed my palace, a lovely and gifted young English girl.

My aim is not to distress you with talk of politics and war, but I wonder whether news has reached you that Paraguay has become involved in a battle against her neighbors who have acted with the utmost lack of candor and disregard for our country's interests. Franco is quite justified in the actions he has taken—your cousin, the Emperor, gave Franco his blessing, for which we will always remain grateful—and my sincere hope is that the peaceful and equitable state to which we aspire will occur without too much delay or strife. I am convinced of the rightness of our position and am certain justice will be served. I could speak at length about this matter but I fear that the geographical distance that alas separates us must necessarily affect your interest in our affairs. So enough of this.

Your devoted friend who sends her best wishes and much affection,
Ella

P.S. I was especially amused by your description of the bathing machine—how I wish I could watch you pedaling it on the lake at Saint-Gratien. Perhaps, I should try to acquire one for my use in the Paraguay River. I wonder what the crocodiles would make of it?

Eleven

HUMAITÁ

For the first time in his life, Frederick Masterman heard a blacksmith frog. The blacksmith frog was aptly named: it sounded exactly like a hammer hitting an iron plate. In his journal he wrote that the sound of several hundred blacksmith frogs nearly deafened him. Frederick Masterman had been sent from Asunción to Humaitá to inspect the field hospital, and while there he also had the opportunity to examine several kinds of fireflies: the *Lampyris occidentalis*, which glowed so brightly he could ride home at night by its light; the *Pyrophorus luminosus,* which gave off an eerie green light (he studied the illuminators under the microscope and noted pear-shaped sacs crossed by several trachealike tubes that determined the amount of light transmitted); but, for him, by far the most beautiful sight was the larva of a beetle. During the day the beetle was an ordinary, ugly gray worm whereas at night, Frederick Masterman wrote, it glowed like a chain of emeralds with a ruby clasp!

Perched on a cliff in a bend of the Paraguay River, Humaitá was a forbidding place. The land was flat and marshy; when it rained the clay soil turned into mud, then into a lake. Narrow roads wound through the *esteros*, the marshes; the higher ground consisted of untended fields, groves of scraggly, neglected orange trees. The barracks were constructed out of mud and thatched with reeds; only Franco had a house made out of bricks. The other houses in the camp were occupied by Colonel von Wisner; Lieutenant-Major Thompson, the English engineer; Franco's brother-in-law, General Barrios; Padre Fidel Maiz, whom Franco had finally released from prison; Dr. Stewart, the surgeon general of the army and Franco's personal physician; and by Ella. (Not knowing how long she would have to stay, Ella brought crates of china, silver, linens to furnish her house, also she had her new Bechstein piano.)

Humaitá boasted more than 300 guns. Frederick Masterman got a good look at nearly all of them: on the land side, he saw 204 guns, 87 of them mounted, which protected three lines of earthworks; another 100 guns defended the center of the fort (among those, a 40-pounder rifled Whitworth recovered from one of the Brazilian steamers at the battle of Riachuelo caught Frederick Masterman's special attention); on the river side, he counted 46 guns—one 80-pounder, four 68-pounders, eight 32-pounders, the rest of mixed calibers.

As for the hospital, Frederick Masterman noted that it was located far too close to the batteries and under constant threat of fire. Several casualties had already occurred. One time a single cannonball ripped through the wall and killed thirteen men as they lay in their beds. Most of the soldiers who were not wounded were sick with dysentery, cholera or the measles.

6 FEBRUARY 1866

I could leave Paraguay tomorrow, I could leave Paraguay today. I could go back to France if I wanted to. I admit I am tempted. (What would I not give for a single day in Paris! To walk down rue du Bac again, to see the chestnut trees around the Tuileries in bloom, to go to a concert and listen to music, to have a proper fitting with Monsieur Worth!) There is a French ship, the *Decidé*, that sets sail tomorrow that would take me and the children—except for Pancho, who would never leave his father. I have already spoken to the captain. All of last night I stayed awake, I could not decide. In the end, I tossed the dice: an even number and I stay, an odd one and I go—it was an odd number!—but already I knew the answer, I cannot leave Franco. My duty lies with Franco—more than my duty, my heart! *[Ella underlined the word "heart."]* Nevertheless, the captain of the *Decidé* has agreed to take a trunk with some valuables, which he will deposit for me with Monsieur Gelot in Paris. Who knows? I may go back to France one day and I must provide for the future. For now, I certainly have no need for jewelry, nor for dresses. Every day I wear the same clothes: riding breeches and a gray cloak. I brought Mathilde to Humaitá—how could I leave her behind?—but more often than not I ride another horse to spare her having to go through the swamps and marshes where the footing is so treacherous. I could not bear it if anything happened to my darling!

"I swear I will swallow it rather than let her get her hands on it. My marriage present from Saturnino." Rafaela sighed and turned the ring around so that the large red stone faced inside her palm. She was dressed in one of Baron de Villa Maria's wife's peach-colored silk bedroom curtains. The bodice fit so tightly Rafaela had had to undo the hooks before she started to eat her meal.

The sisters had refused to comply with the announcement in *El Semanario*, which said that all Paraguayan women, rich and poor alike, had to contribute their jewelry to the State as a means of carrying on the war and protecting the Paraguayan people from the enemy.

Fingering the gold chain and heavy diamond-studded cross that dangled from her fat throat, Inocencia said, "My first-communion present from our dear departed father when I was nine years old. I've never taken it off, not even when I fell off my pony and broke my collarbone—do you remember, Rafaela?" Inocencia was dressed in Baron de Villa Maria's yellow damask drawing room curtains. "I would rather die a thousand deaths than part with it."

"Or be torn limb from limb. Pass the meat, please," Rafaela answered her.

"Doesn't she have enough jewels of her own?" Before passing her sister the dish, Inocencia helped herself to more beef. As she did, the full pagoda sleeve of her yellow damask dress fell into the platter but oblivious of the mess made as her sauce-covered sleeve trailed across the table, Inocencia continued, "Every time I see her she is wearing a new ring, a new bracelet, a new necklace—do you remember the aquamarines Franco gave her? The stones are the size of eggs—parrot eggs."

"As for me, I am sick of always eating beef, beef, beef—why can't the cook buy a different sort of meat for a change? Chicken or pork?" Rafaela took the dish from Inocencia. "And why, pray tell me, are there never enough vegetables?"

"What next?" Inocencia asked. "We will be made to join the army." Their mouths full of food, the sisters laughed.

One Sunday afternoon after attending mass, their only day off, Gaspar and Fulgencio were fishing, fishing more from habit than from pleasure, in the Paraguay River just south of Humaitá, when they spotted a man swimming across the river. The man was struggling so hard in the water that, as the two brothers stood on the bank and watched, it seemed certain the man would be dragged under by the current and drown. And Gaspar and Fulgencio did not know what to do—was the man swimming toward them an enemy or a friend? They had left their bayonets behind in the barracks and they were ready to turn and run.

At last the man dragged himself on to the shore. He lay face-down on his stomach not moving; his wet clothes clinging to his emaciated body. Plucking up their courage, Gaspar and Fulgencio approached him.

"*Hola!*" Gaspar called out to the man.

When he did not answer Fulgencio poked him with his foot. "*Hola!*" he repeated.

"*Cómo se llama usted?*"

The man lifted his head; slowly, painfully, he got to his knees and vomited.

Gaspar and Fulgencio half carried the man to the hospital and arrived just as Dr. Stewart was finishing his rounds and leaving. The surgeon general was late—he and his wife were due to play whist with Ella that evening—but something about how the man looked made him go back in and examine him. Although the symptoms were not yet severe, Dr. Stewart diagnosed smallpox; he also learned that the man, an Argentine, had deserted the Allied army. Dr. Stewart informed General Barrios, but the general neglected to interrogate or send the man away. By then it was probably too late anyway.

When Franco was finally informed, he had the deserter flogged until the man, more dead than alive from both smallpox and the lashes of the whip, confessed to having been sent by President Mitre to introduce and spread the disease among the Paraguayan Army. Dr. Stewart, who was known for his easy and sanguine disposition, no longer felt so sanguine. Despite the fact that he had organized several hospitals in Paraguay that were more efficient and better equipped than those of the Brazilian and Argentine armies, and despite the fact that he had persuaded Franco to hire British physicians, thousands of soldiers in Humaitá had already died of dysentery, measles and cholera, and thousands more, Dr. Stewart knew, would soon die of smallpox.

The following week, Gaspar and Fulgencio, already weak from dysentery and malnutrition, came down with it. Their skin turned black, their throats swelled from the pocks and they could not breathe. After three days filled with agony, when the pain was so severe that the brothers often lost consciousness, Gaspar died. Lying in the hospital bed next to him, Fulgencio was not immediately aware that his brother had died. In his delirium, he kept calling out to Gaspar, a few times he reached out to touch his hand, and it was only a few days later, after his fever had subsided, that Fulgencio suddenly realized that the man lying in the next bed whose hand he had touched was not his brother. His brother was gone.

The state of most of the horses was wretched. There were no pastures— only swamps—and only enough corn and hay to feed the officers' horses. The rest were nothing but skin and bones, and incapable of moving faster than a walk. The soldiers could go faster on foot, except they needed the horses to cross the marshes. Ella made sure there was plenty of grain and hay for Mathilde but Mathilde was getting older and Ella could do nothing about that—the way she could do nothing about the frown lines and the tiny crow's-feet she noticed when she looked closely at her face in the dressing room mirror. Mathilde's withers had sunk and her hipbones had begun to jut out a little; her dappled gray coat was losing its bright sheen. After a day's hard ride, Mathilde's body was covered with flecks of white foam and she stumbled a bit on the way home. According to Ella's calculations, Mathilde was at least fifteen years old.

General Venancio Flores, the leader of the Banda Oriental forces, barely escaped capture when his tent was overrun by the Paraguayan soldiers. The next day, he wrote a letter to his wife describing the situation.

PASO LA PATRIA
3 May 1866

My dear wife,
Good news as well as bad should always be calmly received. Yesterday the vanguard, under my orders, sustained a considerable defeat, the Oriental

Division being almost completely lost. Between twelve and one o'clock my camp was surprised by a powerful column of Paraguayans. It was impossible to resist forces triple the number of ours, and the Oriental Division succumbed, doing honor to its country's flag.

I comprehend the bad position of our encampment. Some days before the event, I went in person to the General in Chief to show him the advantage of removing the camp, but Mitre answered me thus: "Don't alarm yourself, General Flores; the aggression of the barbarians is nil, for the hour of their extermination has sounded." If, therefore, anyone is responsible for the occurrence of May 2, General Mitre is the man.

What is passing here does not suit my temper at all. . . . Meanwhile some of the troops have had nothing to eat for three days. I don't know what will become of us; and if to the critical situation we are in, you add the constant apathy of General Mitre, it may very well happen that going to seek for wool we ourselves may be shorn.

Everything is left for tomorrow, and the most important movements are postponed.

There are no horses or mules for the trains, and no oxen to eat.

I hardly think it worth while to tell you that the Brazilians turned tail in a swinish manner, and there was a battalion that would not charge. My tent was sacked by the Paraguayans. Send me a portmanteau with a few clothes, a large cloth poncho, a straw hat and two pairs of boots.

My beloved Maria, receive the whole heart of your impassioned old
VENANCIO FLORES

P.S. I recommend you, Maria, to send me nothing but camp clothes—no finery, or dress coats. Curious to say, they have lately been even wanting to order me how to dress.

By the end of the month, General Flores had recovered and gathered 45,000 men and 150 guns. From Matto Grosso province, the Brazilians had brought in 2,000 more cavalrymen whose horses were fresh and well fed. The foot soldiers were armed with new rifled carbines and sword-bayonets. Instead of taking advantage of the fresh troops, however,

the leaders vacillated; instead of advancing, they entrenched themselves. Worse, the Argentine and Banda Oriental leaders argued; General
Mitre and General Flores could never agree or see eye-to-eye on any
one thing.

"My dear sir, you should take better care of your person," General
Mitre told General Flores on more than one occasion.

"My person? How so, sir?" General Flores answered.

"You should provide yourself with a proper uniform to keep up the
dignity of your position."

Turning away, General Flores shook his head and mumbled to himself, "Did I not tell you so, Maria?"

The Paraguayans numbered only 25,000 men but they had the one
advantage: the advantage of placement—the impenetrable Bellaco
marshes. The Bellaco marshes extended as far as the eye could see. The
water was choked with rushes—cut and dried, the rushes were used for
thatch—that grew nine feet tall and so close they made the marshes
impassable. In places the water was six feet deep and the bottom was
mud, which made progress still more difficult—even if the horses and
riders got through the rushes, the holes made by the horses' feet made
them sink deeper and get stuck. The only means of crossing the
marshes were a few concealed passes where the rushes had been torn
out by the roots and the mud had been replaced with sand.

But, instead of waiting, Franco struck first and lost his advantage.

The battalion made up of the Paraguayan aristocracy, the men of
Spanish descent, rode their expensive imported thoroughbred horses
into battle and got them hopelessly stuck in the mud and tangled in the
rushes; the horses and the riders became easy targets and nearly all of
them were shot down. Another battalion composed of new recruits tried
to wade across as a group and were picked off like a bunch of sheep; the
same thing happened to older, more experienced battalions. Nonetheless, the Paraguayan soldiers fought bravely and to the death. Lieutenant-
Colonel Ximenez was shot through both feet but continued to fight on

his knees; Colonel Roa, another Paraguayan officer, cut off and alone with a broken sword, escaped by throwing handfuls of dirt in the enemies' eyes and blinding them. One mortally wounded sergeant refused to give up the Paraguayan flag he was carrying to the enemy; he used his last dying breaths to shred the flag with his teeth. But by four o'clock in the afternoon the firing was over and the Bellaco marshes were heaped with Paraguayan dead—six thousand men in all.

"How do I know the bastard is mine?" Franco shouted at Ella.

Ella was pregnant again.

"How do I know he isn't a little Teuton? A little Fischer-Truenfeld?"

"I have never lied to you. I am not going to begin now." Ella's mouth was set, her gray eyes looked black and for once, afraid, Franco stopped shouting.

Miguel Marcial was born two months premature; he weighed less than four pounds. Instead of trying to feed him, Rosaria put the baby in a tub of lukewarm chicken broth. The chicken broth, she claimed, would serve as amniotic fluid and seep through the baby's skin to nourish him. Franco made Padre Fidel Maiz hold a special mass for Miguel Marcial; he prayed and lit a number of candles, in addition he went to visit the baby every day. Taking off his hat and getting down on his knees on the floor next to the tub filled with broth, Franco leaned over and gently kissed Miguel Marcial's tiny head—a head already covered with thick black hair.

When Miguel Marcial died two weeks later, Franco, grief-stricken and guilt-ridden both, accused Rosaria of being a witch and of drowning him. As punishment, he threatened to have her flogged to death.

Her face white with anger, sorrow and lack of sleep, Ella screamed back at Franco: "If you so much as touch a hair on Rosaria's head, I will never share your bed again!" Already she had decided that she would never let herself get pregnant again.

After the enormous losses at Bellaco, Franco ordered that every single able-bodied male be recruited into the army. He would make no exceptions (not even for the son of the farmer, Julio Ignacio, who coughed up blood and was now thirteen years old); he also recruited women to work in the fields and build trenches. He recruited the Payaguá Indians, who spoke neither Spanish nor Guaraní but a totally different language made up of guttural sounds and who ate crocodile meat, and the Guaycurú Indians, who lived in the Chaco and were cannibals.

José de Carmen Gomez, formerly the commandant at Villa Franca, was one of the officers who complained. He said his soldiers would not fight alongside the Guaycurú Indians. The Guaycurú, Commandant Gomez said, were indifferent to the outcome of the war and not to be trusted. Every chance they got, the Guaycurú stole his soldiers' weapons, his soldiers' clothes, their food. No telling, he said, what they would steal next! One incident in particular stayed in the commandant's mind—the same way he said he could never forget having once seen a woman's arm being amputated without proper anesthetic. It occurred one night when he left his tent to relieve himself—something he had to do more and more frequently—and he had stumbled upon a group of Guaycurú. To him it looked like a scene from a bad dream: the Guaycurú were sitting around a fire eating, and no mistaking it, the commandant swore on his mother's grave!, he saw them eating arms and legs and one of the Guaycurú Indians was gnawing on a head—a head with long blond hair! The next morning, Commandant Gomez could hardly believe it himself. Shrugging his shoulders, he took a noisy sip of *maté* through his *bombilla*—who knew, he told himself, maybe it had been a bad *sueño* after all. Only he did not believe so.

Ella too had bad dreams, and in one dream she was eating as well. She ate plate after plate of food and still she was not full and still she was hungry. The food was both familiar and unfamiliar: one plate was filled with food that tasted like chestnuts—the same roast chestnuts she used to buy in winter along the quays of the Seine—but did not look like chestnuts; another plate was filled with what tasted like artichokes but again did not look like artichokes. As time went by, the food that had once tasted good to Ella no longer tasted good and was harder to chew and it tasted like uncooked bark and leaves from a tree. The bark and leaves were raw and tough and she had to chew and chew and chew before she could swallow them; and, in her dream, she realized that what she was eating was a *yatai* palm tree—raw, the heart of the *yatai* palm, Ella knew, tasted like chestnuts, cooked, it tasted like artichokes, but when the heart was removed, the palm tree, she also knew, died.

In the morning when she awoke Ella could hardly speak, her jaws were too sore from chewing all night in her sleep.

Charles Washburn, full of his own sense of justice and importance, took a steamer and went to see Franco at Humaitá. Over breakfast, he tried to flatter Franco into giving up the war.

"What men of modern times have been received with the most enthusiasm and respect?" Too clever for his own good, he asked Franco. "Not the victors with laurels, nor those who have triumphed, irrespective of their cause, by means of superior resources, or even superior genius and ability. For instance, Napoleon"—the American minister knew how much Franco admired him—"was none the less honored for having died a prisoner at St. Helena than he would have been had he conquered at Waterloo and afterward expired in the Tuileries."

"I have no personal ambition. I labor for my country," unswayed, Franco answered Charles Washburn. "I will survive or fall with it. I stand by my acts—*mis hechos, mis hechos,*" he said.

Accompanied by his brother Venancio, his brother-in-law General Barrios, his son Pancho, a staff of about fifty officers and a personal escort

of twenty-four men, Franco rode out to the Allied trenches to meet
with General Mitre. Dressed carefully for the occasion, Franco wore his
best patent leather boots, polished to a high shine by his servant,
Mañuel, his heaviest silver spurs, a scarlet poncho trimmed with gold
lace and lined with vicuña, and a tricornered hat; instead of the mule
Linda, he rode a big white horse.

Franco and General Mitre spoke for five hours. During that time,
they ate nothing and drank only brandy. After several glasses, Franco was
ready to agree: Paraguay was to withdraw from occupied Allied territory;
each nation was to pay for its share of the war; the Allies were to recognize the independence of Paraguay—all but the last provision. When
he heard its words—Franco was to resign and leave the country—
Franco let out a roar and threw down his riding whip. Then, leaping to
his feet and shouting for his horse, he left without another word to
General Mitre.

On the way home, Franco struck his horse with whatever came
under his hand—sharp pointed reeds, thorny branches he ripped off the
trees—forcing the big white horse into a frenzy and making him gallop
and gallop faster, whipping him through the mud and the marshes, and
never once allowing him to slow down or catch his breath. When finally
they reached camp, the big white horse's legs buckled under him and he
fell dead. Franco too could hardly stand. His scarlet poncho trimmed
with gold lace and lined with vicuña was torn, his tricornered hat got
knocked off and was lost, his shiny patent leather boots were spattered
with mud.

The next day, Franco fell ill with malaria, a recurring bout so severe that
his fever lasted over a week. One moment he was cold, freezing cold—
all the blankets, rugs, furs in the army camp were piled on top of him
and still he shook and trembled—the next moment, he was hot, boiling
hot, and within seconds he was drenched with sweat, the sweat pouring
off his body in rivulets and soaking through his nightshirt, his linen, the

mattress. Franco's fever fluctuated so fast and so often that even Dr. Stewart despaired. The whole time, Ella sat by Franco's bedside. She bathed his forehead, she stroked his hand, she spoke quietly and reassuringly to him in his delirium. When he had recovered sufficiently, she had her piano, the Bechstein, brought into Franco's bedroom and she played it for him.

Twelve

CURUPAYTY

"A change of scene" was the reason Lieutenant-Major George Thompson, Franco's military engineer, gave his brother for leaving England and going to Paraguay. He also claimed to have had no previous knowledge of military engineering or artillery; everything he knew he had picked up from Macaulay's *Field of Fortification* and *The Professional Papers of the Corps of Royal Engineers*. He had taught himself, he said: "I took bearings, with a small hand prismatic compass, to all objects I could see, and these bearings I laid down by applying my paper-scale to the proper bearing on the pricked protractor, and carefully shifting it along thence, in a parallel direction, to my station on the paper, and then ruling a line. I then estimated the distance, which I laid down by scale. I surveyed in this manner a great part of the Bellaco. . . . I also made a trigonometrical survey of the River Paraguay, from Curupayty to its fall into the Paraná."

Shortly after he finished building the fortifications at Curupayty—the name was derived from the Guaraní word for the acacia tree—Lieutenant-Major Thompson, along with Captain Ortiz and Major Sayas, the commanders of the river battery, and Captain Gill and Major Hermosa, the artillery commanders, took Franco for a tour. Pancho and Ella came, too.

"We constructed a trench two thousand yards long and six feet deep and eleven feet wide," Lieutenant-Major Thompson explained. Riding ahead, he proudly pointed out each of the gun emplacements; as always, he had a cigar in his mouth—the smoke, he claimed, helped drive away the buffalo gnats and mosquitos, which were a great source of aggravation. "These two eight-inch guns are aimed at the land front, the two over there at the right flank, those four at the river."

Slightly south of Humaitá and across the river from it, Curupayty overlooked a bend in the Paraguay at a point where the water was deep and flowed swiftly. From there the Paraguayans launched torpedoes at the Brazilian fleet. The torpedoes were flimsy homemade affairs—glass capsules filled with sulphuric acid, chlorate of potash and white sugar, all wrapped in cotton wool. Many of them were accidentally exploded by driftwood or by curious crocodiles; one torpedo blew up an American, Mr. Krüger, and a Paraguayan, Mr. Ramos.

"Over here you will find several thirty-two-pounders mounted on both the trench and in the river battery—" Lieutenant-Major Thompson paused to slap at a buffalo gnat that, in spite of the cigar smoke, had landed on his neck. Dark clouds of buffalo gnats rose from the river and descended upon the camp—there were so many that a slap of the hand might kill half a dozen. The sting left a black spot that marked the skin for weeks, Lieutenant-Major Thompson's body was covered with them. "Already the five twelve-pounders and the four nine-pounders are in position in the trench." He wiped the blood where the gnat had stung him. "All in all there are forty-nine guns and two rocket stands. Thirteen of the guns belong to the river battery, the rest to the trench."

Ella could never quite say why she did not like the lieutenant-major. His manner was too dry, too formal. He never looked at her directly.

Finished, he bowed politely to Franco, then lowering his eyes, he bowed ever so slightly to Ella. Lieutenant-Major Thompson did not much like her either. Ella was too flashy, too pretty; he was more used to women like his mother and his sisters back home in England, who served tea and spoke only when spoken to. And a woman did not belong on a battlefield.

Since his bout with malaria, Franco had stopped drinking. He had lost weight and looked fit; for once his teeth did not bother him. Dismounting, with Pancho at his side, Franco walked over to speak with the officers. In an attempt to be friendly, Major Sayas put his hand on Pancho's shoulder but Pancho shrugged it off.

General Diaz, the commander in chief, who had just arrived, rode up to Ella. General Diaz was married to Doña Isidora, one of Ella's ladies-in-waiting. Short and stocky, he was enthusiastic and polite and Ella liked him well enough—more than she liked Lieutenant-Major Thompson.

Taking off his hat, General Diaz said, "This time, we will have them for certain."

"I sincerely hope so," Ella answered.

Reaching up, General Diaz slapped at a cloud of buffalo gnats that hovered over his bare head. "A victory, I guarantee it."

Summer in Asunción was murderously hot and Charles Washburn was determined to move his wife, who was pregnant and suffering from the heat, to cooler quarters. Fortunately, Doña Rafaela, who was kinder and less avaricious than Inocencia, her sister, offered him her own *quinta,* a few miles outside the city. Built on a hill, the *quinta* had a splendid view and large airy rooms that caught the breezes. Also, it had a walled-in garden for Mrs. Washburn's terrier to run in (although, at nearly twelve, Bumppo was a little arthritic and no longer quite so active). Mrs. Washburn spent most afternoons sitting on a balcony, reading and resting, and most afternoons too, unannounced, Rafaela came by to visit and to practice her English.

"American," Mrs. Washburn corrected her. "It's quite different actually." Although blond and fragile-looking, Mrs. Washburn knew how to stand up for herself.

"As different as Guaraní is from Spanish?" There was something childish and naïve about Rafaela and Mrs. Washburn did not dislike her. Also, each time Rafaela brought gifts. The gifts of food, the look and smell of them, made her feel ill; some of the gifts were valuable: a gold chain with a pearl pendant for the baby.

"Oh, but I can't accept this," she started to tell Rafaela.

Rafaela frowned, her lip began to tremble, she looked as if she might cry.

"Oh, my dear," Mrs. Washburn quickly got up and kissed Rafaela. "Of course, I'd be delighted." Then, embarrassed, she called, "Here, Bumppo, here!"

Ella's equerry, Lázaro Alcántara, claimed to be eighteen but Ella guessed he was only fifteen or sixteen years old. He was a quiet, soft-spoken boy, with blond, curly hair. If Ella went out alone, Lázaro rode with her; if Ella needed a leg up—which she didn't—Lázaro helped her mount her horse; if Ella, for some reason, had to dismount, he held her horse. When Ella asked Lázaro questions about himself and his family, he told her that his mother was German originally—it was from her he had inherited his fair hair and curls; his father had died; he had a younger brother and sister to support. Lázaro also told Ella that his dream, once the war was over, was to go to Paris, to study. He wanted to study architecture there, he wanted to build the same kind of buildings in Paraguay that he had seen in books about France.

"I could teach you French," Ella told Lázaro one day as they were riding along the bank of the Paraguay River.

"Do you think I could really learn?" Lázaro's eyes shone with pleasure.

"Of course. We can begin right away. *Bonjour, Monsieur. Comment allez-vous?* You must repeat exactly what I say."

"Bonjour, Monsieur. Comment allez-vous?"
"Très bien. Only you must call me *Madame."*

Standing in his shirtsleeves in front of his quarters at Humaitá, Franco was looking at the battle through his field glasses. It was an exceptionally hot and humid day but Franco hardly noticed (he did not notice until it was almost too late the sound of a stray enemy shell that landed a few feet away from him). He was watching the Argentinian soldiers cross the open plain and then, long before they reached Lieutenant-Major Thompson's trench, get slaughtered at point-blank range by the fire of the 8-inch guns. When he was not looking through his field glasses, Franco was reading the dispatches; Baron von Fischer-Truenfeld had laid down the posts and telegraph lines from Curupayty to Humaitá—there were not enough telegraphs and Baron von Fischer-Truenfeld had had to improvise with an instrument that looked like a knocker. By the end of the afternoon, Franco had received several dispatches confirming what he himself could see: five thousand Argentinian soldiers dead and only fifty-four Paraguayan soldiers and two officers killed, one of whom was Major Sayas. Franco, who had barely moved from his post all day, except to run for cover from the stray shell, stayed where he was a little longer to watch the enemy retreat and his own soldiers go and gather the spoils: rifles, pistols, knives, watches, money, clothes, also saucepans—the enemy had planned on having supper that night at Curupayty. Franco watched the wounded who were lying in the field get shot—only a lieutenant, who had a shattered knee, managed to crawl away as the soldier who was going to shoot him had trouble reloading his musket—or, to save bullets, get hanged from trees. He watched until night fell and until the rest of the Argentinian dead were thrown in the marshes and into the river.

No longer used to drinking alcohol, the champagne to celebrate the victory went straight to Franco's head. All night long, he sang, he danced, he told bawdy jokes. During the battle, one of the officers had gotten hold of a packet of letters from the enemy—letters from General Flores to his wife.

"Old impassioned Venancio, from your beloved Maria!" General Diaz, who also had drunk too much champagne, made as if to read the letters out loud to Franco. He mimicked a woman's high-pitched voice. *"To my old impassioned Venancio!"* General Diaz repeated as he made loud smacking sounds with his lips and shook his hips.

Smoking a cigar and sitting off to one side, Lieutenant-Major Thompson, who was sober, was telling Colonel von Wisner about how the Allies had fired some very beautiful 40-pounder Whitworth rifled balls and percussion shells.

"So beautiful, in fact," he said, "it would almost be a consolation to be killed by one."

"I recommend you, Venancio, send me no finery or silk dresses," General Diaz continued in the high-pitched voice.

"Receive my whole heart, my beloved Maria!" Franco embraced stocky General Diaz to his chest—General Diaz's head barely reached Franco's chin—then, laughing, Franco danced and twirled him around the room in his arms, as if he were a woman, while the other officers whistled and clapped.

"Mañuel!" Franco shouted, "bring us more champagne!"

Frederick Masterman was arrested a month after the battle of Curupayty. Riding home from visiting friends one evening—for him a rare luxury to be away from the hospital—he was absorbed thinking about why the sand flea needed to lay its eggs under the skin of a living animal, and he was not a bit apprehensive for his own safety. He had worked out in his mind that the sac in which the flea laid its eggs was not just a bag of eggs but the developed abdomen of the flea, which absorbed nutritive material from the skin of its host, when all of a sudden he was stopped by an officer and several armed soldiers. He was bound and gagged, and thrown into prison.

Although repeatedly questioned, it was not clear what he was accused of—something to do with the improper delivery of letters not stamped by the Paraguayan post office, a mere pretext for his arrest. Under the threat of torture or, worse, death, he was forced to sign a deposition admitting to his guilt. Guilt for what? Frederick Masterman never found out.

Always damp, his narrow, underground cell was furnished with a bed (a hide stretched over a wooden frame), a broken chair, a candle and a basin; his servant, Tomàs, was allowed to visit once a day and to bring books and wine (later, Frederick Masterman claimed that Monsieur Narcisse Lasserre, a French distiller and a friend who lived in Asunción, saved his life by sending him three bottles of brandy). Tomàs was forbidden to speak to Frederick Masterman—a soldier with a drawn sword always stood between them.

The worst part of his imprisonment was he could not sleep. A sentry stood outside the door of his cell and all through the night, every fifteen minutes, to show that he was awake, the sentry shouted *"Sentinela alerta!"* His cry was taken up in succession by a series of sentries inside the prison and when the last one had finished shouting, it was time for the first one to begin all over again. Also Frederick Masterman feared for his health. Toads shared the cell—each time he got out of bed he put his foot on one. There were cockroaches and he lived in terror of being bitten by a centipede or a scorpion (luckily it was too damp for fleas). There were so many spiders, his cell resembled a giant cobweb. One spider that made its home in a hole in the wall next to his bed became the object of his special attention. He was fascinated by how seemingly effortlessly the spider managed to capture and devour the poisonous scorpions and by how frequently the spider laid its eggs, and as an experiment, to test the spider's fecundity, he removed the ball of eggs, which was almost as large as the spider itself. Each time he did this—six times in a three-week period—the spider produced another ball of eggs.

After *seven months!*—as he himself was later to write in his journal— Frederick Masterman was finally released from prison. He was as thin and as pale as a corpse. His hair, which had turned gray and had not been cut for all this time, hung to his shoulders, his beard was long and tangled. His eyes appeared unnaturally large, the pupils, used only to dark, were hugely dilated. Alone and barely able to walk by himself—his servant, Tomàs, had not been advised of his release—and squinting at the unaccustomed light of dusk, he slowly made his way to the home of the nearest Englishman he knew, Mr. Taylor, the stonemason.

Alonzo Taylor was at supper with his two daughters and his wife— since the war had begun, Mrs. Taylor had decided to leave her bedroom, comb her hair, and take more interest in life.

"More tea, dear?" Mrs. Taylor held up the teapot and was asking her husband when there was a knock on the door.

"Go and see who it is, Elizabeth," she also told one of her daughters.

When Elizabeth opened the front door and saw Frederick Masterman, she started to scream and her father got up from the table so quickly he knocked over his teacup.

Standing protectively in front of his daughter and blocking the door, Alonzo Taylor did not recognize him either. *"Que quiere usted, Señor?"* he asked Frederick Masterman.

Inside Inocencia's aviary, sitting at his table with the same little mean green parrot on top of his head, Dr. Eberhardt was listing the parrots according to their sex. Inocencia had insisted on this. More important to Dr. Eberhardt—he had tried to tell Inocencia but she did not listen to him, she claimed the parrots were molting—was the general state of the parrots' health. The parrots were pulling out their breast feathers—the aviary floor was littered with red, blue, green, yellow feathers. A lot of parrots had abscesses on their mandibles and could not eat properly, others had scaly feet and diarrhea. One poor white-fronted parrot whose nails were bleeding could not perch properly and repeatedly fell down on to the aviary floor. When Dr. Eberhardt caught sight of his favorite parrot, the big hyacinth macaw, he wanted to weep. The big hyacinth macaw's breast was plucked bald and the rest of his usually brilliant feathers were a dull faded blue.

Tea? Profesor, tea? one of the parrots screamed, mimicking his mistress, but Inocencia did not come in and ask, *"Dulce, Profesor?"* the way she usually did. The truth was that, this time, Dr. Eberhardt would have very much liked to have had some tea with plenty of sugar in it and perhaps something sweet to eat as well. He was old and lived alone in a small house in Asunción, with only one servant—he no longer owned a horse—and although he had managed to escape Franco's notice and was left in peace, his life, now that Paraguay was at war, was hard. Like Inocencia's parrots, Dr. Eberhardt did not have enough to eat.

Silly, selfish Inocencia! And what had she said? Male parrots were larger and had flat heads and females had round ones—*bah!* Dr. Eberhardt shook his own head and the mean little green parrot on top of it had to tighten his grip; and what else had the woman said to him?—males tended to sit up on their perches while females sat with their feet spread farther apart on account of the position of their hipbones—*bah!* What did Inocencia know about hipbones? Hers were hidden under layers of fat. And males, she also told him, were louder—she herself was nearly shouting when she said this—and females tended to bite more. He could hardly believe the ignorance of the woman! Old wives' tales, Dr. Eberhardt wanted to tell her.

Holding a squawking yellow-naped Amazon upside down, Dr. Eberhardt counted the red feathers in the parrot's speculum. Males, he knew, normally had five, females only four. This male—Dr. Eberhardt had good reason to believe the parrot was a male—however, had four, the reason perhaps the parrot had been unable to attract a mate. Shrugging his shoulders, Dr. Eberhardt wrote *female* in his notebook. Next he picked up a blue-fronted parrot and counted five red feathers in his speculum—the same theory applied to this species—and, in a pique, Dr. Eberhardt again wrote down *female*.

Tea? Profesor, tea? This time the parrot nearly fooled Dr. Eberhardt, making him swallow hard and making tears spring to his eyes—he could almost taste the sweetened tea. More than ever, Dr. Eberhardt was determined to speak to Inocencia. She had only to take one look at the hyacinth macaw to see for herself that the poor bird had lost half his lovely blue feathers and to see that the poor bird was starving to death.

Every evening before dinner, Ella looked in on her horse, Mathilde—she did not trust the stable boy. Speaking softly so as not to alarm the horse, she opened the stall door and slipped in. After making sure the straw on the floor was clean, the bucket filled with fresh water, Ella put her arms around the horse's neck and rested her head against Mathilde's broad gray shoulder. She stroked Mathilde's head, running her hands down the slightly dished profile, the large flaring nostrils until she reached under the small velvety muzzle, letting the horse nuzzle her hand. "My darling," Ella said to the horse, "my dear, my pretty." One time, reaching into her pocket for sugar, she found an old letter from Princess Mathilde. "From your namesake," she said to the horse, as smiling, she started to read the letter out loud: *"Let me think what you have missed this season—Augier's* Le Mariage d'Olympe, *the revival of Gautier's* Giselle, *a mandolin concert by Velati—I have never heard anyone quite like him and to think that he is blind!"* The crease in the paper made the writing illegible, Ella had to skip a line—*"such a stream of people have come to visit me at the rue de Courcelles: the Duc de Brabant, the King of Portugal, the Prince of Orange and I don't know who else. Of course the Goncourt brothers always come with their sharpened pencils. I am very fond of them both but I admit that sometimes I find their endless scribbling a little tiresome as well as not always accurate. The new faces are Hippolyte Taine and Louis Pasteur, a very pleasant and intelligent man who is a scientist. . . ."* Outside darkness was falling and Ella was vaguely aware of the noisy croaking of frogs—some nights the frogs sounded like hammers hitting anvils—but by now Ella was accustomed to all kinds of sounds, including the sound of gunfire. In the semidarkness of the stall, she folded Princess Mathide's letter and put it back in her pocket. Then, pressing up against the warm and solid weight of Mathilde, she inhaled the smell of fresh grass and horse and breathed deeply. Before leaving, she found the lump of sugar—each day sugar was harder to find—and with a final caress, gave it to the horse.

Charles Washburn was the one responsible for Frederick Masterman's release from prison. He had convinced the Paraguayan authorities for personal reasons. Frederick Masterman was the only European doctor left in Asunción and he had no choice (the truth was Charles Washburn did not much like Frederick Masterman, he thought him queer—he was single and always off on his own examining insects); he wanted him to deliver his wife's child. Not only did Mrs. Washburn have difficulty conceiving, there were signs she would have difficulty giving birth. To make sure of Frederick Masterman's presence, Charles Washburn invited him to live with him and his wife at the American Legation and, to legitimize his position, Charles Washburn officially made Frederick Masterman surgeon to the legation.

Located on Plaza Vieja, the American Legation in Asunción was an old Spanish-style house. It was so large it occupied one side of the square; it had a tiled roof and thick stucco walls decorated with pilasters; the rooms and doorways were so high and wide a horse and rider could easily ride through them. The house was built around a large courtyard with a fountain in the middle that was surrounded by flower beds, and it was there that Frederick Masterman spent most of his days recovering from his ordeal in prison. He was there examining a spider web that stretched between a Cape jasmine and a bunch of orange trees, a distance of nearly twenty feet, when Mrs. Washburn's maid came to fetch him. Mrs. Washburn's water had broken.

The birth of the baby took three days. On the third day, although in intense labor, Mrs. Washburn's cervix was still not fully dilated and Frederick Masterman knew enough about childbirth to be afraid that if the situation continued, he would have to perform a cesarean. He was sweating profusely in the closed-up bedroom; the shutters were shut and the servants kept lighting candles and throwing sickeningly sweet rose water onto the floor. Mrs. Washburn's screams, he guessed, despite the thick stucco walls, could be heard out in the street. (The first day of labor, Mrs. Washburn's dog, at her request, had stayed in the room but, by the afternoon, the dog's incessant barking had gotten on Frederick Masterman's nerves and he had the dog sent out—the dog had had to be dragged out forcibly, snapping and biting.) And what was he to do? Ill equipped, he did not have obstetrical forceps and, except for spirits, he had no anesthetics. Also, he was used to taking care of men, most of them soldiers, and although he had learned to amputate arms and legs, remove bullets and shrapnel, stitch up wounds, he had never before in his life performed such an operation. The grim alternative, which he hardly dared to contemplate, was to perform a craniotomy—he had never done that either—which meant destroying the fetal skull with scissors and crochets, then extracting the fetus piecemeal, but he did not think he had the stomach for that. Better to cut Mrs. Washburn right above the pubic hair line, then cut the stomach muscles and wall, then the uterus. As Frederick Masterman was preparing for the task, the hand holding the scalpel began to shake so hard all of a sudden he was afraid he would drop it, and Mrs. Washburn, who may have caught sight of the scalpel or merely the metal flash of it—by then she was nearly delirious with exhaustion and pain—let out a tremendous scream and, at the same time, a tremendous push and out came her baby.

Ella was right, Lázaro Alcántara had lied, he was only fifteen years old. He had also lied about his family—his mother was not German but Guaraní and he did not know who his father was—and he may or may not have lied about his dream to go to Paris to study architecture and build the same kind of buildings in Paraguay that he had seen in books about France. He did not in fact lie but told the truth about having seen the books about France, along with books about Hungary, since Lázaro Alcántara was Colonel von Wisner's lover.

The victory at Curupayty made General Diaz euphoric and imprudent. The commander in chief also felt he was impervious to danger and he rode around the camp at all hours of the day and night, often without an escort, often unarmed. On a clear moonlit night, against his aides-de-camp's advice, he insisted on getting into a canoe and going fishing in the river. The canoe was hit by a torpedo—probably one of the home-made glass capsules—and capsized. Wounded, General Diaz could not swim and his aides had to rescue him and bring him back to shore. Then Dr. Stewart had to amputate his leg. The leg—General Diaz had insisted on keeping it—once the cut on it was soldered shut, was placed in a little coffin of its own right next to his bed. Ella saw it when she went to the hospital to visit General Diaz; the leg was dressed in a black boot and in a bloodstained white trouser leg with a gold stripe down its side. But a few days later, General Diaz died.

Thirteen

GRAN CHACO

The day Ella and Padre Fidel Maiz rode to the village of Caacupé, the sky turned first purple, then black, before it began to hail. The wind drove a stand of acacia and mimosa trees along the road nearly to the ground. Dismounting, Ella and Padre Fidel Maiz sought shelter inside a small hut; outside streaks of lightning flashed almost continuously, lighting up the countryside.

"A sign," Padre Fidel Maiz, who served as Franco's chaplain, shouted over the noise of the thunder and hail hitting the hut roof. He crossed himself. He was sweating. "We should never have come," he also said.

Earlier in the century, a woman from that village had made a vow that if her daughter who was sick got well, she would give the Virgin all her jewelry; the daughter did get well and the woman kept her promise. Word spread and soon mothers with sick children from all over Paraguay made the pilgrimage to Caacupé.

"Is it true, Father, that in the eyes of God, glass beads and precious stones have the same value?" Ella shouted back. She had not come to Caacupé on a pilgrimage but to replace the jewels with cheap beads. A statue in the village church known as the Virgin of Caacupé was said to be covered from head to toe in precious jewelry. The statue's head was heavy with crowns and tiaras, her neck with pendants and pearl necklaces, her arms, from shoulders to wrists, with gold and silver bracelets, on each finger several rings. Once before the women of Paraguay had been forced to donate their jewelry to Franco as a means of carrying on the war, Ella wanted to get still more.

"The women sacrificed their jewelry to the Virgin of Caacupé as a symbol of faith," Padre Fidel Maiz replied.

"Nevertheless, in the eyes of God, it is the spiritual, not the material, that matters," Ella persisted.

14 JUNE 1867

What a joy to be back home in Obispo Cue, what a joy to have a bath, to sleep in a proper bed with clean linen sheets, and to see the children! Enrique has grown almost two inches since I last saw him. He is turning into quite a handsome little boy. All he can talk about is how he can hardly wait for the velocipede his father has ordered especially for him from Paris to arrive. Carlos Honorio announced that he plans to be a circus-animal trainer when he grows up and he refuses to be parted from a little chinchilla he carries around in his pocket. Leopoldo claims he knows how to read and write! Only Federico seems a little subdued—the boy is too sensitive but what am I to do? He asked me if I thought Maria Oliva was looking down at us from heaven. Certainly, I answered him, and she is holding Corinna Adelaida in her arms. He and I looked through the bag of jewelry I brought back from Caacupé—I was especially tempted by a black pearl ring which fit my finger perfectly but I know where my duty lies!

I found no letters, a huge disappointment, as I had hoped to hear from Princess Mathilde. When I questioned my mayor domo, he answered the standard: *"Non sé nada"*—it is hopeless to try to get these people to speak if they are afraid. I also heard the news that Mr. Masterman has been in prison; I sincerely hope he did not have to suffer too greatly, poor man. Ever since he pulled out Franco's abscessed tooth, I have felt nothing but gratitude for him although I am well aware that he has a reputation for being a bit odd, a bit of an eccentric, but that is not a concern of mine. Apparently he is staying at the American Legation along with an American whose unreliable reputation precedes him, a Mr. Manlove. Rumor has it that he is a spy sent by the Brazilians and I was told by no other than Matias Sanabria himself that he is waiting for the moment when Mr. Manlove abandons the safe haven provided by the legation to arrest him. Under the circumstances, I agree, one cannot be too cautious. Mrs. Washburn, I was also told, finally gave birth to her baby, a girl. If I have a moment, I will pay her a call. I must not forget to go and thank Monsieur Lasserre, who kindly brought over a case of Château Issan. And bless her heart! Rosaria baked me a loaf of *chipa*. Poor Doña Isidora has not once stopped weeping since she heard the news of her husband's death. I do not have the heart to tell her about the general's leg.

One last thing, when I looked out of my window this morning, even though it is midwinter, I saw Doña Iñes, on her hands and knees in the garden, weeding. At first, I mistook her for one of my gardeners. I must speak to her. She could go back as far as Buenos Ayres with Mr. Gould on the H.M.S. *Dotterel*.

Grossly overweight, Mr. Gould, the secretary of the British Legation in Buenos Ayres, needed several hands to help him disembark from the H.M.S. *Dotterel* and proceed on foot to Franco's headquarters at Humaitá. (One of the hands was Fulgencio's, he had to push Mr. Gould up the steep path while another man pulled.) Mr. Gould's mission was to investigate reports that some of his countrymen, their contracts having long ago expired, were being detained against their will and were desirous to leave Paraguay.

"On the contrary," Franco denied Mr. Gould's allegations at the same time as he offered him chocolates, "I have always shown particular partiality toward the Englishmen in my employ and have conferred great benefits on them—here, may I offer you some chocolate truffles that just now arrived from France. In my opinion, the very best." Franco was lying, the chocolates were from Bolivia. "Secondly," he continued, "as you must understand due to the circumstances, I cannot now dispense with the services of these gentlemen or allow any foreigners to leave the country—delicious, aren't they? I admit I too have a terrible weakness for chocolates. Please, help yourself, there is plenty where these came from," Franco said, passing Mr. Gould the box again. "Lastly, I assure you that none of your British subjects have the slightest cause for complaint. To the best of my knowledge and you have my word on this—by all means, Mr. Gould, don't be bashful, have another chocolate truffle—all the Englishmen here are quite content and no one has ever voiced any desire to leave Paraguay."

Mr. Gould was not convinced. Four days later, after he had recovered from an attack of vomiting and diarrhea so violent that Dr. Stewart, Franco's personal physician, had to be called in to attend to him—had he been poisoned? Mr. Gould could not help but wonder—he was finally able to sit up without feeling dizzy and nauseated and write to Mr. Mathew Buckley, British minister plenipotentiary to the Argentine: "Paraguay has for many years past almost exclusively employed Englishmen. The medical service of its army is entrusted to four English surgeons and an English apothecary."

Mr. Gould had to stop writing for a moment to again use the toilet. When he returned, he finished his letter:

It is mainly owing to the exertions of this handful of Englishmen that Paraguay, reduced to its own limited resources, has, under the direction of President Lopez, thus far been enabled to prolong the desperate struggle in

which it has been engaged for upward of two years. Hence the natural
reluctance of His Excellency to part with men whose services are invaluable to
him and whom he cannot possibly hope to replace under present circumstances.

In the end, Mr. Gould had to be satisfied with taking the three wid-
ows of English mechanics and their five children back with him to
Buenos Ayres.

"*Idiota!*" Benigno shouted at his brother Venancio. "Are you so blind!
Didn't you see what I discarded?"

Venancio and Benigno Lopez—at long last Benigno had been
allowed to return to Asunción from his exile at his *estancia* in San
Pedro—played whist nearly every afternoon at the *quinta* of their
mother, Doña Juaña, in Campo Grande. Saturnino Bedoya, their
brother-in-law who was minister of the treasury, played with them; the
fourth player varied according to the day. Gumesmindo Benítez, the editor of *El Semanario,* played on Monday, Wednesday and Friday; the
American envoy, Charles Washburn, on Tuesday and Thursday; Matias
Sanabria, the chief of police, on Saturday (sometimes, if for some reason
one of the players became unavailable, Rafaela was brought in to play
with her husband and brothers). An avid and avaricious gambler—few
people would play with him, it was too dangerous—Benigno kept raising the stakes during the game. Venancio, who worried about his health,
coughed into his handkerchief but did not dare complain. His younger
brother had a terrible temper and Venancio felt too unwell to risk pro-
voking him.

"I, I—" Red in the face, Venancio could not stop coughing.

"Rafaela!" Saturnino called. "Fetch Venancio some water before he
chokes to death."

"So tell me, Saturnino, what have you heard?" Benigno turned to
him.

Saturnino shook his head. "Not good news. Franco's victory at

Curupayty was short-lived. He left Humaitá three days ago, the Allies have the fort surrounded. Franco has crossed the river with his troops into the Chaco."

"The Chaco?" Rafaela had returned with a glass of water, with her free hand she crossed herself. "Good Lord! He'll be eaten by *tigres.*"

"Be quiet, Rafaela," Saturnino said.

"Franco has been forced to retreat. If I could, I swear I would leave the country right now," Benigno said, ignoring his sister and brother-in-law. "Better to leave everything behind. Better to save one's life."

"Ah, if only I had my health," Venancio sighed—he had stopped coughing at last. The minister of war and marine, Venancio was the least intelligent of the three brothers but the best liked; he would have preferred a life of quiet ease, with no responsibilities, on one of his *estancias.*

"And have you heard any news, Don Venancio?" Charles Washburn —it was a Thursday afternoon—who was sitting across from Saturnino Bedoya, turned and asked.

"*Non sé nada.*" Venancio cleared his throat. He hoped he would not start up again.

"That's what you always say." Benigno made a face at his brother.

"I saw Monsieur Cuberville, the new French minister, the other day," Charles Washburn continued, looking intently at his cards and not at Benigno. "He told me that he had spoken to you, Don Benigno. He told me that you had speculated on who could replace your brother, the president."

"Tomorrow, I must see the doctor about my cough," Venancio said to no one in particular.

"*Bah!*" Benigno shouted. "Cuberville drinks too much wine. He is a drunk and a liar! Do you think I've gone mad? Franco would have my head if he heard such talk."

"No doubt, he already has," Charles Washburn said as he trumped the last card, which had been laid down by Venancio.

"*Imbécil!*" Benigno got up from his chair so brusquely that he upset the card table.

⚘

A partial list of the names of the women who offered to take up arms for Paraguay:

Juaña Tomas Frutos
Brigida Chaves
Carmencita Chaves
Doña Carolina Gill
Isabella Carreras
Dolores Bérges
Maria Incarnación Rodriguez
Juliana Mañuela Sanchez
Maria Fernandez
Juaña Pura Mendoza

Rosaria was tired. The children seemed too big and noisy all of a sudden. She had no patience and she shouted at them—and how many times had she told Carlos Honorio to keep his dirty little animal in a cage? Also, her eyesight was no longer what it used to be and she had a hard time threading her bobbins to make lace. From time to time, she still made *chipa*. Kneading the manioc with the melted new cheese, the fat, the salt, the coriander seeds, soothed the stiffness in her fingers, and she got pleasure from braiding the bread into fanciful shapes. On an impulse one day, she baked a loaf of *chipa* with a particularly artful design and gave it to Doña Iñes.

Colonel Enrique von Wisner, Franco's military advisor, could report only what Franco wanted to hear and Franco did not want to hear that the Allied forces numbered over 48,000 men—40,000 were Brazilians, 7,000 Argentines and 1,000 Orientals—while the Paraguayan forces numbered only 20,000 men. Franco did not want to hear that most of the 20,000 were either old men or twelve-year-old boys, that most of the men were either sick or wounded and that the rest of the men were worn out from fatigue and malnutrition. Franco did not want to hear that his soldiers were half starved and half naked—they wore bits of tanned leather and ragged shirts sewn from the fibers of the wild pineapple and when it got cold they made ponchos out of dried hides, hides so stiff they could not move their arms. Franco did not want to hear that paper was scarce and ink had to be made from a black bean paste. Franco did not want to hear that very little drugs or medicine were left in the hospitals and that cholera and smallpox were spreading. And last but not least, Franco did not want to hear that most of the few hundred horses that remained were so weak and emaciated, they could barely carry their riders; the cattle, too, were in a terrible state and dying for lack of pasture.

Ella was watching her children play in the garden; a short distance away, Doña Iñes was kneeling in the zinnia bed. Doña Iñes wore a straw hat and one leg—the injured leg—stuck out awkwardly from under her brown skirt. Ella could see the thick wooden-soled shoe.

Carlos Honorio was shouting, *"Tira le! Tira le!"*

"Matar los macacos!" Enrique shouted back.

Leopoldo yelled, *"Aiii! Una bala me hirió en el brazo!"*

Why, Ella wondered, couldn't the children play something more pacific for a change?

"Doña Iñes, how are you today?" Walking over to her, Ella began, "I see you like to garden."

Doña Iñes pulled up a dandelion green. "When I was a child I used to pick these for my father's rabbits. Before my father was killed at the battle of Vicalváro, my father raised rabbits." Then, looking up, Doña Iñes asked, "How is Mathilde?"

"Princess Mathilde?" Ella could not hide her surprise. "It has been several months since I have received a letter from her. Why do you ask?"

"I was speaking about your horse."

"Oh."

After a moment Ella started to say something else, "Doña Iñes, as you must realize the country is at war and I worry for your safety. Battles are being fought not far from us and each day becomes more dangerous—" But she was interrupted by one of the children's cries.

Once Ella had tended to Carlos Honorio's wound, a bloody nose, and scolded Enrique, she turned back to Doña Iñes, but Doña Iñes was gone. Still later, when Ella returned to her bedroom, she found a vase filled with bright zinnias on her dressing table.

Héctor Varela, the handsome journalist from Buenos Ayres, no longer traveled to Paraguay; there were no more balls or theater performances in Asunción for him to report. Instead he had to report on the battles and revolutions closer to home. One such revolution forced Bartolemé Mitre to return to Argentina (actually that proved to be a good thing, for Mitre survived the war to write a history of the emancipation of his country); another revolution in the Banda Oriental forced Venancio Flores to go back home as well, but he was not as fortunate. He was stabbed in the throat by a Blanco and bled to death in the streets of Montevideo while his wife, Maria, who was with him at the time, tried in vain—an artery had been severed—to stop the bleeding by putting her bare hands on her husband's neck and applying pressure.

His beloved Maria!

A poem published in the *Lambarè*, a popular Guaraní newspaper, that praised Franco and ridiculed the enemy—the Duke de Caxias, Bartolemé Mitre, Venancio Flores (although he had died) and Dom Pedro of Brazil—became so popular, it was set to music. Pancho learned the verses by heart.

Where is Caxias
With all his tortoises?
Why does he not come
With his troop of monkeys?

Pancho was nearly thirteen and, at times, although he would never admit to it, he missed his mother. He missed his brothers and missed playing games with them. At other times, he did not mind so much. He read his books, he did his jigsaw puzzles, he strung up his necklace of ears.

What has Bartolo done,
And that thieving ass
Whom they call Flores,
Those sons of the devil?

One of the women who had offered to take up arms for Paraguay was young and pretty. Her name was Juliana Mañuela Sanchez. Juliana Mañuela Sanchez worked digging trenches and Pancho liked to watch how her small breasts moved inside her blouse when she dug into the ground with her shovel. He thought about how it would feel to touch her breasts and he thought he might give her his necklace of ears if she let him.

To the old monkey Peter
Both have sold themselves;
And have brought to be killed
Very many of their countrymen.

One day, as Juliana Mañuela Sanchez was shoveling earth, Pancho got up the courage to speak to her. He asked Juliana Mañuela Sanchez if she would like to hear him sing. Without looking up at him, Juliana Mañuela Sanchez said she did.

With these creatures like tapirs,
Whom the fierce lion pursues.
Health to our Commander,
And we will go on fighting!

At the American Legation, Ella sat waiting in the drawing room while
Mrs. Washburn got dressed and came downstairs—after her difficult
labor, Mrs. Washburn was often tired and she spent a great deal of time
in bed. Ella also had to listen to James Manlove, the American, who sat
across from her with one long booted leg crossed over the other,
describe his role in a Confederate battle.

"Fawt Pillow ova'looked the Mississippi on the Tennessee side
about fowty miles north of Memphis and was defended by Negro soldiers. We captured most of them and kilt the remainder. Som'a the
Negro tried to escape by runnin' into the rivah—you shud've seen
them, ma'am, I swear they looked just like a drove of hogs—and either
we picked them off"—Manlove placed an imaginary rifle up to his
shoulder and made as if to shoot—"or else they drowned. By the time
the moon came up, the rivah was dyed red with Negro blood."

For once, Ella felt nervous. She had heard how James Manlove had
arrived in Paraguay with neither passport nor papers but with a
scheme to capture Brazilian and Argentine ships. He might be mad. She
shook her head at him. "Mr. Manlove, I'm afraid I haven't understood
a word you've said."

But, as if he too had not understood Ella, James Manlove went on,
"We'd bin ordered to fight everythin' blue bewtixt wind and wahter and
until their flag was hauled down which I don't mind tellin' you, as sure
as I can see you sittin' there, Missus Lynch, we did. From where I was
positioned I made sure to shoot ev'ry Negro that made his appearance
wearin' a federal uniform—"

The door opened and Mrs. Washburn came into the drawing room.

She was holding her baby, she looked fragile and pale. Walking stiff-legged, her dog was at her heels.

"I'm sorry to keep you waiting. My husband, Mr. Washburn, is out riding and Mr. Masterman was called away this morning to attend to Monsieur Lasserre, who was suddenly taken ill—" Mrs. Washburn was holding the baby so tightly the baby began to fuss. "Mr. Masterman says it is cholera. I pray the baby—" Mrs. Washburn bit her lip. "May I offer you some refreshment?" She was close to tears.

"No, thank you. I won't stay but a few minutes. I merely stopped by to see your baby. What's her name?" Ella said.

"Hester."

Mrs. Washburn held out the baby to Ella and Ella, instinctively, took the baby in her arms.

"Oh, she's beautiful!" Again, Ella was thinking of Corinna Adelaida.

Just then the dog began to bark.

From his headquarters at Humaitá, Franco crossed the Paraguay River. Two Payaguá Indians paddled him across in a canoe; one Indian was sitting in the bow, the other in the stern. The Payaguás wore long pieces of wood through their pierced lips and bird wings through their ear lobes; the Payaguá in the bow was wearing a European-style hat—a canvas sun hat. Briefly curious about the sun hat, Franco leaned forward in the canoe and pointed to it—he meant to ask the Payaguá Indian where the hat had come from. Not understanding, the Payaguá took off the hat and handed it to Franco. Franco started to shake his head but he changed his mind; he smiled and thanked the Payaguá Indian instead. He could not refuse the generous offer of the sun hat without offending him.

Always humid and hot, the Gran Chaco was made up of impenetrable thickets of canes, thorny mimosa and jacarandas; swamps filled with dead tree trunks; and fallen branches decked with vines of dark pink trumpet flowers and fetid-smelling orchids. It was also home to tigers, tapirs, wild boar and poisonous snakes; the lagoons, which were almost impassable, were filled with crocodiles, electric eels and piranha.

At sunset, clouds of mosquitos, *vinchucas* and midges descended, biting, pricking and burying themselves in every bit of exposed flesh—one soldier got a jigger stuck in his eyeball and Dr. Stewart had great difficulty cutting it out. Also, the night was noisy with unfamiliar and menacing sounds; the whoop of the tree frog, the cry of the peewit, the call of the turkey buzzard, sounds that disrupted the soldiers' sleep and turned their dreams into nightmares. Nightmares in which the *mboya jagwa,* a thirty-foot snake with the head of a dog, raped their wives and daughters and the *ow ow*, a white ram with tiger claws and tiger teeth, devoured their children.

As they moved deeper into the Chaco, Franco rode the big surefooted mule Linda. Most of the soldiers had to walk and they often sank up to their knees in mud. To cross the lagoons, the soldiers built brushwood bridges. One bridge collapsed just as Pancho rode over it and he and his horse were thrown into water. Franco, who was watching, laughed so hard he nearly choked on his cigar. Wet and humiliated, Pancho had to think hard about something else to keep from crying.

> Where is Caxias
> With all his tortoises?
> Why does he not come
> With his troop of monkeys?

Too late, later, he thought of how surprisingly soft Juliana Mañuela Sanchez's breasts had felt and how easily they had fit in his hands.

Each night, Franco had supper with Lieutenant-Major Thompson, Colonel von Wisner and General Francisco Fernandez—he and not Venancio Lopez was the real commander of the army. Together, they ate snipe and water hens that Lieutenant-Major Thompson had flushed out of the swamps and shot, the birds were cooked over an open fire and were juicy and delicious. Franco always ate several, crunching up the beaks and the small bones, licking his fingers when he was finished and washing the meal down with brandy. While Franco ate, standing at a discreet distance, his band played. Most of the instruments had been lost or damaged and the musicians who had not been killed were forced to improvise. Justo José had been shot in the shoulder at Curupayty and, although he still had trouble lifting up his arm, he had, by some miracle, managed to hang on to his wooden harp and most of the gut strings were intact: *Ta dum ta dum ta dum dum dum, ta dum ta dum ta dum dum dum.*

If there was a moon, Franco rode on until one or two o'clock in the morning. When, at last, he strung up his hammock and wrapped himself in his poncho, he slept soundly and never once dreamed of the dog-snake *mboya jagwa* or the tiger-ram *ow ow.* Franco's dreams were pleasant—in one he was teaching Napoleon, who was wearing a canvas sun hat, how to drink *maté,* in another he was at a ball in Buenos Ayres, waltzing, *uno, dos, tres,* with Doña Dolores, Ella's lady-in-waiting, his arms wrapped tightly around her soft, plump waist. "I've never slept better," Franco boasted to his servant, Mañuel, in the morning. Then after drinking a gourd of *maté* and getting down on his knees to pray—since the death of the baby, Miguel Marcial, Franco had become more devout—he got back on Linda and continued on his way.

One afternoon when it was nearly too hot or humid to take a breath, a flock of parakeets flew directly overhead—there were thousands of birds and for a few seconds the parakeets nearly blotted out the sun—and Pancho, who was riding next to his father, raised his gun up in the air to fire at them. Quicker than he could speak, Franco moved to knock the gun out of Pancho's hands and the shot fell harmlessly to the ground.

"Bad luck to kill a parrot," Franco, who was also superstitious, told his son.

Despite all the hardships, Franco never complained; nor did he lose his confidence. He sat straight and tall in the saddle; he talked and joked with his generals as well as with his soldiers. As far as Franco was concerned, this march was not a retreat. It was a tactical move that would bring Paraguay victory.

Vencer o morir!

Fourteen

SAN FERNANDO

When fifty-four Brazilian ironclad steamers sailed up the Paraguay River to Asunción, the people panicked and fled. The streets of the city were crowded with women and children, the old and the infirm, carrying their bundles of clothes and dragging their carts filled with belongings. Fortunately, Alonzo Taylor owned a carriage. With his possessions tied to the roof, he and his wife and two daughters left Asunción and drove the twelve miles to Luque, the temporary capital, where, unable to find lodgings—Luque was just a small village of mud brick houses—they were forced to sleep inside their carriage.

Alonzo's daughters, Mary and Elizabeth, spent most of their mornings playing in a fast-running stream in the woods near the village. Blond and pretty and in their teens, the two girls had such a good time splashing and dunking each other in the water—although neither girl knew how to swim—that, for a while, they forgot the discomfort of the carriage and the home they had to abandon in Asunción. Also, they felt secure. Their mother, Mrs. Taylor, sat not far away on the grassy bank of the stream and watched them. Occasionally, Alonzo sat and watched as well and, out loud, he teased his pretty daughters and compared them to fish.

"A piranha," Elizabeth, the bolder of the two, replied and made as if to bite her father.

When it began to rain one day—it was the rainy season and often six or seven inches fell in a single day—Mary got out of the water and got dressed while Elizabeth decided to stay in.

"I like the feel of the rain on my head," Elizabeth told Mary, "and, anyway, I am wet already and I still want to wash my hair."

When Alonzo saw only his wife and Mary return to the carriage, right away he shouted at them, "You bloody fools. You should not have left her."

Calling out his daughter's name—Elizabeth was his favorite—and with his heart pounding, Alonzo ran back into the woods. He found Elizabeth lying on the bank of the stream, she was unconscious. Her blond hair was full of soap lather and there was blood in between her legs. Beside himself, Alonzo looked everywhere for footprints and for evidence of a struggle but he found nothing. Later, when Elizabeth regained consciousness, she was confused and hysterical. She talked about seeing a dog in the water and about seeing a snake as well.

"Mark my word, once the Brazilians take Asunción, we shall be safe," Charles Washburn told Frederick Masterman. The two men had climbed up on the roof of the American Legation to watch the Brazilian ironclads steam up the river toward the city. Below them, Asunción looked as if it had been deserted for a hundred years. The empty streets glowed in the sunlight and, except for the occasional barking of a stray dog, not a sound was heard.

"Franco is cut off now. He has no supplies; he and his soldiers will starve," Frederick Masterman said.

"He will have no choice but to capitulate," Charles Washburn answered. Charles Washburn was not particularly fond of Frederick Masterman but he was grateful to him. Also, he preferred Masterman's company to that of James Manlove. James Manlove had caused him no end of trouble and had finally been arrested and shot.

"Look," Frederick Masterman said. He was pointing to Asunción's only defense, a little fort on a hill opposite the city. A few small field pieces and a 150-pound cannon made from church bells were left—the cannon had been hauled up to the fort. The handful of Paraguayan soldiers who remained were unable to operate it and the small field guns fell short of their targets. "The muzzle is lowered properly but the cannon is set too high," observed Frederick Masterman.

The two men watched as the Brazilians returned fire. Their shots looked random. One hit the balcony on Franco's palace, another landed in the empty marketplace and killed a stray dog. After an hour of sporadic firing, the two men could hardly believe their eyes when, as they looked on, the Brazilian ironclads turned around and sailed back down the river.

"Cowards! Come back!" Charles Washburn shook his fists and shouted at them.

"No doubt, the Brazilians will claim a great victory, but what will happen to us now?" Frederick Masterman said.

"You might well ask," Charles Washburn replied.

8 January 1868

Ma chère Princesse,

I cannot express how disappointed I was on my return from Humaitá not to find a letter from you. News from you is like a ray of sunshine especially as, presently, it is the rainy season here and everything in this country is wet, wet, wet—even the clothes in my closet are damp and covered with mold. However there is no point in my complaining, especially since there are more important matters to consider. Franco has had to move his headquarters several

times in the last few months and I have moved with him—no easy matter as
I have had to leave the children (all but the oldest, Pancho, who will not leave
his father's side) behind in Asunción with their nurse. No doubt you would be
surprised if you could have seen me! You might not have recognized me! I
wear the same gray wool riding cloak, the same muddy boots, and my hair is
done up in a single braid. Sometimes several weeks go by before I put on a
dress or have a proper bath! As for my hands—I can't begin to describe how
rough and callused they look from riding and being outdoors all day. I hope I
am not distressing you but life on the front is—

Ella stopped writing. She reread her letter and tore it up. She found it
hard to concentrate but she began again:

Ma chère Princesse,
    Alas, I was hoping to have news of you on my recent return to the capital
and I was particularly eager to hear how you succeeded with your portrait of
Monsieur Mérimée. I envy you your talent and I can well understand the
peace and satisfaction that the practice of art brings you. Likewise, I too find
great solace in playing the piano and the moment my fingers touch the keys I
forget the ordinary cares and burdens of life. And now the thought of you, dear
friend, surrounded as you surely must be (despite Monsieur le Comte's
frequent absences, which you mention in your last letter) by friends and
relatives, including your nephew whom I know has always been more like a
son to you, fills me with happiness. As for my own sons, they too fill me with
joy and—

Again, Ella tore up the letter.

At dusk one evening, Franco crossed the Paraguay one more time—this
time, his canoe nearly overturned when it bumped into the bleached
corpse of a crocodile floating down the river. (For a moment, Franco
mistook it for the corpse of a woman, the pale stomach, the white
breasts.) He established his new headquarters four miles inland on the

banks of the Tebicuary River at the village of San Fernando. High on a hill, San Fernando was situated on dry ground that was covered with a thick flowering foxtail called *aguaráruguai*, which bent and waved in the wind and, from afar, looked like the sea. Except for an occasional palm tree, there were no trees. The country around San Fernando was marshland, flat and wet and uninhabitable; a high road that lay under water most of the year ran along the marshes to Asunción.

Lieutenant-Major Thompson supervised the construction of workshops and lathes to repair the guns; the engineers in his employ had to improvise and both design and make the machines for rifling. He was also in charge of building an arsenal to manufacture gunpowder—there was plenty of iron pyrite in Paraguay—and he put some of the women who had offered to take up arms for Paraguay to work producing saltpeter from urine and decomposed animal substances. The women did not like Lieutenant-Major Thompson—he was humorless and severe and he did not let them sing or laugh while they worked. Whenever he came by to inspect their progress, Carmencita Chaves, one of the women producing saltpeter, made faces and stuck out her tongue at him behind his back. One time, he turned around and caught her with her tongue sticking out at him and without a word he grabbed her so hard by the hair that a handful of it came out. Next time, Lieutenant-Major Thompson told Carmencita Chaves, he would cut out her tongue. He put the rest of the women, Isabella Carreras, Dolores Bérges, Maria Incarnacion Rodriguez, Pancho's favorite Juliana Mañuela Sanchez, Maria Fernandez and Juaña Pura Mendoza, to work stamping percussion caps out of copper.

Before leaving Obispo Cue, Ella told her children that they were each allowed to bring one toy. Enrique, who was nearly ten, wanted to bring his front-pedaled Michaux velocipede—although his feet did not quite yet reach the pedals, Enrique liked to sit on the velocipede and pretend he was riding it—but the velocipede was made of iron and weighed fifty pounds and Ella would not allow it and, instead, he brought three sets of

lead British soldiers (his favorites: the Lancers, the Household Cavalry
and the Light Dragoons); Federico, who was eight, brought a board game
his mother had given him called Wanderers in the Wilderness; Carlos
Honorio took his Noah's ark, which was carved in the shape of a box set
in a boat, with the roof serving as a lid in which 150 pairs of animals as
well as Noah and his wife, their three sons, Shem, Ham and Japheth, and
their wives, had fit originally, but Noah's wife, Shem, Ham and the sons'
three wives, along with many of the animals, were missing (for this, Carlos Honorio blamed Leopoldo); and Leopoldo, aged five, could not
decide between a hobbyhorse, with a real mane and leather reins, and a
humming top, so that in the end Ella let him bring both.

Ella and her family left Asunción on board the *Salto*. Without lights
and under cover of night, the ship took them down river safely, past the
Brazilian ironclads as far as Villa Franca. There, little remained of the once
pretty village of thatch-roofed houses built on a wide lawn that sloped
all the way to the river. Ella could see nothing but burned-out, shelled
façades, wrecked gardens and torn-up trees; the lawn sloping down to
the river was littered with pieces of charred wood, broken carts, wheels,
bones, a horse's skull had been stuck to a pole. In the village, only the
telegraph posts made from hardwood stood intact.

From there they continued the journey on land. Lurching and
bumping along the road, the carriage taking Ella and the children to San
Fernando was so loaded down that it got mired in the mud several times
and everyone had to get out. They also often had to stop and wait for the
other, slower carriage, which Doña Iñes shared with the servants and the
rest of the luggage, to catch up. The bumping and lurching motion made
Leopoldo fall asleep and made Carlos Honorio sick to his stomach and
the carriage had to stop several more times so he could vomit in the
bushes by the side of the road. Federico had spread out Wanderers in the
Wilderness on his knees and he and Enrique, who was sitting across from
him, were trying to play the game. Each time they hit a pothole or a rut
in the road, one of the wooden markers fell to the carriage floor and
each time, too, that Enrique picked up his marker, Federico accused him
of not putting it back in the proper place on the board and of cheating.

"Stupid! It was right here." Enrique pointed to site 22. "Right where the boa is swallowing the jaguar."

"Don't call me stupid. You were over here, where the cayman is eating the Negro!" Federico insisted.

"Hush, children," Ella said. "Stop quarreling. You're giving me a headache."

"Here!" Federico hissed.

"No, here!" Enrique hissed back as, with one swift motion of his hand, he overturned the board and sent both their wooden markers to the floor.

Leopoldo, who had been asleep in Rosaria's lap, woke up and started to cry.

Excerpts from Charles Washburn's journal:

Tuesday, February 25: Silence through the day; I sent Basilio to buy meat and vegetables. Toward evening I took a ride through the streets and met scarcely anybody, the city appearing to be deserted. Hester has now been sick a week.

Wednesday, February 26: Another day of silence, and we know nothing of what has happened since day before yesterday. The child continues sick.

Thursday, February 27: The little one very bad, and the mother has not slept a moment during the whole night. 'Tis said Madam Lynch and the children went on board the *Salto* at twelve o'clock last night. . . .

Monday, March 2: Basilio went to get a passport, but after waiting two hours, without being able to obtain it, returned. From the looks of the people, it seems as if matters were going very badly below.

Tuesday, March 3: At 7 A.M. went to the Ministerio to complain of the treatment of Basilio. . . . There is nothing new from below. Silence only. The ironclads are a little above Humaitá, doing nothing to prevent the Paraguayans from crossing the river. What fools are the Brazilians!

Wednesday, March 4: The weather continues oppressive, with nothing to break the monotony. The days seem very long, but thank God! we are now all in good health.

Benigno Lopez, Franco's brother, had a premonition. The night before he was arrested he dreamt that he was being chased down a long, dark corridor. He never got a look at who was chasing him but whoever it was he knew for certain was intent on harming him, and as he ran, the corridor kept getting narrower and narrower so that Benigno had a harder and harder time fitting himself through it, and just before he awoke, he got stuck in the corridor and whoever was chasing him— Benigno felt a blast of hot breath on his neck—caught up with him.

Minister of the Treasury Saturnino Bedoya had no such premonition. Outside the capital at his *quinta*, he was having dinner with his wife, Rafaela, and sister-in-law, Inocencia, and, as was his custom, he was trying to eat his food and ignore the two women who were talking their usual nonsense, when, unannounced, the chief of police walked into the dining room.

"Have you eaten?" was the first thing Saturnino said to him. He had seen Matias Sanabria just a few days ago, he had played whist with him. Happy for the unexpected company, Saturnino even made a move to make room for Matias Sanabria to sit next to him at the table. "The roast is not so bad tonight and is not overcooked as is the case—" he started to say when, right behind Matias Sanabria, Saturnino saw several policemen. Their swords were drawn.

Their hands and feet manacled, Benigno Lopez and Saturnino

Bedoya were taken to San Fernando in an open cart. It rained every day during the three-day journey and both men got soaked through to the bone. Benigno's too long hair fell into his eyes and he could not brush it back, worse, after one particularly violent lurch of the cart he lost his balance and fell onto his stomach where he lay for the rest of the day unable to move, his head in an inch of water. Next to him, Saturnino had not been able to convey his sudden urgent need in time—no doubt the fault of the undercooked roast—and had defecated into his breeches and although the rain had partly washed away the shit, he could smell it still. Each evening, when their shackles were removed so they could eat, Benigno and Saturnino's arms and wrists were so swollen and stiff, they could barely lift the spoons with the food to their lips. The two men were forbidden to speak but since each one blamed the other for his predicament, they mouthed insults at each other: *Puerco! Perro!* One time when, after another particular violent lurch of the cart, Saturnino was thrown against Benigno and the guard was not looking, Saturnino leaned over and bit Benigno's earlobe off.

"*Perro!*" Benigno screamed at Saturnino.

"*Puerco!*" the guard screamed, beating Benigno.

Two carts followed after Benigno and Saturnino's; the horses pulling them were straining. The carts were filled with Saturnino and Benigno's so-called household gold and silver.

Instead of going to Luque, Dr. Eberhardt had stayed in Asunción. He was old and he had enough dried beef, sugar, *chipa* and *yerba* to last him for a few days. His principal concern, however, was not food for himself but food for the parrots. Already several of the parrots had died of malnutrition: a friendly red-spectacled Amazon; two talkative white-bellied parrots, two yellow-collared macaws and four green-winged macaws—two of the green-winged macaws Dr. Eberhardt had seen born in the aviary—also at least half a dozen parakeets; and every day, filled with apprehension at the prospect of more deaths in the aviary, Dr. Eberhardt walked over to Inocencia's house. The house was shut tight—before leaving, Inocencia had given Dr. Eberhardt the key—and completely deserted, but the moment Dr. Eberhardt unlocked the heavy front door (the aviary was located in the back of the house in the patio) and the parrots heard him, they began to scream and squawk. In spite of his worries, Dr. Eberhardt smiled.

Tea? Profesor, tea?

The day the Brazilian ironclads had sailed up the Paraguay River and fired their guns at Asunción, Dr. Eberhardt, in his excitement, forgot and left the aviary door open. In the front hall, when he returned the next day—fortunately, all the windows of the house were shuttered and shut—he found several parrots perched on top of the marble statue of the woman being bitten by a serpent: a scarlet macaw was perched on her knee, a yellow-naped Amazon on her breast, a blue-fronted parrot on her flung-back head. Several blue-and-yellow macaws hung from the silk curtains (curtains that had once belonged to Baron de Villa Maria and that Inocencia had not made into dresses) and they had ripped the fabric with their sharp claws; a scarlet macaw and a red-and-green macaw were each perched on a mahogany carved pineapple that decorated the headboard of Inocencia's large bed and the parrots were adding their own haphazard carvings. They had also shat on the embroidered monogrammed linen sheets and pillowcases; a couple of parakeets were playing and splashing in the leftover water inside the porcelain basins and commodes; Dr. Eberhardt's favorite hyacinth macaw had gotten inside the larder and his blue feathers—what was left of them—were covered in white flour; from the dining room Dr. Eberhardt heard laughter—like the sound of a raucous dinner party—there he found a single parrot, the little mean green one who used to sit on his head, swinging upside down from an ornate Venetian chandelier, shaking the delicate glass teardrops and mimicking peals of laughter each time one broke off and shattered on the floor.

Collecting all the parrot food he could find—a handful of palm nuts, a cup of sunflower seeds, some peanuts and pine nuts, a few chilies, half a cup of boiled maize, a bunch of berries—Dr. Eberhardt carefully distributed it in the metal trays inside the aviary; he also replenished the water dishes. Then, going back inside Inocencia's big house, he went through each room, opening wide all the windows and shutters wide, and when he was certain that no window or shutter was left closed, Dr. Eberhardt walked back to the aviary and sat at the table the way he always did. He put his head in his hands and wept.

At last a parcel from France arrived; the wrapping paper was torn, the string untied. When Ella opened it, she could barely hide her disappointment. Instead of two books, she found only *Salammbô*.

Ils frappaient au hasard autour d'eux, ils brisaient, ils tuaient; quelques-uns lancèrent des flambeaux dans les feuillages; d'autres, s'accoudant sur la balustrade des lions, les massacrèrent à coups de flèches; les plus hardis coururent aux éléphants, ils voulaient leur abattre la trompe et manger de l'ivoire.

After reading a few pages, Ella shut the book. She had had enough of fighting.

The next time she saw Lázaro Alcántara, she gave him the book.

Pleased with the gift, he asked, "Is Carthage in France?"

"Yes," Ella replied.

"Madame!" Lázaro was running back, he was waving something.

"What is it?"

PARIS
25 April 1868

Ma chère amie,

How I wish you could have been with me at the Odéon the other evening! I am certain you would have enjoyed Le Passant, *François Coppée's new one-act poetic drama. I am even more certain you would have enjoyed the performances! Madame Agar played Sylvie admirably (she is criticized for being too old but how can that be her fault? In my estimation she was*

*excellent); but I must admit I was particularly drawn to a new young actress
by the name of Sarah Bernhardt, who played the lover, Zanetto, to perfection;
she was as supple and slender as any young man and one would have hardly
guessed that . . .*

Ella began to laugh. She laughed so hard she had to stop reading the
letter. Tears were rolling down her cheeks.

Standing next to her, Lázaro was concerned. "Bad news?" he asked.

"Traitor! My own brother!"

Rage consumed Franco. He was dumb and numb with it. He could
not have said what time it was or what day. He was not aware of any person around him or of any person speaking to him; if there were birds
singing or church bells ringing, he did not hear them. Like a black fun-
nel cloud, rage spiraled inside his head, spreading to his neck, straining
the muscles there and settling in his chest, making his heart pound too
fast and loud, forcing his breath out of his ready-to-burst lungs, making
his arms and legs tremble and ache, and his hand shake as he closed it
into a fist to hit Benigno as hard as he could.

Franco broke Benigno's nose. He heard the snap of the bone and
watched the dark blood flow from Benigno's nostrils; it gave him a slight
feeling of release. Once, a long time ago, riding home, he had beaten a
dog on the road and that had given him a similar sensation.

"Speak, traitor!" Franco screamed, hitting Benigno again.

Whirling around, he turned to his brother-in-law Saturnino; like
Benigno, Saturnino sat with his arms and legs chained to the back of the
chair. Rage so fogged Franco's vision that he could barely distinguish
between the two men; he saw only treacherous, featureless shapes.

"Bastard! Piece of *merde!*" Franco yelled, his spit spraying Saturnino
in the face. Shutting his eyes, Saturnino tried not to flinch.

"Here! I have proof! A signed confession by Frederick Masterman,
the Englishman!" Franco continued, waving a piece of paper—the
paper was blank and Franco was guessing. "You think I'm so stupid? You

think I'm so ignorant?" He was working himself up even more. "You think I don't have my spies?" This time Franco hit Saturnino. He hit him so hard that, still chained to his chair, Saturnino fell sideways and the men guarding him had to straighten him back. One of Saturnino's eyes closed.

"Don't think I don't know everything. You dogs! You cowards!" Franco hit Saturnino again. This time the chair tipped over and again the men guarding Saturnino had to right it. "I know what you had planned!" Franco gave a mock laugh. "Also, the date of the evacuation of Humaitá by our soldiers. And do you have the temerity to claim that it was by sheer coincidence that the Brazilian ironclads made their way up the river on the same day?" Franco sneered. "Lieutenant-Major Thompson reported that he saw someone on board trying to signal to the shore. One of the men waved a handkerchief and shouted something—" Franco paused to catch his breath.

"Speak, Saturnino! Say something before I kill you!"

"Please!" Saturnino pleaded. He opened his eyes and tried to focus.

"As for you, scum, vermin, lowest of the low"—Franco went back to stand in front of Benigno—"always the favorite, always indulged. Well, not this time, little brother!" Franco punched Benigno in the stomach hard and Benigno's chair fell over.

"Charles Washburn, the American—" Benigno tried to say when he had caught his breath and was sitting upright again. He had hit his head and blood was dripping into his eyes and frightening him.

"I know all about that meddlesome fool, Charles Washburn," Franco roared. "His servant was in my employ!" Again, he laughed his mock laugh. "Basilio told me how you told Washburn that your secret plan was to replace me and become president in return for handing over the country to the allies. To Caxias—that cowardly bastard!"

Franco paced back and forth in front of Benigno and Saturnino. He could feel his rage diminishing, the black spiral cloud unraveling, dissipating in the air. A part of him wanted to maintain the frenzy, the fury; again, he punched Benigno, but not quite as hard this time.

"From the very beginning, I did not trust that fool, Charles Washburn; nor do I trust the other foreigners who disobeyed my orders and lived at the American Legation, claiming diplomatic immunity. That English pervert, Frederick Masterman! Cowards! I'll have them all arrested. Mark my word!"

Saturnino tried to speak but his mouth had filled with blood.

"What? Speak! What is it that you wish to tell me? Ah, perhaps, you wish to tell me about your wife, my dear sister! She is a traitor as well! Do not worry, Rafaela and Inocencia will soon get their due!" The thought of his fat sisters made Franco lose control of himself again. "Fat cows!" He screamed at Saturnino. "I'll have the fat scheming cows arrested!"

Saturnino tried to form a word but managed only a sound.

Franco stopped his pacing and stood still for a moment. He looked at his two prisoners. Benigno's nose was swollen and he was trying to vomit only it was too painful; Saturnino's eye had disappeared inside the socket and he was spitting blood. Both men were making horrible mewing noises and Franco wanted to be rid of them, rid of the sight of them. Annoyance, irritation, impatience had replaced his rage. He could feel certain things. For instance, a tooth had begun to bother him, there was a tightness in the gum, also a slight throbbing. He looked up as Ella came into the room. For the first time, he noticed the two deep lines on either side of her mouth.

"And what about your mother? Doña Juaña?" Ella was careful to make her voice expressionless.

"No, not my mother. Arrest Inocencia and Rafaela." Suddenly, Franco felt tired. More than anything, he wanted to lie down by himself and sleep—sleep for a week, for maybe a month. "And that lazy, good-for-nothing stonemason who never finished building my palace, arrest him as well. Alonzo Taylor," he added for no reason.

Fifteen

PIKYSYRY

10 September, 1868

My Dear Mother,

Several weeks have elapsed since my last letter to you and although I accept your affectionate reprimand I am also well aware that under different circumstances, my omission would be of no importance. My silence is due in part to my negligent habits but also to the suffering I have had to endure.

I cannot express to you, Mamma, the pain and sorrow with which I read your letter; I expected a more frank and honest reply. Dear Mamma! Perhaps, you do not understand the bitterness I have felt recently without ever daring to speak out or complain. All my endeavors have been useless and my hopes in vain. From the start, all of you have arrayed yourselves against me without a thought to what I may have felt. I am the poor victim! Only the good Lord let the light shine through the darkness to confound my enemies and allow me to

survive. And would to heaven!—would to heaven!—dear Mamma, that I
could help those who turned against me to survive as well.

Venancio and Benigno are in good health.

If I can give you a word of advice, Mamma. I would recommend that you
do not concern yourself overly with the events of the day. Despite your
mother's tender heart, it would not be prudent to show your alarm.

I read your letter as one from a mother to her son, rather than one from a
supplicant to a magistrate. The latter kind would only do harm.

Please convince yourself, Mamma, of all the love with which your blessing
is begged, by

> *Your most obedient son,*
>
> *F. S. Lopez*

Charles Washburn knew that the instant he left the American Legation
to return to the States, Frederick Masterman would lose his immunity
and be arrested—already a half-dozen armed guards had surrounded the
house. Mrs. Washburn, in particular, had wanted to shake Frederick Masterman's hand to wish him luck and tell him thank you—after all, had
he not saved her life? And her baby's? However the baby, Hester, was
screaming—amazing the amount of noise a tiny baby could make!—and,
to make matters worse, Bumppo had gotten so lame with arthritis she
had to carry him in one arm (the baby in the other!), so that with all the
commotion of the departure, Mrs. Washburn felt nauseated and dizzy all
over again and she never even managed to say good-bye. Mr. Washburn
too in his rush to accompany his wife, the baby, the English servants and
secretary, to the harbor to board the U.S.S. *Wasp,* and to spare them the
sight of—who knew?—the guards shooting Frederick Masterman on
the spot, did not have the time to tell him what he had intended to—
that Frederick Masterman was free to accuse him of any crime, if, by
doing so, he could avoid being tortured and secure his freedom. Instead
Charles Washburn had only enough time to wave a hasty farewell
before joining his wife and the others.

In reply, Frederick Masterman had raised his hat and called out after him, "Good-bye, Mr. Washburn, do not forget me!"

Frederick Masterman had sewn a little opium and a little quinine into the seam of his coat. The precaution was useless. As soon as he was arrested, he was stripped of his clothes, the opium and quinine were discovered, iron fetters were fastened to his ankles and he was thrown into a dank, windowless cell. From there, Frederick Masterman, still wearing the iron fetters, was put on a mule and taken to San Fernando. Along the way, as the mule was descending a steep slope, the mule began to trot and Frederick Masterman lost his balance and fell. Unable to free himself—the iron fetters were attached to the mule's saddle girth—he was dragged some distance on the ground on his back while the mule, attempting to free itself, repeatedly kicked him.

In San Fernando, Frederick Masterman endured far worse torture than the bruises inflicted by the mule. His arms were tied tightly behind him and a musket was placed under his knees; his head was pushed down until it rested on the musket and a second musket was placed on the back of his neck and lashed to the first.

"Is it not true that Charles Washburn was the chief conspirator in a plot to depose President Lopez?"

"No!" Frederick Masterman screamed.

"Is it not true that Charles Washburn was in league with the Allied commander the Duke de Caxias?"

"No!"

Two more muskets were added to the back of Frederick Masterman's neck. As the cords were being tightened, he threw his head forward to avoid the pressure on his throat and cut his lip so badly that the blood almost choked him. Then he fainted from the pain.

"Is it not true that Charles Washburn was the chief conspirator in a plot to depose President Lopez?"

"Yes!" When he regained consciousness, rather than be tortured again, Frederick Masterman confessed.

"Is it not true that Charles Washburn was in league with the Allied commander, the Duke de Caxias?"

"Yes!"

After he had signed the false confession, which filled two closely written sheets of paper, Frederick Masterman was given something to eat—he had gone two days without food—and he was allowed to go to sleep, outside, chained to the ground.

Frederick Masterman woke up soaking wet the next morning. Exhausted, he had not noticed that it had rained all night. He recognized Alonzo Taylor, the English stonemason, who was still sleeping lying next to him; on Frederick Masterman's other side, his eyes open and staring blankly at the rising sun, was a young Paraguayan officer who had died unattended sometime during the night. Venancio Lopez, Captain Simon Fidanza, Dr. Antonio de las Carreras, Major Aveiro, Lieutenant Levalle, José Berges, Gumesmindo Benítez were some of the other prisoners at San Fernando. Half naked, beaten and starved, their physical appearances were so altered—Dr. Carreras had his fingers crushed and could no longer use his hands, José Berges had both his ears cut off, Gumesmindo Benítez's spine was broken and he had to crawl everywhere on all fours—that Frederick Masterman did not always recognize them. He did recognize Benigno Lopez, whom he saw being taken away by soldiers carrying muskets and cords, the instruments of torture. Don Benigno returned a few hours later; he could not walk or stand alone. Saturnino Bedoya, Frederick Masterman was told, had been shot in the head the day before.

Inocencia and Rafaela had been taken prisoners as well. The two sisters were kept inside a bullock cart whose sides and windows were boarded up. Every morning, they were made to stand with their dresses pulled up over their heads, their underwear already ripped to shreds, and they were whipped publicly.

"*Misericordia!*" Rafaela screamed, falling in a heap to her knees.

"*Bastardo!*" Although her fat backside was bleeding and she was humiliated, Inocencia would not give in to her brother. Two days before, her husband, Vincente Barrios, had tried to commit suicide by slitting his throat—unfortunately for him the wound was not deep enough—and Inocencia was made to watch while he was bayoneted to death.

"*Bastardo! Bastardo!*" Inocencia kept screaming.

Mathilde, Ella's horse, stood swaying in her stall. Her legs could barely support her, her stomach was horribly distended. When Ella opened the stall door, the horse did not lift her head or prick up her ears or show her usual signs of affection.

"Mathilde, my darling!" Gently, Ella stroked the bloated belly.

"Oh, Mathilde, my Mathilde," Ella whispered. She went to get the horse a pail of clean water, a handful of fresh oats, but Mathilde did not move. Mathilde's breath was labored, her gray coat covered with sweat. Then, as if she could no longer bear her own weight, Mathilde sank to her knees and rolled onto her side on the floor.

"Mathilde!" Ella cried.

Too frightened to speak, the stable boy mumbled the names of poisonous plants: "*Romarillo, chucho, mio-mio.*"

Wrapped in her cloak, Ella lay down on the straw next to her horse. Long out of the practice, she began to pray silently: "Dear God, please, please, I beg you, make Mathilde well again. Please, God, don't let her die. I'll do anything you ask—anything, I promise—" Ella paused. "I'll ask Franco to free those two fat bitches, Inocencia and Rafaela."

Despite her efforts to stay awake and tend to her horse, Ella fell asleep. The next morning she woke to the sound of a loud healthy grunt. Mathilde was getting to her knees, then to her feet, her bloated belly gone. Also thirsty and hungry, Mathilde walked over to the pail of water and drank, then she went to the oats and ate.

"Thank God," Ella said out loud to herself.

Stiff from lying on the ground, Ella sat up slowly—someone else, she realized all of a sudden, was in the stall with her. The person was still sleeping and at first—the light in the stall was dim—Ella thought it might be the stable boy, until she saw a shoe with a thick wooden sole

sticking out of the straw. Doña Iñes had her rosary beads clasped tightly
in her hands, and she was snoring lightly.

"Thank God," Ella said again, resting her head against Mathilde's
neck.

Franco did not like to spend the night alone. Most nights, Juaña Tomas
Frutos, Brigida Chaves, Carmencita Chaves—the two women were
not related—or one of the other women who had offered to take up
arms for Paraguay and were producing saltpeter from urine (Franco no
longer minded the odor on the women's hands) or stamping percussion
caps out of copper slept with him. Ella rarely did. The few times she
stayed and shared Franco's bed, Franco was either too tired or too
drunk to make love to her and Ella was relieved.

In December, the *Wasp*—the same ship that had taken away Charles
Washburn, his family, his servants and secretary—returned bringing the
new American minister, General Martin MacMahon, as well as
Admiral Davis, who had come to negotiate the release of Frederick
Masterman.

"You see," Franco said, showing Admiral Davis the confession
signed by Frederick Masterman, "there is no doubt that the man is guilty
by association."

Franco was most persuasive and Admiral Davis was disposed to
believe him. "I assure you, Your Excellency," Admiral Davis answered,
"that I will receive Mr. Masterman as a criminal and keep him prisoner
until he has reached Washington and can stand trial there."

On board the *Wasp*, the temperature often reached a hundred
degrees. In the evening, as he waited for permission to disembark,
thousands of mosquitos swarmed around General MacMahon and he
spent his time slapping at them. He had brought a copy of *Don Quijote
de la Mancha* to improve his Spanish but it was too hot to concentrate
and too hot to attempt to discover the meaning of *avellanado* and *anto-*

jadizo and *pensamientos* (for some reason, MacMahon had imagined Spanish to be a language of short, one-syllable words). To relieve the monotony, General MacMahon played cards, practiced his marksmanship with the other officers on board and wrote down the events of the day in his journal—events, General MacMahon could not help but notice, that were beginning to bear an eerie similarity to those created by Cervantes:

> The officers amused themselves with occasional shots at birds or beasts on the shore. In one instance a most extraordinary transformation was wrought by the rather questionable rifle practice of a gallant captain, who fired at a white crane on the shore and was astonished to behold the strange bird suddenly assume the shape and proportions of a native of the country, who had been stooping in the bushes by the waterside, and disappear with great rapidity toward the interior.

Pancho was sitting on the ground at Ella's feet, he was eating a slice of manioc cake. Thirteen, Pancho was always hungry and he was big for his age. Already there was the shadow of a moustache on his upper lip.

"Is Paris as beautiful as Asunción?" he asked his mother.

"Yes, Paris is as beautiful." Ella smiled.

"A river, like the Paraguay, flows through the city," Pancho continued, his mouth full.

"That's right, the River Seine. Why do you ask?" Ella answered.

Pancho shrugged. "I'm just curious, I read about it in a book. What about Ireland? Is Ireland beautiful?"

"Yes, Ireland is very beautiful. Don't talk with your mouth full of food," Ella added.

"Will you take me there one day?"

"Of course, I will." Ella leaned down and patted Pancho's hand. "I promise."

Instead of siege and pitched battles, the Paraguayan Army waged a war of entrenchments, but, in view of the vastly superior Allied forces led by the Duke de Caxias, which totaled 30,000 men, Franco was gradually forced to retreat northward—all the while fighting for every inch of ground with amazing tenacity. This time he went upriver to a hill town called Pikysyry. His army was divided into five divisions. Lieutenant-Colonel Thompson—he had been promoted from lieutenant-major and Franco had given him a handsome ceremonial sword with a gold hilt—commanded the Angostura batteries and again he had his men dig a long trench next to the river. This was not an easy task: the mud was slimy and the rope and tackle were as slippery as soap. Major Hermosa commanded the right, Colonel Gonzales the center and Colonel Moniel and Colonel Rivarola commanded the remaining two batteries. The army numbered about 5,000 men, most of whom were boys. The armament consisted of about 100 guns, including the big 150-pound gun brought down from Asunción and the Whitworth Lieutenant-Colonel Thompson had admired. Much of the ammunition had been lost and many of the guns had only twenty or thirty rounds left. The soldiers, too, had to make do with fifty to sixty rounds.

Fulgencio had fewer than forty rounds of ammunition and his musket often jammed or misfired. He was sitting with a dozen men in a small redoubt—earlier they had dug a trench around it and placed chains on posts to keep the horses of the enemy from jumping the trench—and he was sipping cold *maté*. Since his brother, Gaspar, had died, Fulgencio no longer cared much whether he himself lived or died; he no longer felt pain or discomfort—the rain, the mud, thirst, hunger—so acutely. He hardly noticed the host of buffalo gnats that as soon as the sun set swarmed and bit every exposed surface of his body—what little flesh was left on his bones—and his skin was the consistency of leather. And he rarely spoke—everyone he had ever known was dead and what was there left to say? Very occasionally, he thought about his wife but it had been three years since he had last seen her and he could barely recall her face (he remembered that she sometimes wore her hair in thick braids on top of her head and that she put a flower in her hair) and he certainly could not imagine the feel of her body underneath him or how it felt to make love to her. Anyway, he no longer thought about sex although there was a time—it seemed like a lifetime ago—when he and Gaspar used to masturbate before they went to sleep, but he could not imagine doing it now. It would take too much effort. It took all the effort he could muster to sit, to stand, to eat the bit of beef and *chipa*, to drink *maté*, to piss and crap, to raise his gun, aim, fire it. The week before—or was it a month ago?, another thing that had happened was that he had lost track of time—as he was crossing a swamp, his shoe had fallen off in the water. His shoe was not a real shoe but pieces of hides strapped to his feet, and now he was waiting for a man to die so that he could take his shoe but even that did not concern him overly. Instead, he wiggled his bare toes in the mud, and settled himself to sleep a little.

During the night, the Brazilians overran the Pikysyry trenches, stopping short of where Lieutenant-Colonel Thompson was at Angostura, and killed seven hundred Paraguayan soldiers and took nearly half as many prisoners. Fulgencio survived the attack, although the way he was stretched out in the mud he must have appeared dead to the enemy. Most of the soldiers who had been in the redoubt with him were dead—one man was half lying on top of Fulgencio, his arm resting companionably on Fulgencio's shoulder—and the rest had fled. The irony was that in the confusion of the attack, someone, a fellow Paraguayan soldier probably—the Brazilian soldiers lacked nothing in the way of clothes and arms—had gone off with Fulgencio's shoe, his one remaining shoe.

"Mimosa, acacia, a red-leaved hibiscus, and, look, over there's a fuchsia." Ella was pointing out the plants to General MacMahon, who had borrowed one of Franco's horses and was riding next to her—surrounded by the enemy, they could not ride far. "I remember how in front of our house in Cork there was the tallest fuchsia hedge I have ever seen." Ella paused to tighten her reins a little. "Even here in Paraguay, I have never seen a plant like it."

"I remember those fuchsia hedges—purple bells, I called them. They grew along the roads," General MacMahon answered. Tough and unspoiled, General MacMahon had fought in the Union army during the American Civil War. Franco had taken an instant liking to him—as instant as was his dislike of Charles Washburn—and so had Ella. Also, General MacMahon was a good horseman and he was Irish.

"Our house was on an inlet, and one of my first memories is of the tide coming in and out," Ella continued. "As a child, it always amazed me that the mudflats I looked at in the morning—I could cross to the other shore in twenty minutes on foot in my boots—could, by the afternoon, be transformed into glittering deep blue water. With boats sailing on the water! I know, I know, General," Ella said, smiling, "tides have to do with the pull of the moon on the ocean but still I could not help thinking about it as miraculous."

"When I was a boy in Ireland—I was Federico's age—I had a pony," General MacMahon told Ella. "The pony's name was Bibo—don't ask me why—and Bibo was more like a dog, he followed me everywhere, if I had let him he would have come inside the house with me when it was time for my supper. I thought the world of that pony. Then one day my mother asked me to go pick some cress for her from a stream that was perhaps a mile or two from our cottage, so I rode Bibo to the stream, but when I got there the stream had dried up. The stream had turned into a bog, and not knowing any better, I rode Bibo into it—" General MacMahon paused and shook his head. "The bog was quicksand and Bibo got stuck in it. He could not move his feet at all. Also, he was sinking fast. I stood up on his back—in those days I rode bareback—and jumped as far as I could on to dry land, thinking that once I had gotten off him, he would be able to move, but he couldn't. Poor Bibo was up past his knees in the quicksand and he was neighing and shaking his head and getting more and more agitated, which of course made him sink even faster. It was pitiful to watch and from where I was I couldn't reach him or reach the reins to try to pull him out so I decided to run home and get help which is what I did. I ran as fast as my legs could carry me and when I reached home, I got my father and my brothers to go back down with me to the bog—my father brought along a rope and my brothers carried a ladder—and although it had taken me perhaps thirty minutes to do this, by the time we got back to where I had left Bibo, Bibo was gone. There was no trace of him. Nothing. The pony had been swallowed up by the mud."

"Oh," Ella said. "How dreadful."

General MacMahon did not answer right away, then he said, "I swear, in my whole life, that was the worst thing I ever did see or, perhaps I should say the worst thing I never did see."

The Allies kept up their fire for a week. Major Hermosa was crushed to death when his horse was shot and fell on top of him; Colonel Gonzales was killed when the ammunition cart he was standing next to exploded; Colonel Moniel was taken prisoner and Colonel Rivarola bled to death in the field from his wounds. Franco's army was in complete disarray, the number of dead and wounded was huge, still the few obedient and brave Paraguayan soldiers left refused to give up. On December 23, the Allied generals sent a messenger asking Franco to surrender, but that same morning, Dr. Stewart, Franco's personal physician, had pulled out Franco's abscessed tooth, also taking out the tooth next to it for good measure, and Franco had a terrible headache—to make matters worse he had a hangover from the bottle of brandy he had drunk to kill the pain—and he was in no mood to negotiate. Franco cursed the messenger, he threatened him with his sword and, frightened, the messenger rode away without waiting for an official answer.

Christmas Eve a cannonball ripped through Franco's living quarters and missed hitting him and Brigida Chaves by only a few feet. In bed, Franco was on top of Brigida Chaves when the force of the blast knocked them both—surprisingly, Franco did not lose his erection and stayed inside her—to the floor. When the smoke and debris cleared and

Brigida Chaves had left, although it was the middle of the night, Franco sent for General McMahon. The time had come to make out his will:

GENERAL MACMAHON,
MINISTER OF THE UNITED STATES OF AMERICA
PIKYSYRY
24 December 1868

SIR,—As representative of a friendly nation, and to provide against all that may happen, allow me to entrust to your care the subjoined document, by which I transfer to Doña Ella Lynch all my private effects of whatever description.

Concerned about his children, Franco wrote General MacMahon a second letter:

SIR, — As you have the extreme goodness to offer to take charge of my children, I now recommend them to your protection should anything happen to me.

I authorize you to adopt any means in their favor you may consider best for the welfare of those poor little creatures, more particularly Leopoldo, whose tender age fills me with anxiety.

You will thus gain my eternal gratitude, since the fate of those children is what will most trouble me in the terrible period I dedicate to the fortunes of my country. They will be safe under the protection of a gentleman whose qualities I have been able to appreciate, not, indeed, during a long acquaintance, but to me a happy one.

It is thus, General, I venture to trouble you, with motives which make no other call than in that gentlemanly feeling I congratulate myself in having found in Your Excellency, to whom I now offer my friendly acknowledgments.
        Francisco S. Lopez

The Paraguayan line gave way three days later. In the chaos of the battle, Franco could not find Ella. Paying no attention to the bursting shells and rockets falling all around him, he spurred his horse and wheeled past the burning buildings, looking for her and shouting her name. He grew hoarse from both the smoke and the shouting, while his son Pancho, with tears streaming down his face, desperately tried to keep up with his father, until Franco had to abandon the search and retreat. Galloping through the woods a few minutes later, Franco, out of the corner of his eye, caught sight of Brigida Chaves falling off her horse—either she could not ride or she had been shot—but it was too late and Franco did not stop for her. He could hear the Allied infantry right behind him; fortunately, they were firing too high. General Francisco Fernandez and his lancers were covering Franco and although they were vastly outnumbered they bravely stood their ground until Franco was safely out of harm's way and General Fernandez was shot through the heart.

On Christmas Day, two large carriages drawn by horses and several carts drawn by oxen, accompanied by a small detachment of cavalry, made up the convoy that included General MacMahon, the Lopez children— conscientious, General MacMahon was fulfilling Franco's instructions, and paying special attention to Leopoldo, the youngest—Rosaria, Doña Iñes and a number of servants. They were making their slow and arduous way to the new provisional capital at Piribebuy. The carts contained all of Franco and Ella's furniture, silver and china, their clothes and papers; one cart contained Ella's Bechstein piano. The road was a bumpy track, lined with wounded men—more than six thousand of them. Some were walking but most were being pulled in slow-moving carts that the carriages overtook.

"Don't look," Rosaria advised the children.

The children looked anyway. "Did you see him?" Federico whispered to Enrique, nodding to a man lying in a cart. "I don't think he had legs."

"Where? Show me." Curious, Carlos Honorio craned his neck.

"I didn't see him." Excluded, Leopoldo began to cry; also, he remembered he had forgotten his humming top in Pikyrysy. "I want Mamma," he whined.

"Don't cry, Leopoldo. Your mamma will be here soon," Rosaria lied.

Several times they nearly had to turn back. Swollen by the rains, the rivers were difficult to cross. Each time, the horses and oxen were made to swim and the carriages and carts were run into the water until each axle rested inside a canoe; then, wading and swimming, the soldiers pushed the canoes with the carriages to the opposite shore. Midriver, where the current was strongest, they had a hard time keeping the carriages upright and from upsetting into the water. At one crossing, afraid to get into a canoe, Doña Iñes stood hesitating on the bank of the river until, without a word, one of the soldiers picked her up in his arms and, despite her protests, set her down next to Enrique and Federico.

Hot and tired, the two boys were arguing again in the canoe.

"He had one leg, I tell you," Enrique said.

"He had no legs," Federico insisted. "You did not see him."

"I did see him. One leg, I said."

"You must be blind."

"You're the one who is blind!" Enrique half stood up in the canoe and hit Federico in the chest, making the canoe rock.

Federico kicked back at Enrique and made the canoe rock harder.

"*Aiii!*" Doña Iñes cried as the canoe tipped over.

Enrique and Federico were able to grab the overturned canoe and hang on to it as they were swept to the shore but Doña Iñes disappeared under the water. The same soldier who had picked her up in his arms plunged in the river after her—Doña Iñes could not swim and the shoe with the heavy wooden sole dragged her under—and he got her out.

Next, to the sound of church bells ringing from a nearby village, they had to climb the *cordilleras*. The pass over the mountains was cut out of the rock and as steep as a staircase; also it was slippery with water that trickled down from streams. Everyone, including little Leopoldo— General MacMahon put Leopoldo on his shoulders and carried him— had to get out of the carriages and walk; the soldiers had to dismount and lead their horses. Barely had they started when the cart carrying

Ella's Bechstein piano broke an axle. With no means to repair it, the cart and piano had to be abandoned (later, that same village with the ringing church bells was renamed Piano). Less than halfway up the mountain pass, the soldier who had picked up Doña Iñes in his arms and put her in the canoe and then rescued her from drowning—his name was Cantalicio (Doña Iñes understood him to say Jesú Cristo)—again picked her up in his arms and carried her up the steep road. This time, Doña Iñes shut her eyes and did not protest.

At about the same time that Lieutenant-Colonel Thompson had to surrender at Angostura, in Croydon, England, where she lived, Mrs. Masterman received a disturbing letter from her son:

12 September 1868

My Dear Mother:

In my letter to you of the eighth, sent through Mr. Washburn, I mentioned the terrible conspiracy to destroy the government of Paraguay and its President, who by his skill and bravery in this war had defied the power of Brazil and gained a reputation unexampled in America. The conspiracy was suggested and chiefly arranged by Mr. Washburn, who was in league with the enemy. As I was living in his house, I could not help hearing about it; and I am sorry I did not denounce him to the government, but I have done all I could to make up for the neglect. I have candidly confessed all I know of this terrible business; and I hope I will be pardoned by the President. I hope my life may be spared, so I may see you again.

      Your affectionate son,
      Frederick Masterman

Sixteen

PIRIBEBUY

The orange trees that lined the streets of Piribebuy were in bloom and birds chirped and warbled in the branches. All the tidy thatch-roofed houses in the village had pretty flower gardens and the bell in the quaint old church tower in the plaza chimed the hours on time. Looking out at the peaceful scene from her bedroom window and listening to Carlos Honorio, in the next room, naming his animals as he put them inside Noah's ark, it was difficult for Ella to imagine that a war was still being fought and that a few days ago she had nearly been killed.

Colonel von Wisner, Ella and her young equerry, Lázaro Alcántara, left Pikysyry a few minutes before Franco and Pancho. They just missed one another—one time Ella thought she heard a voice call out *"Mamma,"* but she could not see through the cannon smoke. Riding through the woods, they heard several shots, and when Ella turned she saw Lázaro, who was a few paces behind her, fall from his horse. Riderless, the horse galloped past Ella.

"Leave him," Colonel von Wisner called out but Ella had yanked her horse around and was riding back to where Lázaro lay on the ground.

A bullet had severed an artery and a stream of blood gushed like a fountain from his arm. He was trying to stop the flow with one hand, but blood was pouring through his fingers like water. Dismounting, Ella knelt on the ground next to Lázaro and tore off the sleeve of her blouse. She tried to make a tourniquet but the wound was on his shoulder and she could find no place to tie it. Behind her, more shots were fired and she heard Colonel von Wisner, who had ridden back, shout, "We must go at once, or we too shall be killed."

Ella looked up and saw two Brazilian infantrymen with bayonets running toward them through the woods. From where he was sitting on his horse, Colonel von Wisner fired at one; in his haste, Colonel von Wisner fired too close to his horse's head and the horse reared and bolted. Left alone, Ella picked up Lázaro's sword, which lay next to him on the ground, and standing up, she faced the other infantryman. The man was black, a slave probably, and startled to see a woman, he did not fire right away. Ella saw him frown then open his mouth to say something but he was too late. Before the man could shut his mouth or move to defend himself, Ella pursued her next advantage, that of a left-handed fencer, and lunged forward with the sword. She cut him in the neck.

When she turned back to Lázaro, his face was drained of color and his body had gone rigid. He was trying to speak.

"Comment allez-vous, Madame?"

"I have killed a man," Ella picked up her pen and wrote in her diary. "I have killed a black man," she underlined the words. "A Brazilian. A man who no doubt had a wife and children. . . ." Then, pausing, she looked out the window again at the village of Piribebuy. This time, she did not see the flowers that grew in such profusion in the tidy gardens or hear the birds that chirped and warbled in the branches of the orange trees; instead she saw the black man's face and how surprised he

had looked and how for perhaps a second their eyes had met before his
blood, red blood like Lázaro's, had spurted out of his neck and splashed
her clothes and face.

Ella shut her diary.

The Brazilian forces occupied Asunción. They pillaged and looted the
city. Every house was ransacked; furniture, books, papers were stolen,
burned, torn apart. In Calle Liberdad, a dead mule lay rotting in the
middle of the street. The American Legation on the Plaza Vieja had
become the Gran Hotel de Cristo, a misleading name since it was a
brothel. Franco's unfinished palace stood in ruins, the doors and windows ripped out, the statuary broken. The seats, the velvet curtains, the
piano, even the sets—everything that could be carried—were removed
from the opera house modeled on La Scala. Inside Inocencia's house, the
aviary was destroyed, twisted bits of wire lay on the grounds with a few
faded parrot feathers stuck to them; the silk curtains that had once
belonged to Baron de Villa Maria were in tatters; only Inocencia's large
bed with the mahogany carved pineapples still stood in the bedroom,
several Brazilian soldiers kept two or three young Guaraní girls at a time
tied to it. (When one of the Brazilian soldiers slept in the bed, he complained of a recurring dream in which an old man with wings instead
of arms, a sharp beak instead of a nose, flew over his head in a menacing way.) A fire had been set in the front hall and the marble statue of
the woman bitten by a serpent was blackened by smoke, her head was
split at the nose, her marble breasts hacked off. In the Plaza de la Catedral, the center of the town, starving dogs roamed the square, foraging
for food and fighting one another for it. Outside the city, Ella's house,
Obispo Cue, was vandalized and gutted: a broken gilt-framed mirror lay
shattered in the front hall; the hand-painted French wallpaper in the dining room hung down in torn strips; in Ella's bedroom, a chaise longue
covered in pink-and-white toile lay on its side, legless; a pile of human
excrement had dried in a corner. The children's rooms were a mess of
broken toys, even Enrique's velocipede had been completely dismantled

and destroyed—only a single iron pedal remained. The flower and vegetable gardens were trampled and wrecked—the zinnias beheaded, the orange trees uprooted and felled.

Doña Dolores Carisimo de Jovellanos, Ella's lady-in-waiting, had not seen Baron von Fischer-Truenfeld in several months—Baron von Fischer-Truenfeld either was building more telegraph posts or had gone back to Prussia—and she was pregnant. Naturally plump, no one noticed her thickening waist, her expanding bosom; no one noticed that she stood on her bed, then stood higher on the table and jumped to the floor several times a day, that she took scalding hot baths, that she drank salt water—the salt water only made her more nauseated. Every day too, Doña Dolores went and knelt on the hard red tiles of the Catedral de la Encarnación and prayed. All to no avail. At last, she went to seek the advice of Señora Juliana Echegaray de Martinez, who was kind and beautiful, but Señora Juliana was not home. Her husband, Colonel Martinez, along with his five hundred men, who were reduced to skin and bones by fatigue and lack of food, had surrendered at Humaitá and, as punishment, Señora Juliana had been taken prisoner. Next, not knowing who else to turn to, Doña Dolores confided in Doña Isidora Diaz, the third lady-in-waiting. Since the death of her husband, Doña Isidora Diaz had become more absentminded and confused.

"I was the wife of General Diaz," she told Doña Dolores.

"I was speaking of a midwife." Doña Dolores was nearly in tears.

"I was a good wife," Doña Isidora said.

It took Doña Isidora some time before she understood what Doña Dolores was after and before she remembered the name of a midwife in La Trinidad.

Doña Dolores took an early morning train from Asunción. There were no passenger carriages and the wagons were open and piled high with sacks of maize and alfalfa. Two men had to give Doña Dolores a hand up—one from above, the other from behind. The man from behind stuck his finger up her ass. The train swayed and bumped and

Doña Dolores was only faintly aware of the passing countryside, which was dotted with tussocky grass and spindly cotton plants that had gone to seed. She barely noticed when the train went through woods of fig, acacia and mimosa trees. Mostly she felt the hot sun beating down on her head making her sweat.

When Doña Dolores got off the train at La Trinidad, the back of her skirt was damp. At first, she thought she had sat on something wet—the sack of grain; also she thought of the man who had put his finger up her ass, but by the time she reached the midwife's house, she knew the damp was blood and that she was miscarrying. The midwife gave her a glass of hot bitter tea to drink, which burned her mouth and tongue and made the bleeding worse, then she inserted something sharp into Doña Dolores's womb and scraped inside with it while Doña Dolores screamed. Afterward the midwife made Doña Dolores lie down in a hammock wrapped in a blanket while she took her clothes and washed them out for her. When Doña Dolores was ready to leave, she tried to pay the midwife but the midwife would not accept her money.

"God's will." The midwife repeated, "God's will."

In the train going back to Asunción, Doña Dolores started to bleed again. This time the blood between her legs was dark and clotted. The train was nearly empty, an old man drinking *maté* was the only other passenger; occupied sucking on his straw, he never once looked over at Doña Dolores. There were no sacks of grain to sit on in the carriage and when the cramps got bad, Doña Dolores lay down on the wooden carriage floor and wept. Too late, she realized she wanted to keep the baby.

From San Fernando, where he saw Frederick Masterman, whose face he said was covered with blood, Alonzo Taylor was made to march over marshes and impenetrable woods. The marshes were filled with reeds and close-cut grasses whose rough edges were as sharp as knives and cut Alonzo's bare feet; the woods were full of impassable thorny creepers and fallen palm tree branches covered with long sharp spines.

He counted more than two hundred other prisoners. Among the

foreigners were Señor Cauturo, an Argentine; Señor Fülger, a German watchmaker, and Señor Harmann, another German; Lieutenant Romero, an Argentine; Captain Fidanza, an Italian; Señor Leite-Pereira, the Portuguese consul. Also there were four Paraguayan ladies: Señora Juliana Echegaray de Martinez, Doña Dolores Recaldè and the Señoritas Egusquiza, two aged spinsters.

Two bullock carts trailed behind the prisoners, they were said to contain Franco's sisters, Inocencia and Rafaela.

During the march, Alonzo Taylor often walked next to Señora Juliana Martinez. Her body was covered with sores and cuts, her face was badly bruised, on the back of her neck she had a raw spot the size of an orange that oozed pus and blood. Despite his own weakened state, Alonzo tried to help Señora Juliana; he gave her what food he had, sometimes they talked.

"For years Mrs. Lynch was my dear friend. She was always very affectionate and warm," Señora Juliana said.

"She was very fond of one of my daughters, my youngest, Elizabeth. She took her under her wing," Alonzo answered.

"She gave me many gifts—dresses, French silks"—Señora Juliana fingered the tattered and soiled blue scarf she wore on her shoulders—"brocades, furniture for my house, a diamond bracelet on my birthday. She was always generous to me. If only I could see her, speak to her for a moment."

Alonzo nodded. "She gave Elizabeth piano lessons. She told me Elizabeth was quite gifted."

"Tell me the truth, Mr. Taylor. The ugly bruises on my face," Señora Juliana turned to face Alonzo, "do you think they are permanent?"

"No, they will go away, I assure you."

Señora Juliana, Alonzo Taylor knew, had been beautiful and she was only twenty-four years old.

Early one morning, an army officer rode up on a big bay horse who bucked and reared and would not stand still. Jerking at the reins with one hand to try and control the horse, the officer shouted out the following prisoners' names from a piece of paper he held in his other hand: Señor

Cauturo and Lieutenant Romero, the Argentines; Señors Fülger and Harmann, the Germans; Captain Fidanza; Señor Leite-Pereira; Señora Juliana, who was so weak and emaciated she could hardly stand; Doña Dolores Recaldè and Señorita Luisa Egusquiza, who was over sixty and whose sister had died along the way.

Each person answered when his or her name was called and walked forward until a line was formed. Then they were marched off by the guards, followed by three priests who carried chairs for the prisoners' confessions. An hour or so later, Alonzo Taylor heard a volley of shots and a woman screaming. The woman continued to scream long after more shots were fired and Alonzo Taylor shut his eyes and prayed that it was not Señora Juliana Martinez. When the guards returned, one of them was wearing Captain Fidanza's hat and another Señor Leite-Pereira's green cape with the brass buttons; a priest had tied Señora Juliana's blue silk scarf around his neck.

At the Hotel de la Paix in Buenos Ayres, where he was staying, Lieutenant-Colonel Thompson was having dinner with his brother. Eleven years since the brothers had seen each other and at first each did not recognize the other. Lieutenant-Colonel Thompson's hair had turned white and he had lost nearly twenty pounds while his brother had gained as many and had gone bald. During the five-course meal, which began with a cream of pea soup, went on with poached sea bass, vanilla ice and finished with an assortment of local cheeses and a blancmange for dessert, they caught up on family news—births and deaths primarily: a sister drowned in a boating accident off the coast of Bournemouth, a niece both married and widowed in the same year, another relative had had identical twins, two boys whom even the parents could not distinguish, the family dog, a long-haired setter named Samson, whom Lieutenant-Colonel Thompson remembered with affection, had lived to the ripe old age of sixteen but then had had to be put down.

Toward the end of the meal, the hotel proprietor, Monsieur

Maréchal, came over to their table to inquire if everything was satisfactory.

"Excellent, thank you," Lieutenant-Colonel Thompson assured Monsieur Maréchal. "I haven't had such a good meal in years. Eleven to be precise."

Monsieur Maréchal bowed and smiled at the two men. For a moment, he looked as if he wanted to ask something more—news perhaps of Madame Lynch? Instead, he said, *"Bon appétit, messieurs."*

After Monsieur Maréchal had left them, Lieutenant-Colonel Thompson offered his brother a cigar he had brought back from Paraguay—a *pety-hobi* which, despite its rough appearance, was mild. With the cigars, the two brothers drank a sweet Bolivian coffee and poured themselves a glass of brandy. It was only then that Lieutenant-Colonel Thompson began to describe to his brother how, after surrendering at Angostura, he had the good fortune to board the H.M.S. *Cracker*—although he also mentioned how, in his haste, he deeply regretted having to abandon a valuable ceremonial sword with a hilt of solid gold, a gift from Franco—and leave Paraguay.

The two bullock carts Alonzo Taylor had noticed were empty. Inocencia and Rafaela had been released and were on their way to Piribebuy.

In the carriage, Rafaela whined, "I have lost a button on my dress. Will you please have a look, Inocencia." Rafaela was missing all the buttons on her dress, the dress was entirely open in the back and held shut by a piece of rope tied around Rafaela's waist.

"My hair, Rafaela. Is it all in place?" Inocencia answered, patting her head.

"As soon as I get home I am going to sew new buttons on my dress," Rafaela said.

"I wish I could find my comb," Inocencia continued. "The tortoiseshell comb Vincente gave me."

"Silk buttons, bone buttons, brass buttons," Rafaela said in a singsong voice. "From now on I'll have nothing but gold buttons!"

"You haven't seen my comb, have you, Rafaela?" Inocencia was frowning. "If I didn't know you better and if you were not my sister, I would say that you took the comb."

"Don't talk to me about your stupid comb, Inocencia, I am busy looking for my gold button."

"Look for my comb while you are at it," Inocencia answered. Then, all of a sudden, without any warning, she punched Rafaela as hard as she could in the stomach.

"*Aiii,*" Rafaela screamed and grabbed Inocencia by the hair.

The distance between Franco's camp at Cerro León and Piribebuy was only a few miles as the crow flies but Franco had to cross the *cordilleras,* which made the journey much longer. Every two or three days, Franco rode his big sure-footed mule, Linda, first up then down the narrow zigzag path carved into the cliff that was as steep as a staircase to go and see Ella.

Franco looked pale and he had gained weight; he ate large amounts of food not from hunger but from frustration. Also at dinner, he drank too much.

"Open another bottle of champagne," he ordered his servant.

Mañuel looked over at Ella.

"Did you not hear me?" Franco was quick to anger. "You good-for-nothing sneaky pederast!"

Franco listened to no one; occasionally he talked to the American minister, General MacMahon.

"Pass me the dish of meat!" he shouted.

Ella did. "But, *chéri,* you will get indigestion. This is your third helping."

Franco glared at Ella. "Mind your own affairs. I have told you before that if you no longer wish to support me and want to leave, now is the time to go."

"I was talking about the meat. The damn meat! Not the war." Ella was close to tears.

Franco shrugged and continued eating.

Afterward, in bed, asleep, Franco held Ella's hand and snored; he had bad dreams. He shouted out names: "Captain Fidanza!" "Saturnino!" "Lieutenant Romero!" "Señor Harmann!" "Doña Luisa Egusquiza!" "Señor Leite-Pereira!"

His shouting woke Ella up.

"Señora Juliana Martinez!"

Ella remembered how Señora Juliana had helped her dress, had helped fix her hair and clasp the aquamarines around her neck. She could still hear Señora Juliana calling out when she arrived in the morning: *Señora, do you hear the birds singing this morning? They are singing just for you!* Ella's eyes filled with tears—not only was Señora Juliana sweet-natured, she had a lovely speaking voice.

Pancho always crossed the *cordilleras* with Franco. When he reached his mother's house, right away he went to Enrique's room. Squatting on the floor, Pancho played with Enrique's set of lead soldiers. He and Enrique set up elaborate battles between the different regiments, the Lancers, the Household Cavalry, and the Light Dragoons. If Enrique's regiment won, Pancho lost his temper and kicked the remaining soldiers away; one time he kicked Enrique as well.

"*Tonto! Imbecil!*"

Instead of complaining, Enrique laughed, which made Pancho angrier.

In the corner of the room he shared with Enrique, Federico sat reading—or pretending to read. Among his mother's possessions, he had found *The Last of the Mohicans.* The book was translated into French and Federico could make out only a few words here and there; mostly, his eyes were drawn to the colorful illustrations. In one picture, an Indian whose face was painted red, white and yellow had a British soldier by the hair in one hand and a machete in the other; in a second picture, the hands and feet of a pretty fair-haired woman and a fair-haired child were bound by ropes to a post while a group of Indians building a fire with a caldron set on top of it could be seen in the background. Although fascinated, Federico could not help but shudder. The Indians in the book looked to him to be far crueler than the gauchos, far fiercer than the Brazilian *macacos*.

When it was time for Pancho to leave, he, formal, shook hands with his brothers and leaned over in the French manner to kiss his mother's hand—Pancho's lips barely touched Ella's skin—then he mounted his horse and, with his back stiff and straight, rode back up and down the steep path to Cerro León with his father.

Riding through camp one day, Franco recognized Alonzo Taylor among the prisoners.

"In God's name, what are you doing here?"

"Sir, I beg you, a mistake surely. I have committed no crime and my family—" Alonzo started to answer.

But Franco did not want to hear any more. "You are at liberty," he shouted at him, then he whipped his mule and cantered off.

Starving and near death, Alonzo Taylor weighed ninety-eight pounds. He was too weak to go far. Right away, he was captured by Brazilian soldiers, who released him and helped him make his slow, painful way on horseback to Asunción. With no flesh on his bones, Alonzo could barely stay in the saddle, and by the time he reached the house with the fireplace and chimney he had built, he was too ill to speak or say that he was looking for his wife and two daughters. The last thing he remembered was crawling on the floor on his hands and knees to reach the bedroom and calling out for Dolores, the lively girl of mixed Spanish and Guaraní blood who used to sing songs in both languages to him. Afterward Alonzo had no recollection of who took care of him or how he got on board the H.M.S. *Cracker,* and it was also a few days before he could talk plainly or before he learned that his wife and two daughters were safe in Piribebuy.

One morning as Ella was walking down the tree-lined street of Piribebuy, she met Inocencia and Rafaela. The two sisters were holding their prayer books, they were on their way to mass. Since Ella had last seen them, they had aged and lost weight; Rafaela was limping and much of Inocencia's dark hair had fallen out.

"*Buenos días, Señoras.*" Ella felt sorry for them all of a sudden.

Immediately, the two sisters crossed to the other side of the street. Inocencia spat in Ella's direction. "*Puta!*"

"*Ladrona!* You stole my gold buttons," Rafaela shouted at her.

A hundred times Ella had packed her suitcases, a hundred times she had unpacked them. She had made plans to leave, to board a French ship and take her children, Rosaria, her horse, Mathilde, a few of her most valuable possessions: her favorite dresses, her toiletry set of silver-backed combs and brushes, her aquamarine necklace. Now she was determined to stay.

"I've been recalled," General MacMahon told Ella.

"It's too complicated to explain," he said when she asked him the reason. "But one of Ulysses Grant's first appointments when he took office as president of the United States was Elihu Benjamin Washburn as secretary of state."

"Charles Washburn's brother?" Ella asked.

"Exactly. Elihu Washburn was so disliked and his appointment was so controversial that he was forced to resign after only eleven days in office."

"I am not surprised," Ella said.

"However, during those eleven days," General MacMahon went on, "he issued an order which recalled me from my post in Paraguay. Apparently my reports which supported President Lopez were a rebuke to his brother, who is scheduled to appear before a congressional committee called to review his conduct in office."

"His dreadful conduct," Ella also said.

Next General MacMahon rode over the *cordilleras* to inform Franco at Cerro León.

"Not only am I losing the recognition of the United States, but I am losing a good friend," Franco said, clasping General MacMahon to his chest.

"Do not forget us," he also said.

When General MacMahon left Paraguay, he took a large number of boxes and packages along with his own personal trunks and valises. When asked by the Brazilian officials in Asunción what the boxes and packages contained, he answered, "Cigars and *yerba maté*."

In August the Allied forces attacked Piribebuy. The town was bombarded by cannons for four hours; houses, tidy gardens, orange trees were reduced to rubble, dust and ash. The cavalry chased the women and children who tried to escape, trampling them down, driving their lances through them, cutting them up with their sabers. When the hospital was set on fire, all the sick inside burned to death. Fortunately, Ella had been warned in time. A few hours earlier, she and the children had made their escape in a carriage, with Mathilde tied to the back on a lead rope.

Mrs. Taylor and her two daughters, Mary and Elizabeth, sought refuge in the quaint old church with the bell tower. When the Brazilian soldiers broke down the doors, Mrs. Taylor threw herself on top of her daughters trying to shield them but Elizabeth, who had not been herself since the incident by the stream at Luque, struggled from under her mother and ran to the nearest soldier. Snarling like a dog, she lunged at him, biting his face, biting his neck. The soldier, a stout man with a thick black beard, was so startled that at first he did not move, then realizing Elizabeth must be mad, he tried to push her off but, in her frenzy, Elizabeth was nearly as strong as he, and she wrapped herself around him.

"*Ruf!*" Elizabeth barked, she was foaming at the mouth.

"*Argh!*" The soldier yelled, in spite of himself he was frightened of her.

The two rolled around on the church floor like stuck dogs, until, finally, to free himself from her, the soldier pulled out his pistol and shot

Elizabeth in the head. As Elizabeth fell back, her mouth opened and a large wad of the soldier's black hair fell out of it. Mrs. Taylor and Mary, along with the other women who had sought refuge in the church, were raped, then shot or, to save ammunition, had their throats cut. A virgin still, Mary was raped so often she fainted, and, fortunately, did not regain consciousness; the last man to have her, after pulling up his pants, knifed her through the heart. When they were finished, the Brazilian soldiers stole all the silver from the church—the chalice, the candlesticks, the offering plates. They left just as the bell in the tower tolled three.

Instead of going to the church, Alfredo d'Escragnolle Taunay, a captain in the Brazilian cavalry, rode over to Ella's house. Among the possessions left behind, Captain d'Escragnolle Taunay discovered Franco's wine cellar, he opened a bottle of champagne and drank it all down. He also found a beautifully bound edition of *Don Quijote de la Mancha* inscribed to Ella, *With best wishes, from your good friend and countryman, Martin MacMahon.* When later Captain d'Escragnolle Taunay had to go to the toilet, he ripped out the pages and used them to clean himself.

Seventeen

AQUIDABAN RIVER

Justo José's wife named their daughters after the women in the Lopez family: the oldest, Juaña, the second, Rafaela, the third, Inocencia; by the time the fourth daughter was born, the daughter whose arms looked like wings, afraid she had run out of names, Justo José's wife, on an impulse—in spite of her husband's protests—named her Ella.

Juaña was fourteen and she was pregnant. The handsome young soldier who said he would marry her had been taken prisoner at Angostura, then he was forced to take arms in the service of the Brazilians.

(Hearing about this practice while still in Buenos Ayres, Lieutenant-Colonel Thompson was outraged; he wrote the Brazilian minister of war a letter of protest:

I have the honor to address Your Excellency for the purpose of communicating to you that, from various Paraguayans who have lately come from Asunción, I have heard that many of the men who capitulated at Angostura, of which I was the commander, have been obliged to take arms in the Allied army whether they like it or not.

As this is contrary to the written stipulations of the capitulations, and the verbal assurances of the Duke de Caxias, I address myself to Your Excellency to beg you will inquire into and rectify this. . . .

Lieutenant-Colonel Thompson's letter proved useless. The practice of making prisoners fight on the side of their enemy continued and the soldier who was the father of Juaña's unborn child was killed in battle by one of his own countrymen.)

Rafaela, the second girl, died of diphtheria, her throat closed until she could no longer eat or breathe—Justo José, who had returned home to his village of San Estanislao only twice during the war, was still unaware of her death. Inocencia, the prettiest of the four daughters and Justo José's favorite, was twelve and she was employed as a maid in Asunción. No word had been heard from her for over a year; Inocencia did not know how to write and even if she had known, there was no way since the Allies had captured the city that she could have mailed a letter home. The English family she worked for had gone to Luque then on to Piribebuy. According to one rumor Justo José's wife had heard, there was not enough room in the family's carriage for Inocencia but according to another rumor, Inocencia had preferred to stay in Asunción alone. Every day Justo José's wife went to church and prayed for the safety of her daughter; once a week she lit a candle for her. Also, she had hope. A neighbor boy in the village who was about the same age as Inocencia—they had played together as children—told her how, when he had gone to Asunción the week before with some chickens to sell to the Brazilians, he had seen Inocencia. Inocencia was well, he said. He did not say any more or where he had seen Inocencia—on the Plaza Vieja, standing at the front door of the Gran Hotel de Cristo smoking a cigar. He also did not tell her mother how when he went inside the Gran Hotel de Cristo and tried to speak to Inocencia, she had a vacant look on her face and stared at him without recognizing him. Moreover, when the neighbor boy told her who he was, Inocencia just laughed and blew cigar smoke in his face.

Like Justo José her father, Ella, the youngest, was musical; she had a good ear and she was a good mimic. When she walked in the woods she had no trouble imitating birds, their songs, their calls. She could whistle like a duck on its way south, she could scream like a large flight of parrots whirling overhead, she could purse her mouth into the warning sounds of the peewit at the approach of the *carácará* and the *chimangos*, the buzzards and vultures. She could sit so still under her favorite bunchy fig tree, which yielded dark juicy fruit, that a *já-khá*, a wild turkey, flew down from its perch high up in a mimosa tree when she called to it: *chakhan-chaja, chakhan-chaja!* One time, not long after the neighbor boy had seen Inocencia in Asunción, Ella was standing under that same bunchy tree, reaching up with her mouth to eat a ripe fig— her arms were nearly useless, she had two little digits sticking out at the end of each stump—when a parrot perched in the tree grabbed the ripe fig out from in between her teeth.

Instead of being frightened, Ella laughed. And Ella had never seen such a large parrot—with its wings spread out, it was more than a meter long—or such a beautiful parrot: his feathers were a deep violet-blue. The parrot too was looking down at her with his yellow-rimmed, unblinking, curious eyes. After a while, the parrot scrambled up the branch of the fig tree and grabbed another fig, then he scrambled back down holding the fig in his beak. Ella opened her mouth and the parrot dropped the fig into it. Up again went the big blue parrot to get Ella another fig, and another, and another, until Ella had had enough figs to eat. Then Ella waved one of her winglike arms at the parrot and, as if a signal or an action familiar to them both, the parrot—using his beak to balance himself—climbed down from the fig tree onto Ella's shoulder.

"*Kráa, kráa,*" Ella said.

"*Kráa, kráa,*" the big blue parrot answered her.

With the big blue parrot perched on her shoulder, Ella walked back to her house in San Estanislao where her mother and sister—hot and impatient, Juaña was fanning herself with a palm leaf—were in the kitchen waiting. They were waiting for a pumpkin, a sugarcane, a parsnip, a melon, a bunch of oranges—whatever Ella could find in the woods and carry back in her winglike arms—and she had brought them a big blue parrot.

Dropping her palm leaf fan, Juaña made a lunge for the parrot. Quicker, the parrot bit her.

"Aiii!" Juaña held up her bleeding hand.

Justo José's wife was more devious. Standing behind Ella so that Ella could not see her, she took a cloth sack and, with one swift, sure movement, she yanked it over the parrot. Before Ella could turn around and stop her, she set the cloth sack on top of the kitchen table and picked up her wooden mallet. Too late, Ella screamed as her mother repeatedly struck the parrot inside the sack.

When Justo José's wife was certain there was no more movement or sign of life inside the sack, she opened it. The parrot's blue head was crushed; his yellow-rimmed eye was a bit of jelly. Satisfied, Justo José's wife began to pluck the parrot while Juaña filled a pot full of water and put it to boil. Soon bright blue and violet feathers covered Justo José's kitchen floor. Later, his wife would sweep them into the fire, the same fire she used to cook their supper.

After the fall of Piribebuy, Franco lived like a fugitive. He fled through the swamps of the Alta Paraná, first to Caraguatay, then to San Estanislao, to Curuguaty, and finally to Cerro Corá on the banks of the Aquidaban River, never more than a few miles ahead of the pursuing Brazilians. Each battle was more desperate as Franco, who had a thousand men left—boys and old men—a few pieces of artillery, some broken muskets held together with hide and ropes, case-shot made out of screws and chopped up bar-iron, useless beyond a hundred yards, fought to keep from being hemmed in by the enemy. Also, as a result of his drinking, he was more and more unpredictable, more and more unstable and irrational. One day, pleased and proud, he had medals hammered out from whatever pieces of metal were left and ceremoniously distributed them to his troops. He gave a twelve-year-old boy with a broken leg who could hardly walk a medal for not running away, he gave an old man with one eye a medal for being a good lookout. During all that time, Justo José, who hardly had the strength left to lift up his harp and was so hungry that one night he dreamt he ate it—he chewed the cedar wood and swallowed the dozen or so strings, all that remained of the original thirty-six—had to keep on playing, *ta dum ta dum ta dum dum dum*. Then he had to play again the next day when, for no apparent reason, Franco changed his mind and ordered half a dozen of his soldiers flogged, *ta dum ta dum ta dum dum dum,* including the twelve-year-old boy with the broken leg who had received a medal, *ta dum ta dum ta dum*, and the old man with one eye, *ta dum ta dum*. The old man with one eye did not survive the flogging, *ta dum.*

At about the same time, in New York City, Commander Kirkland, captain of the U.S.S. *Wasp,* was sworn and examined by the House Committee that was investigating the conduct of Mr. Washburn as American minister to Paraguay.

QUESTION: In your letter marked "private," you say this: "Mr. Washburn told me that he had never heard of a revolution or conspiracy against the government; but on one occasion Mrs. Washburn, when her husband was not present, stated that there was a plan to turn Lopez out of power, and to put in his place his two brothers, Venancio and Benigno." Please state the circumstances under which you received this information.

COM. KIRKLAND: It was on the passage down the river, two or three days after we left the batteries. Mrs. Washburn said distinctly that there was no conspiracy but that there was a plan. It was at the dinner table. Mr. Washburn had finished his dinner and had gone out for something and, shortly after, came back. This remark struck me as rather singular. I know that she made a distinction between the words "conspiracy" and "plan."

QUESTION: Was any person present?

COM. KIRKLAND: Yes, sir; a Mr. Davie was present.

QUESTION: Did Mrs. Washburn, at the time and in connection with the remarks that you have just stated, say that there was no conspiracy?

COM. KIRKLAND: We were speaking of Lopez and the country and the people, and she said that there was no conspiracy, but that there was a plan to turn Lopez out.

Then Mrs. Washburn was duly sworn and examined by the House Committee and Commander Kirkland's testimony was read to her.

QUESTION: Please state your recollection of that conversation.

MRS. WASHBURN: I do not remember ever to have had any conversation with him about it, more than that we were all conversing about the conspiracy. I could not have said that there was a plan or conspiracy because I did not then believe it; but I may have said that at one time we may have supposed there was, because of the arrest of people, etc. I did not then believe that there was a conspiracy, and, of course, could not have said that there was one. I do not remember definitely what occurred on that voyage, as I was very nervous and suffered a great deal.

Ella could no longer remember where she had last ridden Mathilde. In Caraguatay? San Estanislao? Curuguaty? Nor could she remember when she had last ridden Mathilde. A week ago? a month? a year? a lifetime ago? Mathilde was nearly skin and bones. Her beautiful shiny gray coat was filled with sores, and there were bald patches where the hair had rubbed off. Too tired to lift her neck, her head drooped; one eye was half closed and crusted over with dried mucus. Every morning Ella washed it out with warm water but by the afternoon the eye had closed up again. Worse, when Mathilde walked—months since she had lost two shoes—she stumbled. The boy who looked after her thought Mathilde should be put down; he was also thinking of the horsemeat. If he had dared, he would have stopped feeding Mathilde entirely.

"Oh, my darling," Ella spoke to her horse, "soon this misery will be over. You'll have as much hay and oats as you can eat. More than you can eat. You'll be fat again." At the sound of Ella's voice, Mathilde pricked up her ears. "You'll have straw in your stall up to your knees. Every day, fresh straw." Ella sighed. "You'll see, my darling, we'll go on long rides the way we once did. We'll gallop for hours on green fields bordered by mimosa and sweet-smelling orange trees." Ella stroked the horse's neck. "You'll see, my darling, my dear."

Venancio Lopez, Franco's brother, was nearly dead. Beaten and tortured, he was put inside a cart and dragged along with another prisoner, Commandant José de Carmen Gomez, the no longer handsome commandant of Villa Franca. In the last stages of untreated syphilis, Commandant Gomez was demented and nearly blind. He did not know who Venancio was and when one time Venancio summoned the strength to tell him his name, Commandant Gomez still called him by other names—names of endearment. Two or three times a day with a mad single-mindedness, Commandant Gomez undid his breeches and masturbated in the cart; he rubbed himself against Venancio's leg, against Venancio's thigh, calling out: *"Querida, amor mío, amada, vita mía,"* as his sperm spilled onto Vencancio. Too weak and in too much pain to complain or care, Venancio closed his eyes. At last on a particularly hot day— the wooden cart was airless—on the way to Curuguaty, Venancio died. Left alone in the cart, Commandant Gomez shouted and beat his chest, he gnashed his teeth and tore out his hair. All night long, he screamed, *"Querida, amor mío, amada, vita mía!"*

"Like a cat in heat," said a sergeant, who was barely recovered from the flogging Franco had ordered and could stand the sound no longer. First thing in the morning, he grabbed his old musket and, after several attempts—the gun jammed and misfired—finally shot Commandant Gomez through the heart.

⅍

Even after he drank himself into a near stupor, Franco could not sleep. During the night, he paced around his tent, stumbling in the dark and frightening the tethered horses, waking up the exhausted sentries, before he let himself in Ella's tent.

"*Chéri?*" Ella was a light sleeper.

In bed, Ella tried to arouse him. In the past, it had never taken her long, but now she sucked and sucked on his limp penis until she thought she would gag and until Franco pushed away her head.

"Enough," he said. For the first time in his life, Franco was impotent.

Already eight-year-old Carlos Honorio had decided that he would become a zoologist, or perhaps specialize and become an entomologist or an ornithologist or, maybe even still be a circus animal trainer. In any event, he knew that he preferred animals to people. Since the war started he had owned several pets: a chinchilla, a tame ocelot—Ella teased him, saying that he was lucky it was so hot otherwise she would have made its spotted coat into a muff—and, given him by a soldier, a small spider monkey, who had sat on Carlos Honorio's shoulder, before he ran away.

Every chance he got—when Rosaria was busy or not paying attention—Carlos Honorio slipped away from the tent he shared with his brothers and walked down to the Aquidaban where, in the shade of the feathery bamboo and with a swarm of bright yellow and pale green butterflies hovering over his head, he sat on the riverbank and forgot the time. He watched two water hogs mating—not sure what they were doing, Carlos Honorio guessed the water hogs were fighting. Another time he watched a *capybara*, a large rodent that weighed over a hundred pounds, dive into the river and quickly swim across it; he saw a tapir— Carlos Honorio mistook the tapir for a wild pig—and several anteaters. He saw pheasant, snipe, wild pigeons. A black-and-white royal duck— he had read how it was the biggest duck in the world—swam silently by and disappeared into the marsh. He also saw storks, egrets, ibis and one capped heron. Perched in a tree no more than ten yards from where Carlos Honorio was sitting, the heron had a pale blue face that looked like a mask and two long feathers that sprouted out of the black cap on his head and arched gracefully over his back. Watching it, Carlos Honorio forgot to breathe. There was one other bird he would have given anything to see, given even his wooden Noah's ark: an *ipègtàtà*. Rosaria had told Carlos Honorio how the *ipègtàtà* only fed on fireflies and how the *ipègtàtà* was hard to miss because when it flew, it lit up the sky like a brilliant meteor. But during all the time he spent sitting on the bank of the Aquidaban River—even when he sat there after it got dark—Carlos Honorio never once got to see the *ipègtàtà*.

After listening to Lieutenant-Colonel Thompson's tales, his brother could not help but admire Franco—his energy and his indomitable will. He secretly admired Ella Lynch as well. When he inquired after her, he was told that she was tall and handsome, with gray-blue eyes. In vain he asked to see a photograph. However, while still in Buenos Ayres with his brother, he had occasion to dine with the journalist Héctor Varela, whom he was able to question further about her.

"She was tall and of a flexible and delicate figure with beautiful and seductive curves. Her skin was alabaster." Time had not dimmed Héctor Varela's recollection of Ella. "Her eyes were of a blue that seemed borrowed from the very hues of heaven and had an expression of ineffable sweetness in whose depths the light of Cupid was enthroned."

"You Americans always exaggerate." Nevertheless, Lieutenant-Colonel Thompson's brother was still curious.

"No, Señor. I speak the truth."

"Mrs. Lynch is a clever and ambitious woman," Lieutenant-Colonel Thompson himself was less sanguine about Ella. "She is inclined to stoutness," he also said. When finished with his meal, he offered his brother and Héctor Varela a choice of cigars—a subject of more interest to him. "This variety is called *pety-hobi* and is most prized in Paraguay. This other here is called *pety-para* or spotted tobacco, named for the yellow discoloration that appears on the flower. It grows only in certain places in Paraguay—isn't that so, Señor Varela? The *canala* or cinnamon-colored variety, I am told, is even rarer." Lighting the cigar, Lieutenant-Colonel Thompson also cautioned Héctor Varela and his brother, "Although it appears mild in flavor, it is quite heady."

Smiling, Lieutenant-Colonel Thompson's brother nodded, he was still thinking of Ella. Then, he said, "As regards the reputed atrocities of Lopez—his extorting the testimony from foreign employees by torture, his starving to death women and children; his bayoneting his brothers, his sisters—" Puffing on his cigar, he went on to say something that Lieutenant-Colonel Thompson did not quite catch.

"Sorry?"

"I said how the truth about Lopez and his mistress appears to be entirely unknown on the banks of this river," he paused again to puff on his cigar. "In fact nothing about Paraguay is known outside the country—you are quite right, George, the cigar is quite heady," he also said, interrupting himself.

Ella sat huddled with the children in their tent; the tent was shaking so hard it seemed ready to collapse or blow away. Together they counted out loud the seconds between the lightning and thunder: *uno, dos, tres*. Most times Ella hardly had time to open her mouth and say *uno* before the thunder sounded. In spite of trying to keep a brave face for the sake of the children, she shivered—had not Franco once told her that lightning struck Paraguay ten times more often than it did any other country? The storm was accompanied by the *pampero*, a fierce hot wind that rushed across the country like a tornado, flattening and uprooting trees, knocking down roofs, carrying off livestock, dogs, cats, chickens and flinging them into trees, stunned or dead. In between the flashes of lightning, the sky was as black as night and rain streamed down in sheets.

Rosaria had run outside to bring in the laundry that was hanging up to dry on a line. She barely could make any headway against the wind as all kinds of debris, twigs, leaves, clumps of earth and mud hit her. Her skirt billowed out like a sail pushing her back, her braid came undone and her hair whipped her face. Blindly, she grabbed at the clothesline and struggled to unfasten the soaked clothes—Enrique's shirt, Federico's breeches, another shirt that belonged to Carlos Honorio. As was her habit, once she removed it, she put a wooden clothespin in her mouth before she put it in her laundry basket.

On his way back after the storm from visiting his relatives who lived outside the village of Cerra Corá, Cantalicio, the soldier who had picked Doña Iñes up in his arms and put her inside the canoe and later carried her up the steep path over the *cordilleras*, found Rosaria lying on the ground next to the clothesline. He nearly tripped over her. Rosaria had been struck by lightning; also something was stuck in her mouth. Cantalicio first thought it was a cigar, only when he tried to remove it did he realize what it was. The clothespin was burned black but it had saved Rosaria's life; once she regained consciousness, Rosaria was all right.

Franco's 1,000 men turned into 800 at San Estanislao, then into 500 at Curuguaty—close to home, a lot of men deserted—and at Cerro Corá on the banks of the Aquidaban River, Franco only had 200 men left. Everyone knew the end was near at hand. Everyone also knew that the army could not keep moving from place to place like gypsies, setting up their tents. The children were tired and sick, food had nearly run out; the horses too were nearly dead from exhaustion and starvation.

On her own, Doña Iñes had started to go out and forage for grass along the banks of the Aquidaban. With her skirt folded up to put the grass inside and her white petticoat showing a little underneath, Doña Iñes was not afraid, she said. She liked to garden and it reminded her of how as a child in Toledo she used to collect dandelion grass for her father's rabbits. She wore her hair in a long single braid and she looked almost pretty. Often, girlishly, she stopped to pick a scarlet pomegranate flower or a purple orchid to put in her braid and she smoked one of Rosaria's cigars.

Slowly, Mathilde began to fill out, the bald patches on her coat grew in, her eye cleared. Ella noticed the change, she encouraged Doña Iñes.

"You should go for a ride," she also told her. "You are light and I have no time. And the horse likes you," she added.

When, at last, Doña Iñes got up her courage, she asked Cantalicio to give her a leg up and she sat on Mathilde's back for a few minutes clutching at the horse's mane.

"Bravo!" Ella called out. "Well done, Doña Iñes!"

The next time, Ella and all the children came out to watch as Doña Iñes sat on Mathilde's back a little longer. Proudly, she walked the horse around the campsite as Enrique, Federico, Carlos Honorio and little Leopoldo applauded and cheered her on.

"Hooray! Hooray, for you, Doña Iñes!"

Smiling nervously, the third time, she rode a little way into the forest. When she came back, she was trotting, awkwardly bouncing bareback, her shorter leg dangling at an odd angle against the horse's side. Mathilde, unused to such an inept rider, showed her impatience by bobbing her head up and down.

"Never mind, you are doing very well. Your father—and didn't you tell me he was a cavalry officer and a member of the Progresista party and that he died saving the life of Colonel Garrigo at the battle of Vicalváro—" Ella was tempted to laugh out loud—how had she remembered all that? "I am sure your father would be proud of you, Doña Iñes!" Ella continued to shout and encourage her.

The fourth time Doña Iñes rode Mathilde, she rode her to the village of Cerra Corá and beyond that for several miles and she did not come back.

When Ella found the horse gone, she blamed the boy who looked after her. She hit the boy so hard with her riding crop that he cried out but still he denied it. Later, Ella tried to find Cantalicio and question him. But the soldier was nowhere to be found, he had gone as well—deserted. Ella guessed the rest.

"Who would have guessed?" Fighting back her tears, Ella told Franco.

Before dawn on the morning of the first day of March, Franco woke Ella and his five children and rushed them, half dressed, into a carriage. Pancho, the eldest, refused to get in.

"I am going with you," Pancho told Franco.

Franco shook his head. "Take care of your mother. It's an order."

Franco kissed Ella on the lips; he started to say something to her and changed his mind, then he embraced each of his sons. Again, Pancho resisted, raising his hand, he saluted his father.

Franco had heard the Brazilians coming. He heard the galloping hooves of the well-fed horses; he heard the anticipatory laughter of the overconfident and well-equipped soldiers. No longer able to ford the flooded Aquidaban, and accompanied by only a few of his aides, Franco fled along the river's edge. In the misty early morning light, he had to duck his head to avoid hitting the branches of scarlet pomegranates, white jasmine, flowering orange trees as, with each stride, his big mule's hooves sank deeper and deeper into the mud. Behind him, coming closer, he could hear the Brazilians shouting.

Linda, the big mule, floundered and sank up to his belly and although Franco whipped him, he was forced to dismount. Up to his groin in the mud, he too was stuck in the mire and as he struggled to reach drier ground a Brazilian soldier blocked his path. The Brazilian soldier ordered Franco to surrender. Franco refused. Franco drew out his revolver and fired at him. Another Brazilian soldier hurled his lance at Franco, the lance went through Franco's stomach. Dropping the revolver and falling to his knees, Franco tore out the lance with his hands, then he tried to stand up again. His legs would not support him and he could not see properly, everything looked blurred; instead of one soldier, he saw several as if, all of a sudden, he was surrounded. He saw the flash of lances as they were thrown at him; he heard a shot fired. He tasted blood in his mouth. Slowly, slowly, Franco fell backward into the mud; he saw a large bunch of scarlet pomegranates spinning wildly in the bright blue sky and out of sight.

Eighteen

PARIS

From Paraguay, Ella brought with her:

380 ounces of gold

12,000 worthless dollars (paper money of the Republic of Paraguay)

A promissory note signed by Dr. William Stewart, Franco's personal physician

58 assorted pieces of jewelry including over two dozen rings and an aquamarine necklace made up of exceptionally large stones

20 valuable buttons, including 7 gold ones for waistcoat and 8 gold ones for cuff

14 bracelets, including 2 made from human hair (Corinna Adelaida's and Miguel Marcial's)

1 gold and diamond diadem

Several pairs of earrings

A dozen gold watch guards and chains

Several gold watches

8 silver *bombillas* and gourds for *maté*

6 head combs (2 gold and 4 silver)

1 gold crucifix and 3 rosaries (one particularly pretty gold and coral one)

1 gold cigar holder that had belonged to Franco

3 gold snuffboxes also belonging to Franco

Franco's diamond-encrusted marshal's baton and his whip with his initials, F.S.L., engraved in diamonds.

Ella returned to France in May. She left again almost immediately, before France declared war on Prussia, before the fall of the Second Empire and before the Communards set Paris on fire and the great trees in the Bois de Boulogne were cut down for barricades and all the animals in the zoo—including the young elephant, Pollux, whose trunk was sold for forty francs a kilo—were butchered and eaten; she went to England.

Ella exchanged the 380 ounces of gold for sterling. She used the money to pay for Enrique, Federico, Carlos Honorio and Leopoldo's schooling at Saint Joseph College, a private boys' academy in Croydon, outside London, to pay for the rent of a house in Thurloe Square, and to engage a solicitor to reclaim the 212,000 gold pesos owed her by Dr. William Stewart. Ella felt doubly betrayed—not only had Dr. Stewart been Franco's personal physician, he had been her friend. He and his wife, Venancia Baez, had often dined and played whist with Ella. After they left Paraguay, Dr. Stewart and his wife had settled in Scotland.

In court Dr. Stewart claimed that the proceeds of the sale of a large quantity of *yerba* he had exported to Argentina before the war on Franco's behalf were a gift to him. Ella contended that the proceeds of the sale of the tea were intended for her and her children. She had a letter signed by Dr. Stewart as proof. Under oath the doctor swore that he had been coerced with the threat of torture or death to sign the letter.

The case, known as the Yerba Case, dragged on for more than a year and used up most of Ella's money. Also, in order to testify, she had to make several costly, tedious trips from London to Edinburgh. On one such trip, she ran into Dr. Stewart's wife in the lobby of a hotel. Venancia Baez was just going out the door—Ella was going in—and Venancia did not see her. Ella grabbed her by the arm—Venancia had gained a great deal of weight and the arm felt soft and flabby—and stopped her. "Venancia Baez, I just want to let you know," Ella spoke in a falsely measured and sweet voice, "that I will be the one to stay up half the night dancing—dancing on the head of both your graves!" The court eventually ruled in Ella's favor, but her victory was short-lived; Dr. Stewart had filed for bankruptcy and Ella never received a single penny from him.

With barely enough money left to live on and too proud to admit it, Ella made an effort to keep up appearances. She had sold some of her bracelets and rings and she still dressed well, kept servants, a horse and carriage, went regularly to the theater and entertained in her elegant house. People who saw her remarked on how attractive she was, although her blond hair had begun to turn gray and the lines in her face were a bit more pronounced. In her well-made Parisian clothes, she looked distinguished and more French than English—or Irish, for that matter. What struck people most, however, was that Ella did not appear to look like someone who had suffered great hardships or had known death at such close hand.

No one had spoken as the carriage jolted on the road south from Cerro Corá. On the one side, Ella held Carlos Honorio's hand; on the other, she tried not to look at Pancho, who had tears streaming down his cheeks. In the seat across from her, Rosaria sat with the youngest, Leopoldo, on her lap. Enrique was next to her, a lead soldier clutched in each hand. Then came Federico pressed against the side of the carriage; he too was weeping.

Less than an hour after they had set out, the carriage was overtaken by a Brazilian cavalry detachment and ordered to halt.

Ella looked out the window.

"Lopez's mistress!" the officer in charge shouted at her.

Ella did not answer.

"His bastard children!" he shouted again.

In the carriage, Pancho stood up and went to the window. Pancho had a pistol. Leaning out, he fired it. Hit in the chest, the officer in charge slipped off his horse and fell to the ground. There was a moment of silence, then a soldier rode up and struck twice inside the carriage at Pancho with his long lance.

With her son in her arms, Ella sat back in the carriage, her dress suddenly warm and wet with his blood.

After the Commune was overthrown and the Third Republic established, Ella returned to France. On the train bound for Paris, she was sitting, half dozing, in her compartment when a young man whose hair was very blond and curly walked by in the corridor. As the young man paused and turned his head to glance inside Ella's compartment—his body must have blocked out the light and caused her to look up—for a brief second their eyes met. Ella thought she saw him smile. *Lázaro Alcántara!* Or was she dreaming? A part of her knew that Lázaro was dead but another part of her wanted to believe he was alive—and hadn't he said how *his* dream was to go to Paris after the war? Ella stood up and opened her compartment door. "Lázaro! Lázaro Alcántara!" she called out. The corridor was empty. Determined to find him, Ella ran down the length of the car, then on to the next—a sign in the car said it was expressly forbidden to do this and Ella had to hold the railing and shut her eyes not to look down at the ground underneath her rushing past as she stepped—still no one. In the corridor of the third car, Ella had to squeeze past a man holding a little dog in his arms. The man said something to her she didn't catch and he pinched her buttock—or had the little dog nipped her? On she went to the next car and the next, until she could go no farther, looking inside the compartments, but she found no Lázaro or no young man with curly blond hair who resembled him. On her way back, the train went through a tunnel and the corridor went dark, Ella thought of the man holding the little dog as she waited. When at last she got back to her own compartment, her luggage was gone.

Gone was a great deal of Ella's jewelry, including the aquamarine necklace that Franco had given her and the two bracelets made from Corinna Adelaida's and Miguel Marcial's hair; the gold and diamond diadem; the dozen gold watch guards, chains and watches. Fortunately, the silver gourds for *maté*, the crucifix and rosaries, Franco's gold cigar holder and snuffboxes as well as his diamond-encrusted marshal's baton and his whip with F.S.L. engraved in diamonds, were packed in trunks and were in the luggage car.

Crossing Paris, Ella found that there was a large hole in the middle of Place Vendôme where the column had been and, like the palace of the Tuileries, her old house on rue du Bac was a burned-out ruin; most of the buildings on Boulevard Raspail had been destroyed and there was no sign of the fruit merchant, a big, good-natured man whose name Ella had forgotten. No *fraises des bois* either. The fruit merchant reminded Ella of Marie. If she shut her eyes, Ella could picture Marie exactly: how briskly she walked down the avenue, swinging her hips and holding her shopping basket. She could also hear how Marie both argued and flirted with all the shopkeepers. Afterward, Marie would report back the neighborhood gossip—or some of it—and make Ella laugh. Just then a woman dressed in rags approached Ella; she was begging. As Ella reached into her purse to give the woman a few centimes, she saw that half the woman's face was missing.

"*Vieille conne!*" the woman screamed at Ella, grabbing the money.

When Ella walked down rue de Courcelles, Princess Mathilde's house looked shut and unoccupied. Ella had to bribe the concierge in the building next door before the concierge told her that Princess Mathilde had escaped to Brussels and had not yet returned.

Next, Ella tried to contact Monsieur Gelot about the trunk full of valuables she had sent him from Paraguay:

PARIS

12 September 1871

Dear Monsieur Gelot,

I am writing in regard to the trunk I had sent to you from my home in Paraguay. I am now residing in the city and am eager to recover my belongings. If you would be so kind as to contact me at the address below so that I may do so without further delay I would be most grateful. Meantime, I send my cordial greetings and salutations, etc., etc.

Her letter came back, stamped "Addressee Unknown." When Ella went to the address, a woman answered the door and told her that she did not know of any Monsieur Gelot. The woman looked worn and angry and when Ella tried to insist, the woman told Ella that if she did not leave immediately, she would call her husband, who was in the next room and who was a police officer. Ella did not believe the woman—she heard a child crying in the next room—but suddenly she felt tired and she no longer had the energy or the desire to pursue the matter.

Leopoldo did not feel well. He could not concentrate on the book of arithmetic in front of him; the numbers on the page jumped up and down in a way that made him feel nauseated—the number three and the number five especially, also the number eight. One moment he was sweating, the next he was shivering with cold. In class he kept his head down, he did not want to draw attention to himself. The master, Mr. Phillips, would cane him. His hands too were shaking and Leopoldo dropped his pen.

"Lopez!" Mr. Phillips said.

"Sir?"

"Look at me when I speak to you!" Mr. Phillips said louder.

The room began to spin as Mr. Phillips advanced toward Leopoldo. Mr. Phillips wore some sort of scent—lavender or rose water, Leopoldo could not tell the difference, only that it was too sweet—the scent made him gag. Leopoldo fainted.

Leopoldo was taken to the infirmary and since, when he fainted he fell forward and hit his head on the wooden desk, the nurse of Saint Joseph College attributed his fever to a concussion. In any event, unfamiliar with diseases not native to England, she would not have diagnosed malaria. Although fairly compassionate, the nurse also had certain prejudices. Leopoldo's skin was darker than the other students'; in his delirium, he spoke different languages—the Spanish she was able to recognize but not understand, the other language was even more foreign and guttural—so that when, in the night, Leopoldo cried out as if he were singing:

Tovena Tupa~tachepytyvo~
ha'emi hag~ua che py'arasy

to the nurse, it sounded like a language the devil himself might speak.

Leopoldo died alone in the middle of the night while the nurse was asleep. Ella was informed of her youngest son's death by telegram the next day. Leopoldo's brothers, Enrique, Federico and Carlos Honorio, unaware that their brother had been ill—the reason given that the boys were in different forms—were likewise informed too late. (Had the brothers been told earlier, they might have been able to save Leopoldo, who they knew already had had several malaria attacks in Paraguay.)

During the seven years that Frederick Masterman spent in Paraguay, Mrs. Masterman worried a great deal about her son. His letters—in some he had enclosed sketches—came irregularly, and once the war began, Mrs. Masterman had not heard from her son in three years, when she received the ominous-sounding letter that upset her greatly. She read and reread the last two sentences in particular—*"I hope I will be pardoned by the President. I hope my life may be spared, so I may see you again"*—trying to make sense of them. Thus great was her happiness and relief when finally Frederick Masterman—although ill and half starved—returned to Croydon (coincidentally, Mrs. Masterman lived in the same suburb of London where Saint Joseph College was situated), and she was able to devote herself entirely to the care of her son. Meantime, Frederick Masterman, when he was sufficiently recovered, was able to apply himself to his memoir, which he entitled *Seven Eventful Years in Paraguay*.

As a physician (before he became assistant military surgeon and apothecary general to the Paraguayan Army, he had been a member of the medical staff of Her Majesty's 82nd Regiment), Frederick Masterman felt duty-bound to record and describe the diseases he had encountered in Paraguay: afflictions of the lungs, consumption, pneumonia, influenza, yellow fever, typhus, enteric fever, cholera and measles—introduced during the war by the Allies, cholera and measles cost the lives of sixty thousand persons—and, finally, numerous cases of ague, goiter and elephantiasis. Despite the long list, Frederick Masterman concluded his study on a note of optimism:

> I must add that Paraguay is one of the healthiest countries in the world, if one will but adopt reasonable sanitary precautions: that is to say, live temperately, wear flannel next to the skin, bathe frequently, avoid the sun during the hotter part of the day and keep out of the marshy districts. Except the epidemics I have mentioned, there was scarcely an ailment which could not be referred either to indolence, gluttony, or immorality. . . . I am certainly of the opinion that one has a better chance of a healthy life, and of dying of that malady, not so common with us as it might be, called old age, in Paraguay than in England.

In his study of diseases in Paraguay, Frederick Masterman failed, however, to mention malaria.

In the carriage, Ella remembered, they had in fact spoken a little.

"You'll see, he'll catch up to us," she said, trying to comfort Pancho, her stubborn and grieving firstborn son.

When Carlos Honorio said he had to go to the toilet, Ella said, "Can you wait a few minutes?"

To his shame, Carlos Honorio could not.

A few minutes before the Brazilian cavalry detachment caught up with their carriage, Rosaria, to take Carlos Honorio's mind off his wet pants, softly began to sing:

> Tovena Tupa~tachepytyvo~
> ha'emi hag~ua che py'arasy,
> ymaiteguivema an~andu
> heta ara nachemongevei

Jean-Pierre, the fruit merchant, had a dream that was so vivid and seemed so real that when he woke up he started to tell it to his wife.

"In the dream, I was running down the Boulevard Raspail where I once kept my stall."

"Monique, my cousin, lives nearby on Boulevard Saint-Michel," his wife said.

"And as I ran past each house, the house burst into flames, almost as if it was happening spontaneously."

"I haven't seen Monique in months, I hope she is all right. One of these days I should go and visit her."

"Then I noticed a woman running ahead of me—" Changing his mind, Jean-Pierre stopped telling his wife about his dream.

"What woman?" Suddenly his wife was paying attention.

"I don't know. Just a woman."

In the dream the woman was wearing a red-checkered kerchief but underneath it Jean-Pierre could see that her hair was blond, a beautiful golden blond. She carried a tin can that, he knew right away in the dream, contained kerosene, and she was setting the houses on fire. Jean-Pierre managed to catch up with the woman and when he did he recognized her, although he realized that it had been years since he had last seen her. "Marie," he called out to her in the dream, "why do you burn Paris?" And Marie answered him, "We must start over if we want to live." Her answer made perfect sense in the dream and Jean-Pierre took Marie by the hand. Then he must have kissed Marie and he must have begun to unbutton her dress and make love to her because when he woke up, he had an erection.

From her window, Ella watched Sacré Coeur being built. On Boulevard Pereire, her apartment consisted of two furnished rooms and was situated above a *boulangerie*—the smell of fresh bread early in the morning almost made Ella feel sick with hunger. Ella had had to pawn the rest of her possessions: the head combs, the crucifix and rosaries, Franco's gold cigar holder, the silver gourds and straws (although she did keep a set for herself; one of the few pleasures she still had was to prepare and drink *maté*) and Franco's whip with F.S.L. engraved in diamonds. The whip was considered such a precious oddity that she received several hundred francs for it, more money than for the crucifix and rosaries. She gave Enrique, Federico and Carlos Honorio each a gold snuffbox so that they would have something to remember their father by; the marshal's baton she kept for herself, although she did not need anything to remember Franco by.

In the carriage, while Pancho bled to death on her lap, she was made to drive back to the banks of the Aquidaban, to where Franco lay on his back in the mud. Flies were buzzing around the wounds on Franco's stomach, a swarm were flying in and out of his open mouth. Tied nearby to a mimosa tree, Linda was pawing the ground and snorting impatiently, already someone had taken Franco's saddle off the mule's back. The day was unseasonably warm and steam was rising from the riverbank and Ella was sweating.

While the Brazilian soldiers stood around and watched her (for the time being, they had stopped jeering) and with Rosaria's help, Ella moved Franco's body to higher, drier ground—his body all of a sudden felt small and light—and she laid Pancho out next to his father. Then, with her bare hands, Ella began to cover their bodies with earth. She was halfway finished when Carlos Honorio called out to her and looking up to where he was pointing—by then she could hear their shrill screeches—Ella saw a flight of parrots go by overhead. The parrots were so numerous—hundreds, perhaps thousands—that for a few seconds the parrots mercifully blocked out the sun.

On January 5, 1875, from her box at the gala opening of the new Opéra, Princess Mathilde could survey *tout Paris*, as well as the King of Hanover, King Alfonso XII of Spain, the Ali Pasha, the Prince and Princess of Hohenlohe, the Count of Paris (the Orléanist pretender to the throne), the Duke of Nemours and the Lord Mayor of London; also a Peruvian who, it was rumored, in the fever for acquiring tickets had paid 700 francs on the black market for a box. The Peruvian—Princess Mathilde looked through her glasses searching the boxes for a darker, swarthier face—made her think of Ella. Several years had passed since she had heard from her friend—the reason she assumed was her own flight from Paris—and she hoped that Ella and *her* Emperor or whatever he had become were well. She had forgotten the name of the country: it was not Peru, it was not Brazil—nonetheless, a country that sounded quite agreeable. Her eyes turned back toward the stage and to Madame Krauss, who was playing Rachel in Halévy's *La Juive*—an exceptional performance! Yet, in spite of herself, Princess Mathilde's thoughts went again to Ella. She had a premonition, a vague feeling of unease that something was wrong—had she not perhaps read in *Le Monde illustré* that there had been a battle? a war? Also, she just then remembered the blond woman she had seen in the crowd standing outside the Opéra and how the blond woman had stood out in the crowd—not only was she better dressed than most of the people pushing and shoving trying to catch a glimpse of someone well-known, but there was a stillness about her (Princess Mathilde could not think of any other way to describe her) that had caught Princess Mathilde's eye. At the time, she could not think of who the woman reminded her of; now of course she knew. Ella.

Princess Mathilde could not concentrate on the next act and on Mademoiselle Sangalli's dancing the role of Naila in Delibes's ballet *La Source*. As soon as the curtain came down—the clapping had not yet stopped—Princess Mathilde took the arm of her escort, Monsieur Popelin, with one hand and with the other clutched the *rosso antico* and Algerian onyx balustrade as she almost ran down the white marble staircase and out the door of the Opéra. In the street, the crowd was smaller, a lot of people had gone home, also it was cold—it had begun to snow. Princess Mathilde stood for quite some time, long enough for snowflakes to settle on her velvet cape and on the ostrich plumes in her hair, searching the faces for Ella, until Monsieur Popelin became quite impatient, complaining of the cold, and almost had to force her inside her carriage and home.

When Enrique turned twenty and Carlos Honorio was seventeen, the two brothers went back to Buenos Ayres to make their claim on properties in Paraguay that Ella had signed over to them. Like their mother nearly a quarter of a century earlier, Enrique and Carlos Honorio stayed at the Hotel de la Paix on Calle Cangallo. Monsieur Maréchal was the proprietor still and right away, too, Madame Maréchal inquired about Ella.

"Does she still play the piano?" Madame Maréchal wanted to know. "I remember as if it was yesterday how beautifully she played. We hardly dared to breathe. A sonata by Liszt, I believe."

"These days unfortunately she doesn't have much opportunity to play," Enrique answered.

"What a pity," Madame Maréchal sighed. "I told Monsieur, my husband, that in my opinion, she could have easily been a concert pianist." Madame Maréchal hummed a little tune to herself.

"A very elegant woman. I said so right away," Monsieur Maréchal also said.

Over eighty and very frail, Colonel Enrique von Wisner de Morgenstern lived by himself in a small house on Calle Cuyo near the Italian vegetable market. In honor of his namesake, Enrique, and Carlos Honorio's visit, he had put on his uniform which had grown too large for him—Colonel von Wisner continued to dye his hair a light brown and in the afternoon light his hair looked pink. To celebrate, he offered the two brothers slivovitz, Hungarian brandy, although they would have preferred plain tea.

"Not only was Madame Lynch beautiful," Colonel von Wisner began, "but she was the most physically coordinated woman I have ever met—without being at all masculine, you understand." Colonel von Wisner paused to drink some brandy. "And you should have seen how quickly she learned to fence! Truly amazing! She was far quicker and stronger than most men. Also, she was determined. That was the key." Colonel von Wisner took another sip. "She practiced every day, running forward and backward, extending her arms and legs thus—" Colonel von Wisner extended his thin arms and some of the brandy in his glass spilled, but he did not appear to notice. "This is called *flèching*, a very difficult position because the fencer cannot protect himself and he cannot stop halfway. It's a total commitment to attack."

"What I wanted to ask you, sir, did my mother actually do battle with . . ." Enrique trailed off; Colonel von Wisner was not listening.

"Madame Lynch chose the sabre, which of course is the most difficult weapon and much heavier than the epée. With the sabre I taught her never to swing her arm to deliver a cut, she had to learn to extend it, like this—" Again Colonel von Wisner demonstrated. "The other thing, which I had nearly forgotten, that you reminded me of was that she was left-handed." Colonel von Wisner refilled his brandy glass and, smiling, he shook his head as if in amazement. "The left-handed fencer must always be careful to cover the elbow of his fighting arm against a right-handed fencer, although the left-handed fencer has the possibility of scoring with cuts to the shoulder or to the cheek. But more important—and I told Madame Lynch this—the left-handed fencer has the initial advantage of looking strange to his right-handed opponent." Colonel von Wisner paused to lift the glass to his lips.

"Do you know if she ever did battle?" Carlos Honorio tried to ask again. "If she ever had to kill anyone?"

"How old are you, my boy? Seventeen? Eighteen?" Colonel von Wisner looked over at Carlos Honorio. "Come here and give me a hand, for a minute."

Carlos Honorio stepped up to Colonel von Wisner's chair, his hand extended, and Colonel von Wisner, as if he were fencing, lunged forward and grabbed at the crotch of Carlos Honorio's pants.

"*Touché!*" he cried and fell back coughing into his chair.

"We should be leaving," Enrique said.

When Colonel von Wisner had recovered and had stopped coughing, he frowned all of a sudden. He looked at Enrique and Carlos Honorio as if he was seeing them for the first time. "Who are you anyhow? What are you doing in my house?" he shouted.

Enrique and Carlos Honorio started to answer, "The sons of Madame—"

"I know who you are, you are thieves, you are murderers! I am going to call the police." This time Colonel von Wisner managed to stagger up from his chair. He reached for his cane and brandished it like a sword at Enrique and Carlos Honorio. "Thieves, murderers!" he shouted at them again.

Enrique and Carlos Honorio's claims required expensive and extensive litigation and most of their remaining money was spent on attorneys' fees. Before returning home, they boarded a boat for the upriver journey to Asunción; on their way, they found nothing but desolation. Along the banks of the Paraguay River, the fields were not tilled, the orange trees had been chopped down or uprooted, the houses appeared looted and burned, the walls filled with bullet holes; all the animals they saw—a few cows, some horses, homeless dogs—appeared to be either ill or starving. Of the original population of nearly a million, fewer than two hundred thousand people were left; and there were no men, only women and children.

Enrique and Carlos Honorio had hoped to find Rosaria, their old wet nurse, but when they reached Asunción they were not allowed to disembark. They were ordered back to Buenos Ayres on the next tide.

Ella no longer saw anyone but ghosts. She had lost weight and had become thin—she hardly ate, her stomach hurt and most of the day she was in pain. She herself looked like a ghost—a ghost of herself. From the window of her rooms on the Boulevard Pereire, she watched people in the street go to market, to work, and the children go to school. She watched one girl in particular. The girl was long legged and had black hair, her thick eyebrows nearly met. Ella watched as the girl hurried to school in the morning—the girl was always late—then as she walked back home in the afternoon—then the girl was in no hurry and she often stopped to buy a pastry, she had a sweet tooth—in the *boulangerie* below where Ella lived. Ella thought the girl might be Corinna Adelaida. Each day she was tempted to rush down the stairs to the street and call out to her—tell her who she really was and that she, Ella, was her mother. One day—perhaps tomorrow or the day after—when she was feeling stronger and no longer in pain, she would do that.

"Corinna Adelaida, Corinna Adelaida." Sitting at the window, Ella repeated the name to herself.

There were other people in the street whom Ella recognized.

The *cambâs*, the black Brazilian soldier she had killed with her sabre, had come back. Once a week, Ella heard him calling outside her window. He pushed a cart and sharpened knives and scissors. From time to time, too, she caught a glimpse of Señora Juliana Martinez. Señora Juliana Martinez had not changed a bit; she looked just as pretty, just as elegant, as when she had been Ella's lady-in-waiting. Ella watched her step gracefully out of a carriage, carrying a basket, and watched her disappear inside a house across the street. An hour or so later, Ella watched her come out of the house, still holding the basket—but from the way she held it, the basket looked empty. Clearly she had been visiting a sick or an old relative, proof of her kindness, and, again, Ella wanted to run out into the street and kiss Señora Juliana Martinez's hand.

Several times, it also happened that while Ella was not at her window but was occupied making *maté*—if she was fortunate and Federico had remembered to bring her some—which acted like a mild narcotic and eased the pain in her stomach, and she was grinding the leaves and placing them in the gourd and pouring boiling water over them or perhaps, she had just begun to sip the tea through the silver *bombilla*, she heard a familiar tune: *ta dum ta dum ta dum dum dum*. Quickly, she would put down the *maté* to go to the window and have a look but each time she was too late, she was too slow, the person playing the harp was gone.

Ta dum ta dum ta dum dum dum, Ella hummed to herself.

Always, every day, as well, in Paris, she looked out of her window for Franco, only Ella never saw him again.

AUTHOR'S NOTE

Of course there was an Ella Lynch who was beautiful and misguided, there was a Francisco Solano Lopez who was cruel and ambitious, there were family members, generals, good and bad diplomats and their wives (even so I have taken certain liberties: for instance, I have no idea what Mrs. Charles Washburn looked like, I have her blond and fragile but she might well have been a strapping brunette), and of course there never was a Doña Iñes or Fulgencio and his brother, Gaspar. Nonetheless, I have tried to keep to historical facts where I find them to be important and necessary. The events that take place, especially those dealing with the war, are complicated and, for the most part, not well known, which means that the need to explain and the need to dramatize are often at odds. What then, the reader may wonder, is fact and what is fiction? My general rule of thumb is whatever seems most improbable is probably true. Also I would like to quote a friend who cautions his readers with these words: "Nouns always trump adjectives, and in the phrase 'historical fiction' it is important to remember which of the two words is which."

I am particularly indebted to the following works: *Letters from the Battle-fields of Paraguay,* by Captain Richard F. Burton, F.R.G.S., etc., whose keen observations on flora and fauna and human nature were most edifying; *Seven Eventful Years in Paraguay: A Narrative of Personal Experience amongst the Paraguayans,* by George Frederick Masterman, whose quaint anecdotes and quirky illustrations greatly animate his woe-

ful tale; *The War in Paraguay,* by George Thompson, C.E., to whom I am
grateful for much, including his appreciation of the Whitworth cannon
and Paraguayan cigar; and *The History of Paraguay,* by Charles A. Washburn, where I found much valuable information, including the journal
excerpts quoted.

ACKNOWLEDGMENTS

I am deeply grateful to Terry Karten, Georges Borchardt, Frances Kiernan and Michelle Huneven; and most especially to Edward Tuck.

I want to thank Trent Duffy, Andrew Proctor; Wayne Furman for the use of the Frederick Lewis Allen Memorial Room at the New York Public Library; and Lolin Perera for her translations.

ABOUT THE AUTHOR

Born in Paris, LILY TUCK is the author of three previous novels—*Interviewing Matisse, The Woman Who Walked on Water*, and the PEN/Faulkner finalist *Siam*—and a collection of stories, *Limbo, and Other Places I Have Lived*. Her fiction has appeared in *The New Yorker, Fiction*, the *Paris Review*, and the *Antioch Review*. She lives in New York City.

DISCARD

T.W. Phillips Memorial Library
Bethany College